Made to Be Broken
A novel by Hugh Fritz

Book 1 of the Mystic Rampage Series

Golden Word Books
Santa Fe, NM

Library of Congress Control Number 2019938730

Published by Golden Word Books, Santa Fe, New Mexico.

ISBN 978-1-948749-43-5

–1–

DARREN

It was late August in Chicago, where Darren Raleigh, unemployed and dressed in rags, stood on a curb. He shook a metal cup he hoped people would drop a few coins in as they passed by. His friends usually had tasks for him to do, and he was able to stay busy most days helping them move furniture or paint their homes. Nobody had anything going on today, so he did what he could to hopefully make a few dollars before sunset. It was humiliating asking strangers for pity, but he had a wife and son whom he was determined to look after, even if it meant degrading himself for a few hours.

He still remembered the wedding day. Not long after dropping out of high school, he and Atalissa went to a small church in the city. They didn't have money for a large reception or honeymoon. When they had a child, their financial situation only worsened, which was why every day, the two told their son how important it was that he stay out of trouble and take his education seriously, so he wouldn't be in the same situation when he was their age.

Darren stayed outside until he heard four tolls of a distant bell. Even though he had lived in the city his whole life, he had never discovered what building the sound came from, but it meant that he had been busy eight hours, and he figured it was time to call it a day.

He counted the contents of the cup on the bus. Paying the fare had brought it below $10. He wasn't in the mood to tell Atalissa about his embarrassing haul, so instead he went to a park two blocks from his apartment. There was a round stone table near a tennis court where his friends could usually be found. Darren followed an asphalt trail until he was roughly in the middle of the park. Sure enough, there were four men throwing dice. One of them had a case of beer and was passing cans to the other three. Alcohol was not allowed in the park, but the police weren't usually around to enforce the rule.

Mike made a living as an auto mechanic. He was the one sitting next to the beer, and Darren assumed he had bought it. Danny, sitting next to Mike holding the dice, spent his days behind a counter at a gas station. Juan was unemployed and, like Darren, made most of his money doing favors for friends. But unlike Darren, Juan was unmarried and had broken up with his girlfriend recently. Finally, there was Josh, who worked alongside his father at a family-owned antique store.

The five of them had known each other since childhood. They didn't live near each other and hadn't even attended the same school, but they were all involved in a gang called the Slugs. The name sounded cool when they were younger, but now they thought it sounded dumb. Regardless of that, the gang was large, powerful, and had members in Chicago, Detroit, and even New York. When the five of them were kids, a lot of their time was spent ditching school to play basketball, and when they were older, they had dealt drugs and gotten into fights with other gangs. Darren had gotten in trouble for a few misdemeanors but been lucky enough to avoid prison. Now that he had a wife and son, he aimed to keep it that way, and stayed away from illegal activities as much as he could.

Darren and his friends sat in the park for hours laughing and playing craps. The sun had almost set when they ran out of beer. After finding out Darren had made almost no money, Josh told him he could make some quick cash helping him move furniture into the store that weekend. Darren quickly agreed, thanked Josh, and was about to leave when a voice stopped him. The five turned to see a young man in a black hoodie and baggy jeans approaching. They all recognized him instantly as a new but active member of the gang who everyone called Rookie. He wasn't a bad kid, but Darren tried to avoid him since he was always trying to get him more involved in things like drug sales, telling Darren that having extra legs on the street distributing the product couldn't hurt.

Rookie pulled a crumpled piece of paper out of his pocket. "You guys gotta minute?"

"Me and Darren gonna be busy this weekend," said Josh.

"Don't need y'alls help for anythin' big," said Rookie. "This'll jus' be a sec. Jordan told me to get the word out about somethin' that's been goin' on."

Darren and his friends looked at each other nervously. Jordan was the gang leader in their territory, and when he spoke to someone, it was usually about money. Darren silently prayed that he didn't have a debt to Jordan.

"Jordan got a call from a boy in New York last night," continued Rookie. The five of them relaxed a little. None of them had ever been to New York, so whatever was going on was probably not about them specifically. "Some Slugs got attacked not too long ago. 'Bout two months back, there was another attack in Detroit. We think it was the same guy." He handed the paper to Josh, who laid it on the table for all of them to see. It was a sketch of a middle-aged man. It showed only his face, which had no distinguishing marks like tattoos or scars. The hair was cut to a moderate length and parted to the side. *About 6 feet tall*, and *suit* were scribbled along the paper's edges. There were probably thousands of people in New York who looked like the drawing.

"This the guy?" asked Juan.

"Yeah," said Rookie. "Someone described him over the phone to a friend of Jordan's who got a talent for sketching."

"Don't recognize him," said Danny. The rest of them took a moment longer to study the drawing, then shook their heads. "You got a picture of the Detroit attacker?"

"No," admitted Rookie.

"What makes you think it was the same guy?" asked Josh.

"He's got a pretty unique method. The New Yorkers said some dude in a suit came outa nowhere and started wailin' on 'em. Then there's, well, turn the paper over."

Danny flipped the paper to find another picture. It appeared to be a doorknob in a metal tube that had a wire wrapped around it and a spring at one end holding the doorknob in a pulled-back position. "What's this?" asked Danny.

"That's the weird thing," said Rookie. "The people who were attacked in New York said the guy had that machine strapped to his arm. The people in Detroit said the same thing. The face looks ordinary, but there ain't many weapons out there like this one, so Jordan is asking for any info on it. You guys keep that paper; I got copies. See you around."

"What you think?" asked Mike when Rookie left. "I mean, I work with some people who're good with machines but I never seen no one put together something like this."

"If it was me," said Juan, "I'd jus' use the doorknob like a club."

"Maybe he doesn't want to get his fingerprints on it," said Danny. "Rookie said it was strapped to his arm. Or maybe he's just clumsy and kept dropping it."

"Mind if I take it?" asked Darren. "Tyrell might find it interesting. Maybe he could make some kind of project out of it."

None of them had anyone in particular they wanted to show the picture to, so they did not object to Darren taking it. The sun had set and the sky was getting dark, so Darren guessed it was approaching seven o'clock and figured he should get home. Tyrell had an after-school job and wouldn't be back until much later, but he figured that when he got home, Atalissa would be waiting for him. Having roughly the same academic background as Darren, she didn't have much luck in many professional fields but had landed a part-time job. The money wasn't great but was enough to continue paying their rent and keep Tyrell in school. However, when he opened his door, he found he was alone. He let out a sigh of relief, glad to have extra time to himself.

The apartment was small and had only what the three of them needed. There were two bedrooms, a bathroom, and a sitting area that doubled as a kitchen—not that it could really be called a sitting area, since there weren't a lot of places to sit. In his room, Tyrell had a desk that he had found in an alley, but they didn't have an extra chair, so he'd put a cushion on a milk crate. The cushion had also been found in an alley and had been cleaned several times before Tyrell was comfortable sitting on it. The only other furniture was a plastic table and a couch in front of the television. Darren went to the refrigerator and made a ham sandwich, then went to the couch and grabbed the remote. He didn't enjoy any particular show, but staring at the screen helped pass the time.

It was a few minutes before ten when Atalissa and Tyrell walked through the door. Tyrell went straight to his room, while Atalissa greeted Darren with a kiss on the cheek.

"Hey babe," she said. "Hope you ate already. It's been a long day, and I just want to go to bed."

Darren grinned and tapped his plate. "Yeah, I ate." Atalissa turned toward their bedroom, but he caught her sleeve and pulled her back to give her a goodnight kiss.

As Atalissa left, Tyrell returned and went to the sink. Going straight to his room to empty his pockets when he'd come in and putting everything in its designated spot was a habit he'd had for a while. Drinking a glass of water every night was new. It had started after he'd read somewhere it was good for the heart.

Tyrell sat on the couch next to Darren. Some crime drama was on the television, but the sound was too low for either of them to understand what was happening, which was fine, since neither Tyrell nor Darren was interested in the show.

"How was school today?" asked Darren, eager to break the awkward moment of the two of them staring at a screen and not being able to hear the dialogue.

"Same as always," said Tyrell, apparently too tired to get into the conversation. "What'd you do today?"

Darren didn't want to go into the details of unsuccessful panhandling, so he went straight to business and handed Tyrell the paper. "I have something to show you. Something weird has been going on with the Slugs."

Tyrell stopped mid-sip and looked wide-eyed at Darren. "Are you asking me to get involved in something they're doing?"

"What?" Darren shook his head frantically. "No, no, it's nothing like that. But I thought this was something you might like."

Tyrell tilted the paper up and down as if looking at it from another angle would help him make sense of what he was seeing.

"Believe it or not, that's a weapon," Darren continued. "Someone's been walking around with that thing attached to his arm, and he's been attacking gang members with it."

Tyrell stared at Darren. "That's interesting, but what do you want me to do about it? I've never seen one of these before."

"Nobody's seen it before. That's why I'm showing it to you. What do you think it is?"

Tyrell stared at the picture a little longer. "Well, it looks like a wire wrapped around a piece of metal."

"Yeah," Darren said with a trace of a chuckle. "I'm pretty sure most people got that far."

"What I mean is that it's an electromagnet. We learned about them in school. Passing an electric current through a wire creates a weak magnetic field, but wrapping the wire in a coil makes the magnetic field stronger. Actually, this picture kind of reminds me of a coil gun."

"You learn about coil guns in school too?"

Tyrell suddenly looked sheepish. "Well, no. I was bored one day and did some research on them on my own. The point is that coil guns work kind of like this. They consist of a wire wrapped around a hollow tube with some kind of projectile at one end. An electric current is passed through the wire, and the magnetic field pulls the projectile through the tube. I'm guessing this thing works the same way. The doorknob is pushed back and held in place by the spring.

When an electric current is passed through the wire, the resulting magnetic field pulls the doorknob through the tube and the doorknob hits people."

Darren shrugged. "If it makes sense to you, then it makes sense to me."

"It doesn't make sense yet," said Tyrell. "Hypothetically, this could work the way I described, but the picture isn't complete. If this really is a coil gun, the guy would need some way of generating electricity, and he'd need a lot more than a couple of double A batteries. He must have some kind of power supply with him when he's fighting. Did anyone describe any other devices on this attacker? And who told you all this anyway? It may very well all be made up."

"I wouldn't be the least bit surprised if this was all made up," said Darren. "You should get some sleep. You look tired."

Tyrell finished his glass of water and left. Darren was right behind him, careful not to wake Atalissa as he crawled into bed.

SOLEIL

Miles away from the hustle and bustle of the city was a place where the serenity of nature had been sustained. It was that peace and quiet, and above all the simplicity, that Soleil enjoyed so much. A path followed a river for about five miles until the water flowed underground, then connected a few yards later to a sidewalk that ran along a busy street. Most joggers would reach the end of the trail and then turn around and run back the way they came. If instead they turned right, they would see a gravel parking lot and a small square brown brick building with a green roof. In the front, there was a wooden door with a glass window on either side. The door had a circular window in the middle, but it was impossible to see through since it had been painted yellow and had rays of light drawn around it to make it look like a sun. If anyone took the time to walk up to the building and look in the window, to the right of the door they would see a small chalkboard with the words "Soleil's Cafe" in yellow letters written in a curly font. It was where Soleil worked, as well as where he lived.

Inside, the cafe was clean and organized and had what Soleil thought of as a classic but fun feel. There were ten square tables with yellow cloths, each surrounded by four chairs. The walls were decorated with hundreds of comical bumper stickers Soleil had collected over the years. A wooden counter ran along one of the walls. Behind it, a stove was sandwiched between a refrigerator and a sink. There were no televisions, and the only source of music was a hand-held radio on the counter by the cash register. The radio received only a few channels and had terrible reception, but Soleil could listen to sports as well as a rock 'n' roll station that played music from the 1980s.

He busied himself by sweeping the floor and wiping the tables for the third time that day. The stove was off, but a cast iron skillet was on one of the burners and a stainless steel pot on another. The pot was filled with water ready to be boiled in case any customers came in. The only sound was the radio playing Midnight Oil's "Beds Are Burning." Soleil sang along and danced as he worked, even though he had a terrible voice and was an even worse dancer. When the song was over, he draped his rag over the edge of the sink and went outside to check the time.

In the back of the building, he used an aluminum ladder to climb up to the roof; the sundial there said it was about quarter past three. Soleil kept his calendar on the roof as well. Attached to the sundial, hanging by a string, were a hammer and a leather pouch filled with nails. Painted around the sundial were twelve yellow images that looked like grids; each corresponded to a month of the year. He took the hammer off the sundial and pounded a nail into the roof on the proper yellow square. It was Friday, August 28. Fridays were one of the few times he could expect customers but not for another half an hour or so. He knelt down over the painted calendar and pulled several long strings out of his pocket. Since it was late in the month, he had plenty of nails pounded into the roof to work with. He tied one end of a string to a nail and started weaving the rest of it through the other pegs on the calendar.

In fifty minutes, he had woven his yarn through the nails in a pattern that produced an image of a ukulele. He used brown for the body and white for the strings. He also used the previous month's nails to make an image of a palm tree out of brown and green yarn. He was about to take it apart and make the ukulele bigger when he heard a car approach. A red Mercedes was pulling up to the cafe and two teen-agers with backpacks were getting out. Soleil jumped up from the bed of nails, slipped the hammer back into place, slid down the ladder, and ran to the front of the building. He caught up with the kids just before they walked through the front door.

"Hi, Tyrell. Hi, Lucy. I was just checking the time. You're usually here sooner."

"Traffic was bad," said Lucy. "And I'm so getting you a watch for Christmas. Seriously—they're not that expensive, and you really need to catch up with modern technology."

Every once in a while, a few people would stop in at the cafe for a quick bite to eat, but Tyrell and Lucy were Soleil's only regular customers. They had been coming by long enough for Soleil to know a lot about them. He knew Tyrell had discovered the cafe by chance three years ago when some members of the Slugs were making crack at his apartment. His father didn't want him around while the drugs were being cooked, so he told him to find something to do outside for a while. Tyrell decided to hop on a bus, not caring where it went. Eventually he got off near the nature preserve, followed the trail, and found Soleil's Cafe. Tyrell enjoyed the style there and thought the food was great, so he returned every week. The only problem was he didn't have a car, so his best friend always drove. Lucy enjoyed the cafe as much as he did, so it didn't take much to convince her to join in on the tradition.

Lucy and Tyrell had been friends since they started high school together. Both of her parents worked in the pharmaceutical industry, and her family had much more money than Tyrell's. Her appearance made it clear that there was a difference in their lifestyles. While Tyrell wore old, worn clothes that didn't fit properly and likely had been purchased at a thrift shop, Lucy's were clean and pressed. Even today, they looked like complete opposites. Tyrell was wearing faded jeans and a black T-shirt with an image of a mushroom cloud on it while Lucy was wearing dress pants and a white polo shirt.

The three of them went straight to the counter, where Tyrell and Lucy sat down and took some of their books out of their bags. Tyrell ordered a grilled ham and cheese with a strawberry-banana smoothie while Lucy ordered a glass of water and a dish called a Noodle Tapestry. The two started their homework and talked while Soleil went to work. He couldn't join in the conversation, since the sizzling slices of ham he put on the skillet and the hiss of the fire drowned their voices out as it heated the water for the noodles. The ham and cheese sandwich wasn't as simple as the menu made it sound. Soleil preferred serving fresh ingredients and put lots of seasonings in his dishes. He placed slices of mozzarella on two pieces of rye bread and heated them in the same skillet as the ham. Meanwhile, he cut slices of fresh tomatoes and lettuce while mixing pepper, olive oil, and lemon salt in a small bowl. Lucy's noodles were pre-prepared. The dish was called the Noodle Tapestry because of the colors. There were plain yellow egg noodles, green noodles made by mixing wheat grass with the flour; red noodles that he made by incorporating diced beets; and black noodles that got their color from squid ink. When the noodles were cooked, Soleil put them all on one plate, then expertly separated the colors and put them in small piles to make the dish look like an edible painter's palette. He topped the mounds of noodles with parmesan cheese and stacked peppered tomato slices in the center of the plate.

When Soleil brought Tyrell and Lucy their dishes, he expected them to be talking about school, but instead their books were set aside and they were looking at a crumpled piece of paper on the counter.

"Tell me what you think of this," said Tyrell as Soleil handed him his plate. "There's some guy attacking members of the gang, and apparently this is the weapon he's using."

Soleil looked at the picture and saw the image of a doorknob in a metal tube with a wire wrapped around it. He didn't want to show any emotion, but seeing the picture nearly made him gasp. He felt his face drop into a look of disappointment, and he was relieved when Tyrell mistook it for a look of confusion.

"I call it a Wrist Cannon," Tyrell said between bites. "I think it's an electromagnet."

Lucy laughed. "You're such a geek sometimes. A 'Wrist Cannon!' You make it sound like something out of a sci-fi movie."

Tyrell washed his food down with a healthy gulp of his smoothie. "I'm more curious about the person behind the cannon. Why would he make his own weapon? Why not just use a baseball bat or something? It would be so much easier to get his hands on and would probably be easier to use."

"Maybe he's just looking for attention," said Lucy.

"But he's attacking people that he knows won't report it to the police," Tyrell countered. "No gang members are going to report an assault. Most of them are probably guilty of assault themselves. I think he wants to avoid being noticed."

Lucy gently cut a segment out of her top tomato. "Then he's probably trying to prove something to the gang."

"Or to himself," said Tyrell. "I think this guy is an inventor, but he never got any appreciation for his work. Maybe he tried to put this machine on the market but for some reason never got a patent, or maybe it went to the market but didn't sell. The point is he's been down on his luck, and he's using his invention as a way to prove to himself that his talent wasn't wasted."

"That's quite a story," said Soleil.

"Thanks," said Tyrell. "I came up with it in English class."

The two of them talked a little longer about the Wrist Cannon and the mysterious person in the picture. Soleil tried to avoid the topic and busied himself by cleaning the stove and pans in the sink. When he was done, he asked if they needed any help with their homework. The two slid their books back in front of them and told Soleil which parts of their assignments they were having trouble with. When it got late, Soleil suggested the two should go home. Once Lucy and Tyrell left, Soleil locked the door and let his mind wander back to what Tyrell had shown him. He knew exactly who was responsible for the unreported attacks on the gang, and had a fairly good idea of why he was doing it.

"Damn it, Flarence," he said aloud in the empty cafe as he turned off the lights and watched Lucy and Tyrell drive away.

FLARENCE

He had been indoors too long. His hotel room had a balcony, but even the fresh air didn't alleviate the feeling that the walls were closing in on him. In the past, he'd tried going to the gym and running in the park but didn't find that exercise relieved his stress. For the moment, he paced back and forth along the rail with his phone in one hand, anxiously awaiting the call.

On a calm night, he'd be able to hear the soles of his dress shoes connecting with the floor, but tonight the wind drowned them out. The breeze was strong and made his khaki pants slap against his legs. His gray suit jacket flapped about in spite of being buttoned, but that was the case even in gentle wind. The jacket was intentionally large to hide the bulge of the weapon resting in the inner pocket. It wasn't lethal but was one that only he could use.

After what felt like hours, the phone finally vibrated. The name Claire flashed on the screen, but he didn't need to check it to know who was calling. He flipped it open before the first ring was complete.

"Are you hurt?" he said before Claire could speak. The question was just a formality. Claire was his friend as well as his partner, and he was concerned about the dangerous situations the two of them constantly found themselves in.

"I'm fine, Flarence. I spotted Jeffery. He was in a car with three other people. They just pulled into a garage. The address is 1670 LaSalle St. I saw some people playing cards and drinking in there before the door closed, so he might have joined in with them."

Jeffery was the target they'd been following for the past three weeks, after Claire noticed he had been reported missing. Flarence and Claire tracked down Jeffery's parents and, as with all their clients, approached them privately. They introduced themselves as private investigators. Alice, Jeffery's mother, sobbed while she told them stories of how her relationship with Jeffery had been going downhill until he finally snapped and stormed out of the house and had not returned. Flarence told Alice he would take the case, and would collect his $30-a-week fee when he successfully returned Jeffery home.

Flarence and Claire had located Jeffery immediately but spent the next three weeks taking turns stalking him. This was partly to find out if Jeffery spent a great deal of time at any particular locations where it would be easy to grab him, and partly to let Flarence's fees accrue. Neither of them knew why Jeffery had left home, but once he did, he hardly spent any time alone. Flarence figured the garage was as good a place as any. Besides, he was worried that if they delayed any longer, the police might close in on Jeffery and bring him home themselves. He might as well act now and take the money.

"How many?" asked Flarence.

"I saw three when the garage door opened. I don't know if they're armed or not."

"Thanks," said Flarence. "Stick around in case I need you."

He took the Fister from the inner pocket of his suit coat. The copper tube with its two round brass knobs was attached to a black leather glove. With the Fister securely attached to his arm, he took a deep breath, and disappeared in the blink of an eye.

He reappeared inside the garage three miles east of where he'd been standing a moment ago. Jeffery and the others Claire had mentioned were still inside. Four of them were drinking beer and talking around the car they had just ridden in on, while another three were placing cards and betting money on an upside-down bucket. They were having such a good time that they didn't notice Florence's arrival.

Florence, knowing their obliviousness to his entry would last only a matter of seconds, sprang into action immediately. He lunged for one of the people playing cards, who was aware enough of his surroundings to turn his head before being hit. Florence brought his right hand down on the person's face. A moment before his fist made contact, electricity surged through the wire. The iron bar shot forward like a piston against the resistance of the spring, and when Florence's fist hit the man's lower lip, the brass knob simultaneously struck him in the nose. He sprawled backward on the floor, his face dripping with blood. Florence did not waste any time gloating. Before his first target hit the floor, he landed a kick in the jaw of another of the card players.

By now, the third person who was sitting around the bucket had dropped his cards and risen to his feet with his hand in his pocket. Florence could only assume he was reaching for a weapon but wasn't going to give him the chance to pull it out. He grabbed the man by the shoulders and threw him into the group standing by the car. As he did so, he noticed that one of the people by the car was now holding an opened switchblade. The one with the knife sidestepped as Florence completed his throw, and Jeffery and two others caught the man before he fell headfirst into one of the car windows. They helped straighten their comrade up, which Florence was counting on, as it left them vulnerable.

He struck one of them with his right hand and the Fister once again activated just before making contact, which resulted in Florence's knuckles digging into his opponent's ribs and the brass knob striking him in the liver. Florence turned on the other person and delivered a left hook to the jaw, followed by a kick to the knee. Florence then turned his attention back to the bent-over man and finished him off by driving his elbow into the spine. All that was left was Jeffery and the man with the knife. Jeffery was closer and tried to punch him in the face, but Florence bobbed and drove forward, shoving Jeffery away.

The armed man gritted his teeth and waved his knife back and forth. Florence held his hand out to his side, and the bucket that was being used as a poker table flew toward him. Florence caught the bucket and threw it at the man's head. The man brought his hands in front of his face so the bucket bounced off his arms rather than his nose, and Florence attacked. He took one long stride forward before he dropped low and swept his leg at the man's knees. The man with the knife fell but was able to grab the side of the car for balance before he hit the ground. From his crouched position Florence threw a cross with his right hand. This time Florence's fist did not make contact with his target. The piston activated and the brass doorknob struck the man's chin. His head snapped to the side, and he fell in a heap on the hard floor.

Florence turned around to face Jeffery, who was on his feet with his fists clenched. His right hand, along with the right sleeve of his shirt, was dirty. An open bag of potting soil lay by Jeffery's feet. He must have grabbed a handful of dirt after Florence shoved him.

"Your parents are worried about you," said Florence. "They've asked me to bring you home alive, but that's all they've asked me to do. I could easily knock you out and drag you home. And don't start whining about how this is police brutality or something. I'm not a cop."

Jeffery didn't say anything. He threw the contents in his hand at Florence's face. The dirt stopped in midair, remained suspended there for a moment, and then each clump fell to the floor as if it weighed a hundred pounds.

"Now you're gonna get it," said Florence. He ran across the room and thrust his palm forward, striking Jeffery in the nose. As Jeffery bent backward, Florence moved with him and executed a hip throw. There was a thud as Jeffery's skull struck the cement floor. He groaned once and lay still.

Behind Flarence, the garage door rose on its own. He flung Jeffery over his shoulder and carried him into the alley. As soon as they were both outside, the garage door went back down. A moment later, he heard a rustling in a nearby tree. Claire jumped from a branch and landed on a wooden fence, which she ran across gracefully. When she reached the edge she propelled herself forward, somersaulted and landed elegantly on her feet in front of Flarence.

"I didn't hear any guns go off," she said.

"Only one of them pulled a weapon," said Flarence as he removed the Fister from his arm and placed it back in his inner jacket pocket, "and it was a knife."

"Are you upset?" asked Claire.

Flarence ignored her. "He resisted so I had to pound him a little. Do you want to take him home now? He'll just be trouble when he comes around. If we brought him back to our place, we'd have to watch him in shifts all night, and I don't feel up to that right now."

"Neither do I. It's getting late and I could really use some sleep. Chasing a car on foot isn't as easy as it sounds." Flarence smiled and took her hand in his. He vanished from the alley, taking Claire and Jeffery with him.

The three of them reappeared beside a fence in the back yard of Jeffery's house. "Care to join me?" Flarence asked as he adjusted his grip on Jeffery.

She considered it a moment while her eyes drifted over the house and settled on a low window. "You go ahead." She jumped, grasped the window ledge, and started doing pull-ups.

Flarence walked to the front of the house and pounded hard on the door. Morgan, Jeffery's father, who was groggy and apparently suspicious of visitors late at night, had armed himself with a baseball bat. He dropped his weapon when he saw Jeffery.

"I found your kid," said Flarence. "Can I bring him in?"

Flarence carried Jeffery into the living room and dropped him on a couch. Morgan immediately rushed to see if his son was breathing.

"He'll be fine," said Flarence with a shrug.

The mother rushed into the room in a nightgown. "Oh my God, Jeffery! Sorry, we didn't expect you this late. Wait here while I get my purse."

"You could have called us," said Morgan. "You could have told us where he was, and we could have picked him up."

Florence didn't say anything. He just stood in the room and waited for the mother to return.

"I-i-it's been three weeks since we hired you," she stammered when she entered the room with a small leather bag. "You said twenty... no, thirty a week... oh my... I'm afraid this is all I have." She pulled a wad of bills out of her bag and tried to hand them to Florence, but her hands were shaking. Some of the money slipped between her fingers and fell to the floor. Florence picked it up and counted it. Thirteen dollars.

"This'll be fine," he said and started walking toward the door. "I'm just glad I was able to help."

"Thank you," said Jeffery's father. "We'll be sure to tell the police what you did."

At the moment, the only thing on their minds was joy at having their son back, but that would run out soon, and they would probably start asking Florence for more information about his work. He jogged to the door to get out before the questions started.

Claire dropped to the ground when she saw Florence coming. "Were these people actually able to pay you the full amount?"

"Does it matter?" said Florence. He passed two of the bills to Claire. As he held them, the ink smeared and the images on the paper changed. Each transformed into a one hundred dollar bill. Claire pocketed her share, and Florence did likewise. He then took Claire by the hand, and the two vanished for the final time that night.

Florence and Claire appeared next to a wall in their hotel room. Claire instinctively turned on the lights, and the two caught their breaths when they found they weren't alone. The surprise only lasted a second, and they both relaxed when they realized who it was.

"Hi, Soleil," said Flarence. "Not that this is a bad time, but don't you usually wait for me to visit you?"

"This is a special circumstance," said Soleil. "I know what you've been up to."

"You've known what we've been up to for a while," said Claire. "Nothing's changed since we last saw you."

"I'm not the only one who knows anymore," said Soleil. "Word has been spreading in Chicago about some mystery man who's been beating up members of a gang. There are people walking around with a picture of your Wrist Cannon and asking for information about you. It's bad enough that you use your powers for violence, but now you're getting sloppy. You won't be able to keep a low profile much longer."

"First of all," said Flarence, "I'm not targeting any gang. I help people with their problems. The fact that a lot of problems are connected to the Slugs is just a coincidence. And second, "Wrist Cannon" actually has a nice ring to it. I might have to start using that."

"Good," said Claire. "I never liked calling it the Fister."

"This isn't a joke!" Soleil shouted. "There's going to be consequences for what you're doing."

Flarence sighed and shook his head. "Soleil, I love you, but one of these days I'm going to knock your gullible, naive head right off your shoulders. Nobody's coming after me."

"What if I'm not naive?" said Soleil. "I know you've been frustrated with the secrecy, but what if it is true? Do you really want to risk it?"

Flarence's face became stern as he looked Soleil in the eye. "Absolutely. Nothing would make me happier than seeing one of the big guns face to face."

Soleil was silent for a moment. "Just be careful," he said, and then he disappeared.

Flarence turned to face Claire. "You know I'm not just doing this to prove a point, right? I really do care about the people we're helping"

"I know," said Claire. "I do too. And hey, even if the Council is real . . ."

"They're not."

Claire held a razor blade between her index finger and thumb. "Good, because they'd be in for a world of hurt if they tried to get between us."

—2—

DARREN

As September rolled in, the weather created a dull, gloomy feeling. The rain had been falling non-stop for several days, which meant Darren was not in the mood to stand on the street with a cup. As luck would have it, there was plenty else to keep him busy. Mike had invited him to stop by the garage to help with some work. Darren didn't know a lot about cars but could follow instructions and avoid embarrassing mistakes.

Josh had also been asking for Darren's help particularly often lately. The antique shop he and his father operated was busier than usual, with a lot of large items like dressers, desks, and cabinets needing to be moved. Since Josh's dad was old and not always up to the task, Darren helped load them onto the truck. Josh was very insistent about not letting Darren come along in the truck when he was transporting antiques, which Darren found a little odd, but he didn't argue as long as he got paid.

It was another wet Sunday, and Darren had no intention of leaving the house. Atalissa was out shopping, and Tyrell was at Soleil's Cafe working on his homework. Darren was bored out of his mind with no one to talk to and was thankful when he heard a knock at the door. Josh's father, Andrew, was standing outside.

"Sorry to bother you," said Andrew, "but I have a desk to deliver and need help moving it."

"Is Josh around?" asked Darren.

"He's sick," said Andrew. "He either got a nasty cold or he got food poisoning. I don't know. All I know is he says he can't work today."

Darren agreed to help in exchange for Josh's share of the sale. Andrew drove slowly because of the rain as they took the truck to the store to pick up the desk. He had the windshield wipers on full speed but still had to squint to see the road. Darren figured his age had made his vision worse, and that soon the old man would need glasses. Andrew droned on about what transportation was like when he was young, when gas was cheap and cars were bigger.

The antique store looked disorganized inside, but Andrew knew what he was doing. All kinds of items were sprawled around the rooms, which made them seem like a mesh of sofas, desks, lamps, and tables at first glance. But if one were to stand still and take in the scenery, patterns in the mess would become apparent. There was still room for people to move among the furniture, which turned the store from a pile of old junk into more of a maze. As they moved about, Andrew expertly avoided all the furniture, while Darren, not as familiar with the layout, stumbled trying to keep up, and nearly knocked over a lamp. Finally the two approached a simple but elegant writing desk near a wall. There were two drawers on top, and in the middle was a small, hollow mound with a hole in the center large enough to hold a pen. There were no drawers under the desk, but the legs were curved and had grooves carved into them.

"It doesn't look all that heavy," said Darren.

"Don't say that until you've tried lifting it," said Andrew.

The only way to move the desk out of the store was to lift it over their heads. Darren found the weight manageable but had to be patient, as Andrew's old arms struggled to keep it elevated. He took small steps, and before they were halfway across the room, Andrew's breaths became quick. Three times during the journey, he needed a break. When they finally made it to the front door, the rain was still coming down hard. They put the desk down so Andrew could find a tarp to drape over it. He also used the opportunity to take a fourth break. When they finally hoisted the desk into the truck, Darren slammed the doors shut, and the two jogged back into the shop.

"I know it's asking a lot," said Andrew, "but could you drive this for me?"

Darren didn't answer right away. He didn't want to spend his day driving a desk through the city in the pouring rain. Andrew dug two sheets of paper out of his pocket and waved them around until Darren took them. They were hand-written directions to the buyer's address. The papers were a little damp, but the instructions were still legible and detailed, with turn-by-turn directions and the amount of miles to go for each step.

"This is going to take an hour," said Darren.

"Hour and a half," Andrew said, "given the weather and traffic."

"Look," said Darren, "I know you said you wanted my help moving that desk, but this is a little much."

"Oh, come on," pleaded Andrew. "I'm an old man. I don't have the energy I used to. Besides, someone has to watch the store." Darren still didn't answer. "Look, I'll up your cut of the sale," Andrew said with a sigh. "I'll give you some cash for gas too."

Darren was still reluctant but didn't want to turn down the chance at extra money. He folded up the instructions, threw his hood over his head, and once again ran outside into the rain. Through the rearview mirror he watched Andrew waving goodbye as he drove away.

The drive was long, but at least the buyer lived in one of the city's better neighborhoods. Darren didn't go to the suburbs often but enjoyed the opportunity when it came along. Seeing all the big houses with nice cars parked out front gave him something to dream about. While he knew there was no chance of his being able to afford such a house, there was still hope for Tyrell, who was smart, took his studies seriously, and had the potential to do whatever he put his mind to.

As much as dreaming about Tyrell's future success lifted Darren's spirits, it did very little to improve the weather. The dark clouds forced Darren to turn the headlights on, and the rain was still coming down too hard for the windshield wipers to help much, even at their highest setting. In addition to hindering his vision, the rain also made the roads slick and difficult to drive on, especially in the old truck, which was in need of an inspection and probably a tune-up. Darren made his way to a section of the city where the traffic was light, but he was still moving at a snail's pace.

As he pressed the gas pedal passing by a four-way stop, Darren suddenly felt something wrong when he was halfway through the intersection. He looked out the passenger window and saw a pair of headlights coming at him. It was too late to avoid a collision as the other car blew through the stop sign and came barreling toward him. Just before the collision, Darren could see through the rain well enough to notice the driver looking down, the glow of a cell phone illuminating his face. Darren felt a jolt from the impact as he heard the windows crack and felt the airbags deploy. He was wearing his seat belt, but his body jerked sideways, and he felt a shot of pain as his head hit the side window.

He sat still, momentarily stunned, before moving his hand up to the side of his head. When he pulled it away, his fingertips were red. He looked in the mirror and saw he had a cut just above his left eye. Without thinking, he tried to stop the bleeding with the closest thing available: the papers with the driving directions. He turned off the engine, unbuckled his seat belt, and slid outside.

Darren inspected the damage before dealing with the other driver. The door was caved-in and looked like it was holding onto the truck by a thread. The damage to the car that had hit him was nowhere near the condition the van was in. The driver emerged, a little shaken but not injured, and walked quickly toward Darren.

"Didn't you see me coming? Don't your brakes work?" Darren said. The other driver seemed more frightened than angry, and Darren had a feeling he knew the crash was his fault.

Darren pulled the papers away and craned his head up, letting the rain wash away some of the blood.

"Oh man, you're hurt. Here, let me see your face." The other driver leaned a little closer to Darren and squinted, then backed away. "You'll be fine."

"Are you a doctor?" said Darren.

"Well, no."

"Then shut up."

Darren went back into the van. He closed his eyes and was about to put the papers back on the wound until he realized it was a bad idea. He unfolded them and examined the directions. They were covered in blood, and the rain had smeared the ink. No matter how long it took to get this mess straightened out, the delivery was going to have to wait for another day. Darren pushed the thought out of his head and leaned back against the seat. Considering the headache he was developing, the smashed truck that Andrew was going to definitely yell at him about, and the fact that the delivery was going to be delayed, he felt he should enjoy a brief moment of silence. Unfortunately, the moment was briefer than he would have preferred. He heard a tapping and slowly opened his eyes. The other driver knocked at the window and held a few cards in his left hand.

"We need to exchange insurance information. You have insurance on this thing, right?"

Darren had no idea if Andrew had insurance on his van, or where he kept the information if he did. He tried the glove compartment first, but all he found was receipts. He grabbed a handful and looked through them. Most were for food, and a few were from movies tickets. Darren decided to put the glove compartment in the "maybe" file of his list of where the insurance information might be. He checked under the visors, with no results. The driver was still outside and had started tapping at the window again as he said something to Darren about how he wasn't supposed to be driving without insurance. Darren considered taking the time to thank the other driver for pointing that out. He also considered telling him to shut up again, and maybe open the door on his face. Before he could do any of those things he became aware of flashing lights. A cop car had shown up.

Darren abandoned his search for the insurance information and exited the van. He didn't want the other driver talking to the officer alone for fear that he would change the story to convince the cops that Darren was the one who blew through the stop sign.

Two police officers stepped out of the car and took a quick visual inventory of the damage, then one of them walked away with the careless driver while the other stayed by the truck with Darren.

The officer stood up straight and didn't squint in spite of the rain that was still falling. The man introduced himself as Officer Tymbir. He was large enough to be intimidating but his face was calm. He didn't look kind, but he didn't look angry either. It was an assertive look that made it clear he was in control of the situation.

"Someone on this block called as soon as they heard the crash," said Tymbir. "They mentioned someone looked like they'd been hurt. Paramedics are on their way. The cut doesn't look that bad though. You'll be fine."

Darren wished everyone would stop telling him he would be fine. Hearing that his injuries weren't severe didn't make the pain go away. The officer asked for Darren's version of how the accident had happened. Darren got straight to the point and told the officer about how the other driver went right through the stop sign with his eyes off the road. When he was done, Tymbir started inquiring about Darren's reason for being out. He took Tymbir through the explanation of the antique shop and how Josh was sick, so his father needed someone to take his place.

Tymbir walked to the back of the truck and asked Darren to open the double doors. Darren wasn't sure if Tymbir was trying to stall until the paramedics got to the scene, or if for some reason he didn't believe the story. He wanted to ask Tymbir why anyone would make up a story about being a delivery driver for an antique store but held his tongue and opened the back of the truck.

He understood the reason for the distrust. He knew he looked out of place wearing his hoodie and sagging pants in a suburban neighborhood like this one. He didn't like the way strangers instantly assumed the worst of him based on the way he dressed, but if there was one thing he had learned in his youth, it was that resisting police officers only made situations worse. He had told Officer Tymbir the truth. He had done nothing wrong, and the crash was entirely the other driver's fault. He figured that as long as he played it cool, things would work out fine.

Tymbir started climbing into the van. He paused with one foot resting on the ledge. "Mind if I have a look inside?" Darren nodded. Tymbir swept the tarp off the desk and ran his hand over the wooden top. "This is pretty nice," he said. Darren only shrugged. He wasn't an expert on antiques and wouldn't know a nice desk from one a friend of his threw together in a day. Tymbir tried to open the two letter cabinets, but they were locked. He gave Darren a suspicious look. Darren shrugged. Tymbir brushed his hand along the underside of the desk and paused. A moment later he removed a key that had been taped to the bottom of the desk. Darren hadn't noticed it before because he was too busy trying to avoid bumping into furniture and worrying about whether Andrew was going to make it to the van without having a heart attack.

Tymbir put the key in one of the locks on the drawers and turned it. He opened the letter compartment, and when he looked inside, his face changed from focused and calm to cold and intense. He leaned out of the door and called to the other officer to meet him in the van. Darren started to climb inside, but Tymbir held up his hand and said "Please stay where you are, sir," in a stern voice that made Darren stop dead in his tracks. The other officer approached the van and climbed into the back. Tymbir motioned for him to look into the letter compartment. The other officer glanced inside for a moment and then backed away. He looked at Tymbir first with a look of shock, which quickly turned to excitement.

Tymbir motioned for Darren to join them in the back of the van, and the moment he entered, Tymbir snapped a pair of handcuffs on Darren's wrists. Darren had enough of a view of the desk to see the bag of white powder sitting in the compartment while Tymbir recited the Miranda rights speech. "That's not mine!" Darren shouted in panic as he was dragged toward the police car. "I didn't know that was there! I swear, that's not mine!"

SOLEIL

Tyrell held his phone above his head as if he was going to throw it across the cafe but instead put it on the counter and groaned. Soleil was silent and let Tyrell collect his thoughts before asking what was wrong.

"That was my mom," he said, now sitting with his head in his hands and his elbows on the counter. "Apparently dad's been arrested. The cops busted him for carrying drugs." Soleil still didn't say anything. He thought about giving Tyrell a free smoothie but decided that wouldn't help. "My mom grew out of that phase," Tyrell continued. "I was able to stay away from that life altogether, so why is it so difficult for him to quit and move on to something else?"

"I'm sorry," said Soleil, "but he's doing it because he cares about you. We all need a source of income, and your dad's just trying to make a living the only way he knows how. Not everyone is born with a wide variety of talents."

"I wasn't born good at math," said Tyrell. "I chose to practice a skill that might come in handy. Dad keeps this up because he doesn't want to change. He doesn't care about us. He's lazy and selfish."

There was another period of silence, which Soleil hoped Tyrell would break. He knew the situation wasn't exactly new. Since Tyrell had started coming to the cafe on a weekly basis, he had opened up about everything that had happened to him, all the times he was bullied by kids in his neighborhood, when he was worried about his dad, how he had a difficult time making friends, and if it wasn't for Lucy, he would feel completely alone. Tyrell was Soleil's closest friend, who deserved a lot more than he'd been given. Now he was on the verge of being separated from his dad. That was too much. Tyrell deserved a break, and Soleil knew he was the only one who could provide it.

"Listen, Tyrell, if you want, I can keep Darren out of prison." Soleil didn't make eye contact with Tyrell just yet. He still wasn't entirely sure Tyrell could be trusted with the information he was about to give him. Soleil had revealed his secret to some of his closest friends before, but all those times had ended in heartbreak and occasionally death. Tyrell was just a kid, though, and he had a good heart. After all these years of Tyrell's opening up about his life, the least Soleil could do was be honest about his own.

"You know a lawyer?" Tyrell asked.

"No," said Soleil, who had now found the strength to look Tyrell in the face. "I mean I can physically remove your father from jail. I can even destroy any records the police have of whatever crime he committed. I can do all this before tomorrow morning, and I can promise nobody will be hurt."

Tyrell leaned back in his chair and crossed his arms. "Really? If you had those skills at your disposal all this time, how come you never offered to help before?"

"It's complicated," said Soleil. "I can't offer these kinds of services to just anybody. I'm telling you this because we've been friends for a few years now, and in all that time, you've had to live with a lot of trouble. But you never let it hold you back. I admire you for that, and I don't want to see you worrying about your father anymore. Just this once, you deserve a get-out-of-jail-free card."

"But how're you going to spring my dad?" said Tyrell. "Is this going to be like an action movie where the seemingly calm cafe owner presses a secret button under his counter and a hidden panel in the wall opens up revealing an arsenal of military-grade weapons? Are you going to put on a pair of sunglasses and pull out a box of grenades, then say some catch phrase before charging into the police station guns blazing but conveniently not making any kill shots, and in a few hours, I'd see footage of you on the news carrying my dad out of the burning police station moments before it collapses?"

Soleil closed his eyes and inhaled deeply. "Tyrell," he said, "I'm a Genie."

Tyrell stared at Soleil for a moment, his arms still crossed, and then he got up and walked toward the exit. The door had a deadbolt lock connected to an oval-shaped latch, and when Tyrell approached the door, the latch snapped into a horizontal position.

"I wasn't joking," said Soleil.

"Yeah, right," said Tyrell, who turned around to face him. "You had that lock automated. You flipped some switch under the counter and the door locked itself."

Soleil raised his hands above his head. Behind Tyrell, the deadbolt clicked open and then closed again. "See?" said Soleil, "No switches. I can use my magic to manipulate gravity. I can make one half of the latch heavier, causing it to fall sideways." There was another click, and Tyrell turned around to see the latch was once again in the vertical position. When Tyrell turned around again, the chairs had risen off the ground. They flipped, hovered for a moment, and came to rest hanging over the table ledges. "It's magic, Tyrell. I swear."

Soleil walked around the counter. "Come on. I'll give you a lift home." He put his hand on Tyrell's shoulder and gripped tightly enough to make him wince, but before Tyrell could tell him to let go, they were off the ground. There was the familiar feeling of pressure crushing his body from every angle, and then the cafe was shrinking in the distance. There was a moment of relief when they paused on various rooftops. Then, suddenly, the experience was over. The two were now standing in a dark room, and Tyrell squirmed out of Soleil's grip before he extended his arms and found a wall. He ran his hands along it and soon found a light switch. When he turned it on, a single ceiling bulb revealed a wooden frame bed, some biology books on a cheap plastic desk, and a poster on the wall with a picture of Albert Einstein sticking his tongue out above the words "As a child, he was no Einstein." They were in Tyrell's apartment, standing in his room. Tyrell stared at Soleil speechless.

"I summoned us here," said Soleil. He pointed to the wall Tyrell had been running his hands along. "Or, more specifically, I summoned myself to this wall and carried you with me." There was a creaking of floorboards on the other side of the door. "It sounds like your mom's awake," said Soleil. "Maybe this isn't the best place to talk." Neither of them touched the light switch, but the lights went out as if an invisible hand had flipped the switch. Soleil grabbed Tyrell's shoulder again, and before Tyrell could object, they were both back in Soleil's cafe, standing in front of the counter. The chairs were still resting upside-down on the tables.

It took Tyrell a moment to collect himself. He stared at Soleil with a look of awe and fear, and then lifted a chair off the nearest table, set it on the floor, and sat down. "All right," he said. "I'm listening."

Soleil grabbed a chair for himself and sat directly across from Tyrell. "You should start. It's probably best if you get the important questions off your mind first."

"You said you summoned yourself to my apartment," said Tyrell. "Why don't you start by explaining the details about that?"

Soleil raised a hand above his head. Behind him, a saltshaker on the counter flew across the room and landed in his palm. He placed it on the table in front of Tyrell. "I can cause objects to become attracted to each other," he explained, "and I don't need to summon them to myself." The saltshaker took flight again. It moved to the right and landed gracefully on top of another table on the other side of the cafe. "When I perform a summoning spell, the object of lesser mass is the one that moves. If I summon a pencil, the pencil travels to me, but if I summon my body to a car, or a wall of your apartment, I travel to it."

"We didn't open the door when we were traveling," said Tyrell. "It felt like we went straight through the ceiling. How did we pass through the building without damaging it?"

"Summoning is just the tip of the iceberg," said Soleil. The table the two were sitting at became a heap of sawdust. As Tyrell brushed it off his pant legs, it didn't settle to the floor but remained suspended in the air as if being held by invisible strings. Then the dust began to organize and took on the shape of the square table it had been previously. It became rigid, transforming from a cloud to a solid table once again. "I can manipulate matter at the molecular, atomic, and subatomic levels. I can control chemical reactions and influence a metal's magnetic state, or push electrons through a wire to generate electricity without a power source. I can also manipulate physical states. I can boil or freeze water on demand, or dismantle and reconstruct walls in seconds just by thinking about it. It takes a great deal of focus to do this when moving as fast as we were when summon-traveling to your apartment, but I was able to make temporary holes in anything that stood in our way. As we were moving, I reconstructed everything I broke down by the time we arrived at our destination."

"We were flying across the city," said Tyrell. "How come nobody noticed us?"

"A trick of the light, and I mean that literally. Think of me as a psychic prism." The table they were sitting at once again served as an example of Soleil's power. It vanished from sight for a moment, and then in a flash became visible again. "I can alter a photon's wavelength, driving its frequency outside the visible range, which renders the object imperceptible to the naked eye. While we were travelling, I pushed the light reflecting off of us into the infrared region. This takes an incredible amount of focus, and I can't keep large objects invisible for very long, but in our case, we were traveling fast, and we only needed to be invisible for a moment. Not that it would matter unless someone was looking up. It helps to live in the city. I didn't summon my body to your apartment directly. I summoned us to rooftop antennas and air handling units. We jumped from building to building."

"How fast do you move when summon-traveling?"

Soleil shrugged. "It depends on the mass difference. Your wall is much heavier than I am, so we moved very quickly. Lesser difference means slower travel."

Tyrell began rubbing his eyes. "Could we stop talking for a minute? This is a lot to take in."

There was a pause before Soleil broke the silence. "I'm sorry I didn't tell you sooner, but I need to keep this a secret from everybody I know for as long as possible. Every time I tell someone what I am, it ends badly."

Tyrell said, "My parents and I have been going through difficult times for as long as I can remember. You could have snapped your fingers at any time and made all our problems disappear, but you didn't because you were worried I'd stop being your friend?"

"You've experienced seventeen years of discomfort," said Soleil. "I've been alive for centuries, and most of my relationships have not gone smoothly. My family and I don't always get along, and I've lost more than one significant other. I've also lived in villages of people who noticed I was different from them and blamed me for their suffering, assuming I brought some kind of curse upon them. I think you should cut me some slack for being reclusive."

"I thought Genies lived in bottles and couldn't use magic until they were set free."

"Not everything in the stories is accurate, but the idea is the same. The bottles mentioned in the stories are common objects that most people will pass by without noticing. In my case, I live in a small cafe that few people know exists, and of all the customers who come in here, you're the only one who really talks to me. Genies don't want to be noticed."

"And the part about your master being given three wishes?" said Tyrell.

"I don't approve of the words 'master' or calling my services 'wishes.' All Genies are given autonomy when their client asks for help. I'm only here to give you what you need, and it's very important that you understand that. If you wish for money, I'll get you enough to pay your bills and rent, but I will not make you a millionaire just because you ask me to. If your wish is for your father to return home safely tonight, I'll remove him from jail and destroy all records of him ever being there, but what happens afterward is entirely up to him. I will not force him to get a job or break off contact with the gang. Those choices are his to make."

"You said you didn't like the word wish," said Tyrell, "so how do you decide when you've completed your services? Are you agreeing to help me with three problems?"

"I don't know where the three wishes myth came from," said Soleil. "There is no limit to how many times I can help you. If I choose to be your Genie for the rest of your life, that's my choice, and I can help you with any problem you might encounter. However, I reserve the right to end my services at any time with or without any reason, as do you. If you ever feel I've overstayed my welcome, you may tell me to leave, and I will. Most people keep me around for about a year before getting sick of me. My longest employment was for a decade."

"The way you describe being a Genie makes it sound like a business," said Tyrell.

"In a way it is, but I'm not exactly a self-employed man. I have bosses."

"So, do you have a contract for me to sign or something?"

"There's no paper contract," said Soleil, "but there are certain rules I need to follow. For example, as I explained earlier, there is no cap on the amount of times I can use magic to help you. There is, however, a commitment issue to be taken into account." Soleil held his hand out with his palm facing up. A small silver ring floated out of the back pocket of his jeans, hovered through the air and came to a rest in his upturned palm. "This represents the commitment to my clients," said Soleil. "If you accept this, it means you alone have the right to ask me for help. I cannot use magic for anyone's sake but yours."

"A ring?" said Tyrell. "No offense, but I'm not really a jewelry kind of guy."

Soleil placed the ring on the table. "The last services I performed were for a woman," he explained. "I had feelings for her and incorporated my magic commitment into our wedding vows. It seemed like a romantic idea at the time. The object doesn't have to be a ring, though. I can transform it into anything you want. Here, try this."

The ring broke and became straight so that it was now a flat piece of metal which remolded and formed a key. It was a blank key with no teeth to fit into a lock, but it had a hole that would fit in a key ring. "There," said Soleil. "Carry that with you. It's nothing fancy, but at least you won't be likely to lose it."

"Let's get on with the important issue," said Tyrell. "What are you planning to do about my dad?

"You let me worry about that," said Soleil. "I promise you that by morning your dad will be home safely. It will be as if he was never arrested." He held his hand out to Tyrell. "I'll summon you home if you want, and then I'll get right on it."

"No way," said Tyrell. "When you summoned me, it felt like I was being sucked into a vacuum."

"Fair enough," said Soleil. "Where's your dad being held?"

Tyrell told him the name of the police department. He stood up and walked out of the cafe.

Soleil focused on the police station. He had never been there, but it would be easy for him to locate. Without getting up, he turned off the light and locked the door. He closed his eyes and separated his mind from his body. His senses left him one by one. The sound of cars passing by outside became faint, he could no longer smell the coffee beans behind the counter, and before long, he could no longer feel the chair he was sitting on. Soon he felt weightless, as if he were floating above his own body. Physically, his eyes were still closed, but his sight had returned. He looked down at himself.

Soleil wasn't sure what an astral projection looked like. He didn't cast a reflection in a mirror, no camera could capture a picture of him, and no one could see or hear him when he was in this form. He could travel anywhere but could feel nothing. He couldn't interact with anyone, and objects passed right through him. He figured it was the next best thing to being a ghost.

Soleil's projection floated straight up away from his body, passed through the ceiling, and continued to rise until he had a view of the whole city. He knew he would find the police station if he trusted his feelings. When he was in his astral form, he developed a sixth sense that helped him find what he was looking for. This was the trade-off for separating his mind from his body; by surrendering all his other senses, his intuition became nearly perfect.

At the moment, he felt the need to travel north. He didn't know how far, but he knew it was the right direction. Below him, the cars were tiny spheres of moving lights, while trains rushed along beside them. A flock of geese crossed his path and passed through him without noticing. Before long, he felt he was close to his destination. His projection descended gracefully to the ground. As he was sinking, he noticed a large building with a parking lot full of police cars. He floated around the building until he found a sign on a door that confirmed it was what he was looking for.

Soleil's projection hovered around the area and looked for surveillance systems. There were cameras by the entrance and in the parking lot. There were also police officers standing outside talking. His projection traveled to the roof, where he found an air-handling unit. It traveled back through the city to his cafe, floated back into his body, and his senses returned.

He summoned his body out of the cafe and launched it to the post of a power line near the street. From there, he summoned his body to the wall of a building, and to a billboard advertising an insurance company. Tyrell might have been uncomfortable with the sensation, but it was nothing compared with what Soleil went through himself.

In addition to focusing on his destination, he also needed to be aware of any solid objects in his path. If he was traveling toward a building, he only had a fraction of a second to dismantle the wall and reassemble it the moment he'd passed through. Additionally, he needed to bend the light around his body to maintain his invisibility. Every centimeter he moved required millions of adjustments. Sometimes he wondered if staying invisible was really necessary. He was moving too quickly for any human to be able to follow him, but he needed to take every precaution for the sake of keeping his secret.

In no time, he landed on the roof of the police station. The next step was to locate Darren. His astral projection could have searched all the holding cells, but Soleil's psychometry abilities would be much faster. Once he made physical contact with an object, he could mentally see past events and learn its history. If he felt a building, he would know every person who had ever been inside it, how long they had stayed, and what they had done while they were there. He knelt on one knee, placed his hands on the roof, and searched the building's past. In his mind, he saw Darren being brought into the police station by two officers. His wrists were handcuffed, and he struggled while being dragged to a holding cell labeled C-6. Soleil broke his psychometry and walked across the roof until he was directly above the room, which was two levels below him.

Soleil turned his attention to the wires in the building and paid close attention to those connected to light fixtures. Not only could he feel the electricity flowing, but he also could control it and make it weaker or stronger at will. Soleil curled his hands into fists as he amplified the power flowing to the lights. There was a flash throughout the building as every bulb burned out simultaneously. He knew a power surge would not keep a building full of police officers distracted for long, and he needed to act fast. He disintegrated the section of the roof he was standing on, creating a hole directly below his feet. He fell to the level below him, and reconstructed the roof the moment he'd passed through it. Before he hit the ground, he had already created another hole in the floor, which he fell through and subsequently reconstructed. He landed in the holding cell; Darren was standing in front of the door.

"What's going on?" he shouted at nobody in particular. "Is this a blackout?"

"It's not a blackout," said Soleil. "It's a breakout."

Darren spun around and looked for the source of the voice but couldn't see Soleil in the dark. "Who said …" he began, but Soleil didn't give him a chance to finish. He grabbed Darren by the shoulders and summoned his body out of the building. In seconds, the two of them were standing by a dumpster behind Darren's apartment. Darren nearly collapsed when his feet touched the ground, but Soleil still had a tight grip on his shoulders, and he forced Darren to stay on his feet.

"You're home," said Soleil. "Go be with your family. If you want to know what happened, go to a place called Soleil's Cafe tomorrow. Tyrell knows where it is."

Soleil summoned his body back to the roof of the police station, leaving Darren alone in the alley. It was still dark inside, as people were busy replacing light bulbs. There were criminals inside who were taking the opportunity to give the police a hard time, kicking at their cell doors and shouting in the dark. It wasn't a riot, but there was enough chaos for Soleil to take advantage of. Once again, he deconstructed a spot on the roof and fell to the level below, landing in an empty office that had not had its lights replaced yet.

Soleil walked behind a desk and placed a hand on the wall. Once again, he performed a psychometry spell and saw Darren being brought to his cell as if it was happening right in front of him. This time, Soleil focused on what the officers did after they locked Darren up. One of them went outside and smoked a cigarette while the other one went to a desk and started filling out paperwork on Darren's arrest. The officer had still been working on it when the lights went out. Soleil considered making the documents invisible and summoning them to his body, but there was a camera in the room that would notice a pile of papers suddenly disappearing. He would need to do something about the cameras before collecting the files.

Soleil focused on a cup of pens and pencils on the desk, removed them, and used his powers to melt the empty cup's metal, flatten it out on the desk, and then remold it until roughly the shape of a police badge. He wasn't exactly sure what the badge was supposed to look like, but in the dark, it wouldn't matter. His tie-dyed shirt also had to be altered. It contained every color imaginable, and Soleil smeared the ink, mixing it and focusing particularly on expanding blue portions until his entire shirt was roughly the color of a police officer's uniform. To complete his disguise, he broke small fragments of rubber off the soles of his shoes, made the fragments hover in front of him, and mentally molded them as he had done with the metal cup until they resembled buttons, which he attached to his now-dark blue shirt along with the fake badge. He wouldn't pass for a police officer very long, even in the dark, but he wouldn't need much time to complete what he was there to do.

Soleil left the office and started walking down the hall to the nearest stairway. Emergency fixtures were providing some light but not enough for anyone to notice how fake his uniform and badge were. Two officers were in the middle of the hallway, one standing on a chair unscrewing a bulb while the other held the chair and a flashlight for him. The one standing on the chair glanced at Soleil as he passed by but went back to work without paying much attention.

Soleil made his way to the first floor and was soon standing in front of the room that contained the paperwork on Darren's arrest. The room was empty, with most of the officers probably still looking through storage closets and grabbing as many spare bulbs as they could. Soleil could hear the camera attached to the ceiling humming softly. Outside the camera's field of vision, he focused on the screws connecting it to the ceiling, and slid the camera out of its position, mount and all. It fell to the floor with a thud. Soleil laid the papers in a row, and focused on raising the temperature of the ink on the pages. Letter by letter, the writing began to smear, and the words bled together until none of the documents were legible. Soleil then forced the liquefied ink off the pages, and it ran like rivers along the desk and onto the carpet, leaving only the blank documents behind as if they had never been written on. He then increased the temperature of the ink further until it vaporized and the stain rose from the carpet, dispersing throughout the room as a dark cloud. That took care of the paperwork, but there was still security footage of Darren's being brought in.

Soleil went to the room that contained the recorded footage from the security cameras. He didn't have much time left. By now, many lights had been replaced, and the building was not nearly as dark as it had been. *Almost done*, he thought. *Just a little longer.* When he found the footage room, one man was sitting in a chair with a few computer monitors in front of him, each displaying a different part of the building. Soleil focused on the monitors and distorted the images, making it appear that the cameras had gone out. The man slapped the screens a few times, trying to restore the footage. When it didn't work, he grumbled something under his breath and left the room to check the cameras.

The moment he was gone, Soleil went in and restored the screens. He found the one that showed footage of the front door of the station, focused on the screen, and forced the recordings to reverse until they had rewound to the point where he saw Darren being brought in. He altered the image by rearranging the pixels and expanding the bodies until they blended into the background. Soleil advanced the recording to the next frame and repeated the process over and over. He was working as fast as he could, but there were a lot of frames to move through.

More lights had been replaced, and the hallway outside the recording room was now fairly well lit. It also wouldn't be long before the officer Soleil had lured out returned. He rushed through the images, advancing and altering frame after frame. When he had advanced the recording to the last one containing Darren and the two officers and fast-forwarded it to the current time, he left the room as fast as he could without making it look as if he was in a hurry. But the moment he left, he found the officer who had been monitoring the screens earlier at the other end of the hall. Soleil did not make eye contact. He turned and moved in the opposite direction, not realizing that he was running.

"Hey," the officer called out as he started following Soleil. "Hey, who are you? Get back here!"

Soleil knew he could not summon his body out of the station with an officer behind who had him in sight. There would be enough confusion when no one would be able to find out what had caused the blackout. The officers who'd arrested Darren would also be very upset when they found their paperwork destroyed and no video evidence of the man's ever being brought in. Despite the strangeness of the events, no one would likely blame what happened on magic.

However, if an officer saw Soleil disappear into thin air, this would lead some to suspect paranormal activity. Desperate for cover, Soleil went into a bathroom at the end of the hallway. But in his haste, he didn't realize it was a women's room, which only brought him more attention. Fortunately, it was unoccupied. Once the door was closed, he performed another summoning spell.

Back in his cafe, he restored his shirt so it was a mesh of different colors again and reattached the buttons to his shoes. He realized he still had his fake badge but didn't feel like going back to the station to replace it. He took off the badge and molded it again, this time turning it into a metal figurine resembling a turtle, which he placed on top of his cash register.

"That was for you, Tyrell," he said out loud. "You're welcome."

"Who's Tyrell?"

Soleil spun and saw Florence and Claire sitting at a table in the cafe. "I guess it's my turn to pop in uninvited," said Florence.

Claire held up a few newspaper sheets. "There's a guy on a crime spree," she said. "He's been robbing convenience stores at gunpoint. He's struck three places in the past two months. I thought it would be worth looking into."

"And as long as we were in the neighborhood, I thought we'd stop by," said Florence. "We let ourselves in when we saw you weren't around. I hope you don't mind."

"My house is your house," said Soleil. "Can I get you something to eat?"

Florence ignored the offer. "I know you don't have a car, and you're not much of a jogger. I also knew you couldn't be out having fun with your friends because I don't remember the last time you did anything fun or made any friends. Then I find you summoning yourself into your own cafe saying you've just performed a favor for someone named Tyrell."

"Please stay out of this," said Soleil.

"No," said Florence. "You like talking about how I use my powers. Now I want to talk about yours."

"Fine," said Soleil. "I have a new client."

Flarence smirked and folded his arms. "What did you tell him about your abilities?"

"I haven't told him anything yet," said Soleil. "All he knows right now is that I'm not human."

"But you'll tell him soon, right?" said Flarence. "I'm assuming you're going to tell him that same ridiculous story you told all your other clients."

Soleil approached Flarence and pounded his fists on the table. "I'm so sick of you talking about our history like it's a fairy tale!"

"That's exactly what it is," said Flarence, still sitting calmly in the chair. "You're basing your actions on events that have never been proven to have actually happened."

Soleil took a breath and regained control. "It's not I'm the only one in the world taking a leap of faith. Millions of humans do it every day."

"At least humans have scriptures to guide them and buildings where people who share their beliefs can meet," said Flarence. "What do we have? A bedtime story our dad told us."

"Just go," said Soleil. "Go find your robber and please don't make this complicated. I'm going to tell Tyrell the story as soon as possible, and I'd appreciate it if you stayed out of the way."

Claire stood up first, and held her hand out to Flarence, who took it, and the two disappeared.

FLARENCE

Flarence summoned them to an old pickup truck that had stopped working years ago and was now sitting in a junkyard. They were still for a moment and listened for anyone who might be around. "I want to know more about Soleil's new master," said Flarence when they were sure they were alone.

"Don't you think the armed robber is more important?"

"Maybe, but I worry about Soleil sometimes. I know he only wants to use his powers to help the less fortunate, but there are bad people on the loose, especially in this city, and he's letting them tell him how to use his magic."

"Fine," said Claire. "So do you want to save the robber for another time?"

"No, we should take care of that tonight. Do you think you could take care of him yourself?"

Claire nodded.

"All right," said Flarence, "keep a lookout."

He sat on the ground with his back against one of the truck's rear tires and performed an astral projection. He had explained to Claire how important it was for her to keep watch for anyone passing by when he was performing the spell. When he was in his astral form, someone could beat him up and rob him, and he wouldn't know anything had happened until his projection returned to his body. Claire crouched by the truck and listened for footsteps as Flarence's spiritual essence was severed and floated high above the city.

His projection focused on what he had read in the newspaper. The robber wore a hockey mask when he hit a convenience store, but one of the clerks had fought back and removed the mask long enough for a camera to get a shot of the man's face. The clerk had been shot, but the police had been able to use the footage to identify the robber as Charles Bradley. Flarence and Claire would have let the police handle the situation, but Bradley was still robbing stores and had become more violent since being identified. He didn't wear the mask anymore and didn't hesitate to shoot the people he was robbing. Maybe he was frustrated or figured he didn't have anything to lose, since the cops now knew his name, and he wanted to have some fun before being caught.

Flarence's projection flew eastbound, away from the junkyard. As he flew over the streets, one car in particular caught his attention. It was a black Toyota that had just pulled into a mostly empty 7-Eleven parking lot. Flarence's projection descended into the car and looked at the driver, who opened the glove compartment and pulled out a 9-mm handgun. There was no time to look for Soleil's new master. His projection returned to his body.

When he physically opened his eyes, he was glad to see Claire was ready for action. The baggy long-sleeved shirt she'd been wearing was now tied around her waist to reveal a dark blue undershirt with a series of chains attached to it, stitched tightly to the fabric to prevent them from jingling when she walked. She still had her jeans on but underneath she was wearing leggings that also had chains stitched to the front. Before, she'd had chains stitched to the back as well, but that had made sitting too uncomfortable. Her hair was tied into a ponytail, and in the center were two pointed metal rods approximately ten inches long. A short scarf was tied around her face, covering her from nose to chin. Sewn to it were leather pouches arranged in zig-zag patterns, each one containing a razor blade about an inch long. Though they were not designed to be deadly weapons, when used properly, they could be effective in a close combat fight. Flarence had seen Claire in many fights and could testify that she knew how to use them properly. She was also wearing black leather gloves with extra padding on the fingertips so she could use the razors without cutting herself. Each finger had a ring with a small metal plate and a different letter embedded into it. On her left hand were the letters R-A-Z-R, and on the right were the letters P-U-N-K. Razor Punk was the nickname she'd come up with years ago, and when she wore her scarf and chain mail shirt, she liked Flarence to use it.

"We don't have much time," said Flarence. "He's about to attack again." He grabbed her wrist and summoned the two of them to a wall of the 7-Eleven. They were standing at the back of the building on the opposite side of the parking lot. Flarence led Claire to the edge of the wall, and the two peeked around the corner. They could see Bradley's car, and inside they could hear him shouting at the clerk.

"I didn't have time to find Tyrell," said Flarence. "I'm going to project again. Don't stand around waiting for me to come back."

"You'll be vulnerable," said Claire. "You'll be out in the open with nobody watching out for you."

"There's nobody back here. I'll be fine." There was a bang inside the store. A moment later, Bradley ran to his car, carrying a small bag that probably held the money. "Go!" Florence shouted to Claire.

Claire ran around the building and launched herself at the car as the door closed. She landed on the hood and brought her right hand down on the windshield, cracking the glass where the metal letters on her glove struck it. Claire punched another section of the windshield with her other hand to create even more cracks and make it harder for Bradley to see. She broke off one of the side mirrors. From his position, Florence couldn't see inside the car, but Claire leaped off the hood an instant before there was another loud bang and a bullet tore through the windshield. The car's engine roared to life and lurched backward as Bradley drove away. He tried to turn out of the parking lot, but couldn't see well enough through the cracked windshield and drove into a lamppost. He stumbled out of the car holding his head and waving the gun around. He fired a few shots in Claire's direction, but she had run back behind the wall near Florence, and the bullets hit only brick. Bradley started running, and Claire pursued him, not bothering to look in the store at the man behind the counter. She had never taken first aid classes, and there was nothing she could do for someone who'd been shot.

Florence stayed behind and watched Claire chase Bradley. Inside the 7-Eleven, he could hear someone repeating "Oh, my God!" and describing the location of the store. Someone else inside must have called 911. Florence decided to let the professionals handle the situation, and he projected again, focusing on the name Tyrell. Without a full name, it took longer than usual for him to have an impulse, but eventually it worked. His projection flew through the city and found the small apartment, which he floated inside of and surveyed. All three people there were asleep.

His projection returned to his body just as the ambulance arrived. Florence could see the flashing lights of the police cars around the corner of the building. The man who'd been shot was being wheeled to the ambulance, while the witness who had called was describing the scene, including the strange woman who had appeared and smashed the shooter's windshield with her bare hands.

Florence summoned his body to the wall of the bedroom where the boy slept. The kid definitely tossed and turned in his sleep, because half the covers were lying on the floor. Near the bed was a desk with books and papers on it. Florence looked at them and found they were stacks of homework labeled Tyrell Raleigh, confirming that he was indeed in the right room. He crept around as quietly as possible, trying to get an idea of what kind of person Tyrell Raleigh was. Most of the room was a mess, which was normal for teen-agers. It was littered with empty soda cans and dirty clothes, but the desk was neat and organized. There were also milk crates next to the desk full of notebooks and folders. Each crate was labeled with a different year.

He noticed a yearbook on top of the milk crates containing the folders. Florence expected to find pages of signatures and jokes by Tyrell's friends inside, but when he flipped the pages, he saw that most of them were empty. It was only the last page that was full of writing: the words "What Makes You Great" written in large letters followed by a column of bullet points that filled the rest of the page. On the bottom was a heart followed by the word "Lucy." So Soleil's new master was a slightly messy teen-ager who didn't have many friends, but someone named Lucy had a high school crush on him.

Florence put the yearbook down and approached the bedroom door. From what he had seen, there was nothing dangerous about Tyrell, and he didn't want to leave Claire on her own too long against a man with a gun. He would have to perform another projection to do it, but not in the apartment. There was no denying that this was a bad neighborhood, and if Tyrell or his parents woke up to find someone in their home, they would probably attack before asking questions. He also couldn't go back to the 7-Eleven. The cops were probably still there, and he wouldn't be able to find any privacy.

He crept through the apartment and made his way to the nearest exit. The streetlight coming in a window wasn't great. When Flarence closed the door to the apartment, he sensed that he wasn't alone. Down the hallway, two men were leaning against the wall drinking beer; one was smoking a joint. Flarence took a blank key out of his pocket and held it near the lock on the door. He molded the metal as he slid it into the lock, forcing teeth to fit into the tumblers to turn the latch. The click of the door locking was loud enough to get the attention of the two men at the end of the hall. He heard them put their beer cans down and walk toward him. He started going the other way and was grateful to come across a door labeled "Stairwell." Before going down, he glanced back and saw the two still approaching.

Flarence closed the door behind him and focused on the spindle connecting the two knobs. As he had done with the key, he molded the metal into a new shape, rounding out its edges to make it circular. On the other side, one of the men tried to open the door, but the knob just turned uselessly. Flarence hurried down the stairs. He could probably knock out both of them with a single punch, and would if they got through the door and caught up with him, but he was not in the mood to draw unwanted attention. Other people might hear the commotion if a fight broke out, and he would quickly find himself in a situation he wasn't prepared to handle. Unfortunately, he soon found that the situation had gotten out of control the moment he entered the apartment building.

Sitting in the stairwell was a group of people drinking beer, smoking cigarettes, and playing cards. Some were teen-agers but others looked to be in their late 20s. All of them were wearing black and blue clothes that needed to be washed, which made Flarence appear out of place in his khaki pants and suit jacket. There were six of them, and the space was so narrow he couldn't pass through without awkwardly stepping over someone. He took a chance and tried to walk through the crowd as casually as possible, but one of them stood up and pushed him back. Flarence saw it coming and was able to keep his balance, but didn't retaliate. He felt it was best if the group didn't see him as a threat. Maybe they were just trying to look tough and would let him go after threatening him a little.

"You lost?" said the man who had pushed Flarence.

"I'm just leaving," Flarence replied as he backed up a step higher to put some distance between him and the group. "I have a friend in this apartment a few floors up."

"No, you don't," said another member of the group. "Everyone knows everyone around here, and everyone knows everyone's friends. If we don't know you, no one here does."

"Hey! Stop that guy!" a voice called from behind Flarence. He didn't have to turn around. The two men from the hallway had caught up with him. Flarence turned sideways and tried to keep one eye on the two people above him and another on the group below. He could feel a fight approaching.

"We saw 'im upstairs," said the man who had been smoking the joint. "He came out of Darren's apartment. We didn't like the look of 'im."

Darren's apartment. Flarence hadn't looked into the other bedroom. Darren must be Tyrell's father.

"You do look familiar," said one of the members of the group below Flarence. "Yeah, there's been a picture goin' round. Somebody's been going after our group. You look like the guy in the picture."

At that moment, a thought occurred to Flarence. He didn't know why it hadn't hit him immediately. He had been around people wearing black and blue clothes before. It had happened in Chicago as well as Detroit and New York. These people were Slugs. Black and blue were the gang's colors. Not only had Flarence walked right into their territory, but they knew he had attacked them on multiple occasions. The possibility of finding a peaceful way out of the situation was gone.

At that moment, Flarence also considered what the situation said about Tyrell. Soleil's new master was a messy teen-ager with a crush on a girl named Lucy, and now it turned out he was involved with a street gang. It wasn't clear how deep Tyrell's involvement went, but at some level, Soleil was going to be granting wishes for a group of lowlifes and misfits.

Flarence stopped thinking about Soleil and focused on the matter at hand. There were eight gangsters in all. He was surrounded, and didn't have the element of surprise he had had when he went after Jeffery in the garage. For the most part, the group appeared to be pretty focused, but it was late at night, one of his opponents was high, and a few of them appeared to be drunk. There was no way of knowing if any of them were armed, but based on his experience, he guessed at least one of them had a knife. Flarence had his Wrist Cannon in his pocket, but the second his hand went under his coat, one of them would jump at him. If anyone was going to make the first move, it had to be Flarence.

Someone was talking about how they should call Jordan for advice, but Flarence wasn't listening. He lunged backward and grabbed the stoned gangster by the collar and threw him down the stairs to the group below. The pot smoker's friend tried to throw a punch, but Flarence countered. He twisted the gangster's arm and took him hostage just as one of the gangsters below pulled out a gun.

"You better put 'im down," said the man with the gun.

Flarence had been hoping one of them had a firearm. He focused on the bullets and forced their temperature to rise. Every bullet reacted at once, which caused a deafening bang and a flash as the gun was blown to pieces. The group all fell to the floor disoriented and holding their ears. A piece of metal struck Flarence's hostage. Flarence bolted down the stairs, avoiding the group as he made his way to the ground floor as quickly as possible. When he was out of the building, he dove under the nearest car. He projected and focused on finding Claire.

It didn't take long. She was only a few blocks from the 7-Eleven where he had last seen her. His projection hovered over a bloody scene involving her and two other people. Bradley was lying on the sidewalk with a broken leg and cuts all over his face. A police officer was standing a few yards away pointing a Taser at Claire, who was on her knees with her hands on her head. The officer pulled out a pair of handcuffs and approached her, but before he could put them on, she pulled one of the needles out of her hair, stabbed him in the hand, and ran. The officer staggered back against a mailbox. He put his bleeding hand into his armpit and started yelling into a walkie-talkie.

Flarence's projection returned, and he summoned his body to the wall of a building Claire was running toward. He flew through the city and appeared next to the wall in front of her. "Time to go," he said. Claire ran to him and jumped into his open arms. Soon they were miles away, standing under a bridge over the Chicago River.

Claire took off her gloves, and the two took a moment to relax. Flarence wasn't even winded after the excitement of the night, but Claire needed a moment to catch her breath.

"Soleil's new master is a kid," said Flarence. "He's in high school, and he lives in Slug territory. It's possible he's in the gang."

Claire took off her scarf. She looped the ends through links in her chains and tied them before putting her long-sleeved shirt back on. "Sounds like he's worth looking into," she said.

—3—

DARREN

Nobody in the apartment had gotten a good night's sleep. After Darren had seen Soleil disappear, he went upstairs and demanded answers. All Tyrell could tell him for sure was the location of Soleil's Cafe, and he promised to take his father there as soon as possible. Since Tyrell had been born, there was a no swearing policy in the apartment, but in this situation, Darren made an exception. Atalissa eventually calmed him down and convinced him to go to bed, but a few hours later, there was a pounding on their door. When Atalissa answered, their friend Brodie ran in and shouted something about an accident on the stairwell.

Apparently, J.J.'s gun had malfunctioned, and he had shot his brother. Brodie got in Darren's face and almost punched him. He said the man J.J. was pointing his gun at when it happened looked like the guy in the picture that had been circulating in the neighborhood, and he had been seen leaving Darren's apartment moments earlier. All Darren could do was tell Brodie that he had no idea who the stranger was or why he had been seen leaving the apartment.

The situation would have become violent, but the ambulance arrived, and when Brodie heard the sirens, he left to be with J.J. and his brother. Atalissa left with him, leaving Darren and Tyrell alone. They didn't say anything, but both understood that they needed to go to Soleil's Cafe as soon as possible and get more information on what was going on. They would have left at that moment, but the busses would not be running until the morning.

Atalissa did not return that night, and Darren assumed she was still at the hospital. It was seven in the morning when he had rolled out of bed. He knew he had to meet Soleil but was also afraid to leave the apartment. If people misunderstood the situation and thought Darren had something to do with a member of the gang getting injured or killed, his life was in danger.

If word about last night traveled fast enough, it was possible he would be mugged the second he went outside, but it was more likely that the people who had witnessed the incident last night would go to Jordan first and ask him what to do about it. Jordan would call for Darren soon and hear his version of what had taken place. Hopefully, after talking to Soleil, he would at least have enough information to come up with a reasonable excuse for the strange things that had happened.

Darren and Tyrell met at the front door. Neither brought up the fact that it was Monday, and Tyrell should be in school. The two of them took the stairs to the main floor, relieved that they didn't see anyone on the way. The excitement in the apartment house had died down, and everyone was likely either still at the hospital or back in their apartments.

The sky was clear that morning, but the sun was still low, and it was a long, cold wait for the bus. After a thirty-minute ride and a ten-minute walk, they came to the nature preserve, where every once in a while, they passed a jogger wearing skin-tight clothes designed for cold temperatures.

Darren was freezing and beginning to become impatient. He was about to ask how much farther it was when the trail suddenly ended and he saw the small building in the gravel parking lot and the chalkboard sign in the window.

"I know it doesn't look like much," said Tyrell, "but this is really where he lives."

Darren and Tyrell walked in and found two people sitting at a table. One was Soleil, but Darren had never seen the other before. The stranger was older, with dark, wiry hair. He had bushy eyebrows and was wearing odd clothes. His shirt was light brown and had no sleeves. It looked like it was made out of some kind of fur, and the sides were held together with leather straps fed through a series of holes and tied together. His pants also looked homemade: dark brown, thick, and seemingly made of leather. Whoever he was, he made Darren uncomfortable, and Tyrell's face suggested he felt the same way. Soleil motioned for them to sit.

"Can I get you anything to eat?" he asked.

"I'll have a ham sandwich," said Tyrell.

A plate flew across the cafe, and Soleil caught it. Like the plate, slices of bread, tomatoes, ham, and cheese flew to him and landed on top of one another. When it was finished, Soleil slid the plate across the table to Tyrell. There was a sizzling sound as the food began to heat up. The cheese melted, brown streaks appeared on the bread, and the smell of cooked ham filled the room.

"Does anyone else want one?" asked Soleil after the sandwich was ready. Darren shook his head.

"Dad, this is Soleil," said Tyrell as he took a bite and wiped the crumbs from his mouth with his sleeve. "He's the guy I told you about. He's the person who helps me with my homework on weekends." He looked at the other man. "I don't believe we've ever met."

"Tyrell, this is my father," said Soleil. "He taught me everything I know."

"My name is Mohinaux," said the old man.

He didn't look like Soleil's father. There was a noticeable difference in skin tone as well as eye and hair color. In addition, Mohinaux seemed to have an accent when he spoke, although Darren couldn't place where it was from.

"You don't look like you're related," said Darren.

"I know, and I'm here to help my son explain everything," said Mohinaux. "Soleil tells me you are very different from his usual clients."

"It's true," said Soleil. "The world has changed a lot since I last offered magical services. People have become more inquisitive, and I'm sure you have many questions about why I use my powers the way I do. Dad and I are just going to give you a brief summary of our history. Stop us any time if you have questions."

Mohinaux jumped in. "As you have probably inferred, my son and I are incredibly old. I've honestly lost track of how many years I've been alive. However, I was not the first magical being to exist. Our kind began with a group of sorcerers scattered all over the world. When non-magical beings witnessed their power they began to worship the sorcerers. All the ancient myths you've heard, from Greek gods to shamans and witch doctors; they were all sorcerers."

"You and Soleil are related to gods?" asked Darren.

"We're not exactly related," continued Mohinaux. "Our powers were given to us as a gift. I'll get to that part later. As time passed, sorcerers from around the world met each other but disagreed about the proper way to use their powers. Some kept their distance from non-magical people but did their best to control nature and the well-being of crops. A few interacted more closely with ordinary folk and produced a variety of demigods and monsters.

Many of them were eventually overcome with their power, feeling they had complete control over non-magical people's lives, and some reached the point where they demanded human sacrifices. Others felt their powers should be used to help the less powerful and were against using magic in violence or as an excuse for bloodshed. These differences resulted in a debate that lasted many, many years. As the debates on uses of magic continued, they began to turn violent. Unfortunately, when sorcerers fight, the results can be catastrophic. The Titans who fought the Greek gods were actually created and sent by sorcerers who lived in what is now South America.

It became clear that if the war continued, the planet would be destroyed, so all battles were suspended, and every magical being convened to reach an agreement once and for all on the proper way to use their powers. Eventually a set of laws was established. The driving factor was that being treated as gods had led to corruption and caused sorcerers to abuse their abilities, but many still believed that their powers should not be wasted. The decision was made that all parties, magical or not, should have a say in how sorcerers use magic.

Therefore, a sorcerer would be allowed to use his powers as much as he wanted, so long as he was given a human's consent. This agreement resulted in the establishment of Genies. Sorcerers are allowed to offer their services to individuals on the condition that their wishes do not interfere with the other laws that resulted from the debate. Genies are forbidden to show off. We need to keep our powers secret till we're ready to accept a client. This is to reduce chances of the wrong kind of person seeking Genies out and trying to take advantage or us. To make sure the rules were followed, a Council of Elders was established. They watch over the Genies and step in when there is foul play."

"How do you know all this?" asked Darren. "Were you around during the debate?"

"No," said Mohinaux. "This was all explained to me after I became a Genie."

"How exactly did you become one?" asked Tyrell.

"Sorcerers live long," Mohinaux explained, "but are not immortal. Despite the extreme punishment we can withstand, it is possible for us to be killed in battle, and though it takes millennia, it is possible for us to die of old age. All the sorcerers who wrote the original laws are deceased. However, in order for the organization of Genies to continue, they were allowed to pass their powers on to someone before they died. When a Genie transfers his or her powers, the non-magical person is said to become Enchanted. I had an old Genie in my service for several years who I convinced to Enchant me before he passed away and Soleil . . ."

"I was given less of a choice in the matter. I've had powers for as long as I can remember."

"He was born a Genie," said Mohinaux. "I knew that having powers would result in me outliving my family, and I did not want to live alone. The sorcerer who granted me my powers also agreed to give me two Enchanted sons."

"Two?" said Tyrell, looking at Soleil. "You have a brother?"

Soleil nodded. "We don't see each other as often as we used to, but he still drops in once in a while."

"Anyway," said Mohinaux, "that's the story of how my son and I became Genies. I hope this has shed some light on the situation."

Darren leaned forward and rested his elbows on the table as he stared at Mohinaux. "Just to be clear, you're saying you can give me your powers."

"I said I have the right to choose to pass my abilities onto another person before I die," replied Mohinaux. "I don't need to give you magical abilities, and neither does my son."

"Fair enough," said Darren, "but how does it work? How do you pass your powers to another person?"

"I'm glad you asked," said Soleil, "and Tyrell, it is very important that you remember this when making your requests. Magic is contagious, and direct exposure is all it takes for someone to become Enchanted. Simply altering the color of your hair would give you a sorcerer's powers. I will not perform wishes that involve using magic directly on another living thing."

"But you used magic on me last night," said Darren. "You dragged me out of jail and dropped me off in front of a dumpster."

"Not exactly," said Soleil. "I did that summoning spell on myself and was holding onto you while traveling. My body was exposed to magic, not yours, so you weren't Enchanted."

Tyrell's brow furrowed like it did when he was processing a difficult homework problem. "Can magic be used by all living things or just humans?"

"Any living creature can become Enchanted," said Mohinaux, "but each species is affected differently. One example you might have heard of is an Enchanted wolf. When a wolf is Enchanted, it cannot perform spells the way humans can, but its size, senses, and hunting abilities are increased. Its metabolism is also slowed to the point where it only needs to eat once a month. It spends most of the month dormant and only a few days searching for food."

"You're talking about werewolves," said Tyrell.

Mohinaux nodded. "All the stories of monsters came from sorcerers' Enchanting their animal companions. An Enchanted wolf is a werewolf, an Enchanted bat is a vampire, stories of fairies are based on Enchanted moths, a Minotaur is an Enchanted bull, and the list goes on. That's the common effect of magic. It makes creatures harder, bigger, faster, and stronger. However, Enchanted animals needed to be watched closely. When they got loose, they caused lots of trouble among non-magical people, so for safety purposes, the rules forbid the Enchantment of animals. I'm happy to say there hasn't been a werewolf on the loose in centuries. To be honest, even I was nervous when I saw them."

The door to the cafe opened, and Darren turned to see a middle-aged man and woman walk in. The woman was wearing loose, faded jeans and a baggy flannel shirt with a checkered pattern of gray and brown squares. The man was wearing khaki pants and a gray suit jacket over a white button-up shirt with no tie. Darren couldn't place the man's face but felt he had seen him before. However, his curiosity about Soleil and Mohinaux was greater than his curiosity about the newcomers. "We're kind of in the middle of something here, could you come back later?" he asked.

"It's all right," said Soleil. "They can stay."

Darren looked back to see that Soleil was slouching. The man and woman grabbed chairs from other tables and sat near Soleil and Mohinaux.

"Tyrell," sighed Soleil, "this is my brother, Flarence, and his friend, Claire."

"It's nice to meet you," said Flarence. "Soleil told me about you. What have we missed? What have you told them so far?"

"We were explaining the rules of sorcery to them," said Mohinaux. "We've been through the importance of keeping magic secret and the process of Enchanting other living beings."

"And have you been through the Council of Elders?"

"We've brushed over it," said Mohinaux.

"Flarence, don't," said Soleil. "Please, just don't."

"Fine, I won't," said Flarence. He looked at Tyrell. "Do you have anything to say about the story? I'm sure you've got questions."

Tyrell paused and looked at Darren. He then looked at the Genies. "Where is the Council of Elders located?" he asked.

"There is no single meeting place," said Mohinaux. "It was part of keeping the existence of Genies a secret. The Elders need to move, or they would be too easy to find."

"So where are they now?" said Tyrell.

Flarence spread his arms out to his sides and made an overly exaggerated shrug. "Nobody knows."

Soleil glared at Flarence. "We don't know exactly who or where the Elders are, but they watch us. They make sure we don't break the rules."

"Us?" said Tyrell. "How many Genies are there in the world, and how many of them are Elders, and how many of them are performing magical services for people?"

Flarence shrugged again. "Nobody knows."

"It's true that I've never met another Genie outside of my own family," said Soleil, "but they are out there. They're just keeping their existence a secret. Trust me—we aren't the only Genies in the world."

"What happens if you break the rules?" said Darren.

"No. Body. Knows," said Flarence. He didn't shrug this time, but he shook his head left, then right with each word. Everyone at the table other than Claire was becoming annoyed and glared at him.

Soleil sighed and rubbed his temples. "He has a point. There's a lot that I haven't seen before, and for the most part we take the existence of the Council on blind faith."

"Let's rephrase that," said Flarence. "Soleil takes the existence of the Council on blind faith. Dad says the Council members have the ability to take away our powers, and that fear prevents Soleil from bending the rules. I don't have that problem. I don't have a master, and I don't ask for anyone's consent before using magic. I'll be watching both of you very closely, and if I don't like what you're asking of my brother, I'll step in and stop you."

"Where did that come from?" said Darren. "My son hasn't even known about magic and Genies for a day, and you're getting suspicious of him."

"We don't know either of you personally," said Claire, "but both of us are very familiar with your gang."

Tyrell reached into his pocket and pulled out the piece of paper with the drawing of the Wrist Cannon and the face of the man who had been seen using it. He had meant to ask Soleil if he knew anything about it, figuring it was possible the device actually had no physical power source and was operated by magic. He held up the drawing so it was next to Flarence's face and compared them side by side. The drawing wasn't perfect, but there was a clear resemblance. Darren took the picture and did his own comparison. He stood up and pointed at Flarence. "You broke into my apartment last night!"

Flarence didn't flinch at Darren's sudden outburst. "Technically, I didn't break anything to get in. I even locked the door on my way out. You're welcome."

"J.J. shot his brother last night," said Darren. "That wasn't a malfunctioning gun, was it?"

"You didn't tell me you killed someone," said Claire.

"You did what?" said Mohinaux.

"It wouldn't be the first time," said Soleil.

"Okay, can everyone cut me some slack?" said Flarence. "I wasn't the one who pulled out the gun. All I did was heat up the bullets a little. It's not my fault someone got in the way of the blast."

"Of course it's your fault," said Darren. "Why didn't you just get out of the building without fighting anyone off? You could have just summoned yourself out of the building, right? Why didn't you think of that?"

"It's because he didn't want to be seen using his powers," said Soleil. "It's all an act. He's not as tough as he wants people to think he is." He looked directly at Flarence. "You're not breaking the rules. You're just bending them a little. That keeps you safe from the Council. You used magic on a gun, but you did it in a way to make it look like an accident. Admit it; you're just as worried about the Council as I am."

"You're missing the point," said Flarence. "Your new master is involved with a gang."

"I was aware of that when I told Tyrell about my powers," said Soleil. "And Tyrell isn't involved with the gang, only Darren is, and he doesn't participate in a lot of their illegal activities anymore."

"I'm still going to be keeping my eye on you," said Flarence. He held out his hand, which Claire took, and the two of them disappeared. Darren rushed around the table and tried to catch them. He swung his arms wildly as he paced about the room, hoping to hit one of them.

"Don't bother," said Soleil. "They're long gone."

"I had no idea he was so out of control," said Mohinaux. "I had no idea he had become a killer."

Darren was breathing heavily. "He's your son! Don't you keep in touch with him? I haven't seen my pop in a while, but at least I give him a call once in a blue moon."

"We Genies take the rule of secrecy very seriously," said Mohinaux. "Even when we see each other, we don't talk about our powers much, especially in public."

"Your son is a murderous vigilante," said Darren. "That seems like something to be concerned about. Why isn't the Council stepping in?"

Mohinaux tapped his fingertips on the table. "I'm sure the Council is aware of the situation and is considering the proper course of action."

"How did Flarence even know where we live anyway?" said Tyrell.

"Genies have ways of finding things," said Soleil. "We can take on what is called an astral form which allows us to find anything we focus on."

"Why doesn't Florence use it to find the members of the Council?" asked Tyrell.

"It wouldn't work," said Soleil. "Genies have a sort of natural protection from incoming spells. I could use a projection to find you, Darren, or Claire, but I wouldn't be able to find dad or Florence. At least not directly. If I used an astral projection to find Claire and she was with Florence, I would be able to observe him through observing her."

"But the members of the Council watch you," said Tyrell. "Can't you feel them?"

"The Council of Elders are more powerful than average Genies," said Mohinaux. "They can use their powers in ways Soleil and I don't know about, including the production of an undetectable astral projection which can find other Enchanted beings."

"I'm going home," said Darren.

Soleil stood up and held his hand out, "I'll give you a ride."

Darren knocked his hand away. "Back off—I feel like walking. Tyrell, I'll see you there." He stomped out of the cafe and slammed the door behind him. He swore out loud every few steps as he walked quickly along the trail. He still had to explain to people why Florence had been seen leaving his apartment the previous night, and nobody would believe a story about his son being involved with Genies. He increased the length of his stride to relieve his stress as he considered the situation. A lot of people in the gang were going to be angry with him, but his friends would stand by him. Mike always had his back, and Josh owed him for neglecting to tell him about storing drugs in the furniture he was transporting. The next few days were going to be rough, but he would get by with a little help from his friends, as well as from his family.

The sun was almost down when Darren arrived back in his neighborhood. He could feel people watching him. By now, the story had spread and had probably been twisted to make Darren seem more responsible for the shooting than he actually was. Fortunately, nobody attacked him. Darren walked into his apartment, never wishing so badly that the elevator worked. He entered the stairwell and walked the five floors to his apartment. On the way, he passed the group of people who usually hung out there. They were talking among themselves, but when they saw him, they stopped and stared at him as he walked by. Darren just passed quietly and avoided eye contact.

When he walked into his apartment, Tyrell and Atalissa were sitting on the couch. Atalissa looked at him and turned away quickly, but he noticed that her eyes were moist.

"He didn't make it," she said, holding a tissue to her eyes as she sniffed.

Darren sat next to her, and the three of them said nothing for a few minutes. "Have you told her about Soleil and the others?" he asked Tyrell.

"Yeah," said Tyrell. "Soleil and I summon-traveled here and gave mom a demonstration of what he could do. I filled her in about the Council and the rules after he left. She's all caught up."

"Jordan came by while you were gone," said Atalissa. "He wants to see you Wednesday at 6." They all looked at each other nervously.

"Look," said Darren, "I'll admit that we've never been in a situation more unusual than this one, but we have been through worse. We're going to be okay."

SOLEIL

The door was unlocked and the lights were on, but the blinds were closed. Soleil didn't want to open the cafe and risk having to deal with customers. He spent the morning and most of the afternoon thinking about the situation with Tyrell, Darren, and Flarence. When he finally found the energy to go downstairs, he still had trouble clearing them from his mind. Resorting to his usual distractions, he cleaned the restaurant. Every table was immaculate, the stove was spotless, and the inside of the refrigerator had been scrubbed. He grabbed the broom that was resting against a wall and turned on the radio. He sang along quietly with the songs he knew, but when Jethro Tull's "Aqualung" played through the light static, he couldn't contain himself. His head bobbed wildly, and during the chorus, he jumped onto one of the tables and shouted into the broomstick. He froze when the door opened and Lucy walked in. The two stared at each other awkwardly.

"Sorry," said Lucy, "I can come back some other time."

Soleil hopped off the table. "No, it's all right. Can I get you something to eat?"

"No, thanks. I'm sorry for bothering you. It's just that Tyrell was acting weird today, and I was wondering if you knew anything."

"His dad's in kind of a rough spot," said Soleil. "Has he told you anything about it?"

"No," said Lucy. "He was really distant today, and wasn't in school at all yesterday. It isn't like him. I tried talking to him after school, but he left in a hurry. I tried calling him, but he didn't pick up his phone. I figured he might have come here, so I thought I'd stop by."

Soleil leaned the broom against the wall. "Have you been to his house yet?"

"No," said Lucy. "I'd never tell him this, but his neighborhood kind of creeps me out. I guess I'll go there next though."

"Do you mind if I go with you? I noticed Tyrell's been acting differently too, and I'd like to talk to him." Lucy nodded and the two left the cafe together. Traveling with a summoning spell was quicker than driving, but Soleil took any chance he had to ride in a car. There wasn't time to take in the passing scenery when summon-traveling, but as he rode in the passenger's seat, he savored the view even when there was nothing but buildings and streetlights passing by.

The two didn't speak until they arrived at the apartment. Lucy dug through the change in the car's cup holder. "Don't bother," said Soleil, "no meter maids ever come down this block." Lucy ignored him, not wanting to risk getting a ticket. When they were inside, she instinctively went to the stairwell.

Even if Tyrell doesn't want it, I'm doing something about that elevator, thought Soleil. The two of them walked up the stairs and passed a group of people drinking beer and smoking cigarettes on the second floor. Soleil's Grateful Dead shirt and ponytail hair didn't look right next to the black and blue attire and buzz cuts worn by the stair gang. Lucy looked even more out of place, being the only girl present, and she received several leering looks as well as a whistle. Her hands grabbed the hem of her skirt as she climbed the stairs and she forced it down as far as it would go to hide as much of her legs as possible. Soleil helped by walking behind her, doing all he could to block the group's view as they ascended.

Yeah, I'm definitely fixing the elevator.

Atalissa answered when Soleil and Lucy reached Tyrell's apartment. "Hi," said Lucy. "Is Tyrell here? I kind of want to talk to him."

Atalissa looked at Soleil. "He didn't come home from school yet. I figured he was with you."

"That's all right," said Lucy. "Sorry to bother you. See you later." She turned to walk back to the stairs.

"Wait," said Soleil. He was silent for a moment, not knowing what to say. "Can I use your bathroom?" he muttered just loud enough for Atalissa to hear. She stepped aside and allowed him into the apartment.

He sat on the toilet and performed an astral projection, which was guided to a small, shaded house by a stretch of train tracks where Tyrell was tied to a chair. He wasn't bleeding, but his head was slumped into his chest. His eyes were closed, but he was definitely awake and struggling at the ropes binding his wrists to the chair. Soleil's projection saw two other people in the room, both wearing sweaters and work boots with pistols in holsters around their waists.

Soleil's projection floated around and took stock of the number of people in the house. He also looked for something to summon his body to. His projection found a kitchen with a refrigerator in the corner that would do nicely. The rest of the house was empty, but someone in a car in the front yard was talking on a cell phone. His projection returned to his body, and he stood up, flushed the toilet, and joined Lucy in the hallway outside the apartment. "We should go," he said. "I'm worried about Tyrell. He should have been home by now."

"There's a library near here," said Lucy. "He might have gone there to do his homework."

"Yeah, maybe," said Soleil. He turned to Atalissa and silently mouthed the word "no."

"I'll try calling him," said Atalissa as she went to her bedroom and got her cell phone from her bedside table. She walked back into the main room while dialing Tyrell's number, close enough to Soleil and Lucy for them to hear the ringing on the other end of the line.

"Come on," Soleil said after there was no answer, "let's try the library." The fear in Soleil's voice was enough to get Lucy's attention, and she followed him without question. The two raced down the stairs two at a time. Lucy didn't bother adjusting her skirt as they passed the people in the stairwell again. Once outside, Soleil let Lucy rush to her car. "You go ahead to the library. I know some other places he might have gone that I want to check. If I find him, I'll tell him to call you."

"What if I find him first?" Lucy called after him.

Soleil waved his arms in a gesture that said, "don't worry about it" and kept walking. He heard Lucy start her car. Once she had driven away, he turned down an alley, hid behind a garbage can, and summoned his way to the house. When his feet touched the floor in front of the refrigerator, the boards emitted a soft creaking sound, which made him freeze and listen for footsteps. Satisfied that his entrance had gone unnoticed, he explored the kitchen. Near the refrigerator was a stainless steel stove with a drawer on the bottom. Soleil opened it and found an assortment of cookware from which he selected a cast iron skillet.

Tyrell was being held in a cellar which looked as if it had been used for storage and had scratch marks all over the floor. Soleil opened the door leading down to it. The wooden staircase looked as old and loud as the kitchen floor. He kicked off from the top step and manipulated the gravitational pull on his body to make himself lighter than air, floating to the basement without touching any of the steps. To the left, he saw rows of wooden wine racks filled with bottles. On the right was an out-of-date washer and dryer next to a wooden door leading to the storage room where Tyrell was tied up. Soleil approached the door and pressed his ear against it.

He wasn't a doctor, but over the centuries, he had picked up some information on human physiology, including how ears perceive sounds. He used his powers to make the bones in his middle ear move more freely, making them more sensitive to soft noises. He also focused some of his magic on his olfactory nerves, which optimized his sense of smell. Without his seeing inside the room, his improved senses provided a good idea of the layout.

The two gunmen were standing side by side. One was talking about something that had happened between him and a girl at a bar, while the other laughed. The smell of the guns in their holsters hit Soleil's nose, rich with the scent of gunpowder and oil. The weapons were definitely loaded. In addition to the gunmen, Soleil smelled Tyrell's sweat and heard his heavy breathing. He even heard the rustling of the ropes as Tyrell tried to loosen the knots. He was sitting behind the gunmen, and Soleil guessed there were about eight yards between him and the chair Tyrell was tied to. Soleil pulled his face away from the door and allowed his senses to return to normal.

Knowing he'd likely need a distraction, he reached into the back pocket of his ripped jeans and pulled out a few coins before he turned his attention to the door's old, rusted hinges, forcing their temperature to rise. Soon, they were glowing bright red and beginning to melt, dripping slowly down the wooden frame. He held his breath, lifted the skillet to chest level, and gave the door a swift kick. It swung sideways and fell to the ground with a dull thud. The gunmen spun around and drew their weapons in a smooth motion. They paused for a breath, realized they didn't know the intruder, and opened fire.

Soleil crouched to make himself a smaller target and positioned the skillet in front of his head. As the two men pulled the triggers, he focused his magic on the bullets and summoned each one to the skillet. All the bullets struck the metal and left Soleil unharmed. He shifted the skillet's position to make it appear as if he was really judging the path of the bullets and using the cooking device as a shield. After a few seconds, the shooters ran out of bullets and the concussive bang of gunfire was replaced by soft clicks.

"I just want to talk," Soleil shouted as the shooters reloaded their guns. Behind them, Tyrell's head was up, and he was struggling harder than ever with the ropes, but he didn't speak. Soleil could have deconstructed the ropes from where he stood but wanted to maintain his focus on the bullets in case one of the men fired again. "He's just a kid," said Soleil to keep the shooters focused on him instead of Tyrell. "Let him go. Untie him now, and we'll walk out of here peacefully. We won't tell anyone about this."

"You're not his dad, are you?" one of the gunmen asked.

"No, I'm just a friend." As soon as he said it, three more shots rang out. Again, each bullet struck the skillet.

"Stop aiming for his shield," said one of the gunmen.

"I'm not aiming for it."

"Then you're the worst shot in the world." Two more bangs filled the room as Soleil ducked and two more bullets ricochet off the cast iron.

"Oh, you're one to talk."

"Everyone just calm down," said Soleil. "What do you want with him anyway?" He never heard an answer. There was a creaking behind him. He didn't need to turn to know that the man in the car had heard the shots and come inside the house to check it out. Without turning, Soleil focused on the wooden steps and deconstructed the top three. There was a yelp and a crash as the man behind him fell to the ground below. Soleil deconstructed the coins he had taken from his pocket and threw the metal shavings into the shooters' faces.

He ran into the room as the two gunmen attempted to rub the metal out of their eyes. He focused on the skillet and molded a section of its rim to form a sharp edge. "Hold still," Soleil said to Tyrell, who was still struggling to break free of the ropes. He held Tyrell's wrists with one hand and cut the ropes with the sharp edge of the skillet. Tyrell was freed from the chair before the two gunmen had recovered, and Soleil ran for the stairs, pulling Tyrell behind him by the wrist.

"Careful," he called back to Tyrell, "the stairs are broken." The two leaped over the gap.

"Why don't you just summon us out of here?"

"Soon. I want it to look like we ran." As soon as the front door was open, he spun around, grabbed Tyrell tightly by his shoulder, and performed a summoning spell. Once they were in Tyrell's room, Soleil let go of his shoulder and allowed him a moment to catch his breath. Soleil looked down and realized he was still holding the skillet. "Do you want this?"

Tyrell and Soleil went to the main room, where Atalissa and Darren were sitting on the couch. His mother ran to hug him, and Darren smiled and put a hand on his shoulder for a moment. Then the two broke away and turned to Soleil.

"What happened?" Darren asked as Soleil took a step back. He opened his mouth but didn't know where to begin. He didn't even know who had kidnapped Tyrell or why.

Tyrell walked to the couch and collapsed on the cushions. "Don't blame Soleil. None of us saw this coming. I got off the bus, and the next thing I knew some guys grabbed me and threw me in the back of a car. They took me to a house and tied me to a chair until Soleil showed up and got me out of there."

"They weren't holding you for ransom," said Atalissa. "They would have called us and demanded money or something if they were."

"Actually, they tried to call," Tyrell admitted sheepishly. "I was trying to get my phone out of my pocket when they came after me, but I dropped it."

"I'll find it," said Soleil.

Darren started pacing the room. "It was probably someone in the gang. By now, the story about J.J's brother being shot is all over the neighborhood, and the detail about Flarence being seen leaving our apartment before it happened has probably been highly emphasized. No doubt there are people around here blaming us for the death of a member."

"It wasn't anyone in the gang," said Tyrell. "For one thing, they weren't wearing the gang's colors. Also, all three of the kidnappers had guns. Gang violence is a problem here, but guns are expensive and usually cheaper methods are used, like baseball bats or switchblades. I don't know who those guys were, but they weren't gang members."

"So we have other people to worry about?" said Atalissa. "Who else has a reason to come after us?"

All three of them turned to Soleil who shook his head and crossed his arms defensively. "If those guys were Genies, they would have used magic, not guns."

"Flarence uses weapons," said Darren. "Maybe the guns had some magic in them. Maybe Flarence was the one who sent them. He made it very clear that he doesn't have a high opinion of us."

"Flarence didn't send them. With the exception of Claire, he doesn't have any friends, and trust me, those guys were not Genies. If they were, I wouldn't have been able to get Tyrell out of there so easily. I took one of them down by disintegrating some stairs. Any Genie would have seen that coming a mile away."

"So they weren't Genies or Slugs," said Tyrell. "Who else hates us?"

The four of them were silent as they thought about it.

"Do you want me to stay here tonight?" said Soleil. "You know, just in case there's more trouble."

"We'll be fine," said Darren. "You can go home now."

Soleil placed the skillet on the kitchen counter. "Whatever you say. I'll find your phone and have it back to you by tomorrow." He summoned his body back to his cafe.

FLARENCE

Flarence sat alone on the balcony of a hotel room with a newspaper in his hands. Most people were starting to leave for work, which caused the usual commotion of rushed drivers blaring their horns in the hope that excessive noise would make the car in front of them move faster. It made him smile. He craved early mornings in busy cities filled with the sound of thousands of people hurrying frantically through the streets in a panic.

In Flarence's line of work, he made his own hours, his office was wherever he wanted it to be, and his only deadline was finding his targets before the cops did. There was never any need to rush in the morning or fight traffic. It made him feel as if he was one step ahead of the world. In the distance, someone ran after a bus, shouting and waving his hands in the air as the driver ignored him and drove away. Flarence grinned and turned his attention back to the newspaper.

Claire had woken up a little earlier and was in the shower. After the conversation in the cafe on Monday, the two had wandered around until night, when they found a fairly crowded bar with low security. Flarence ordered drinks while Claire made small talk with people at the bar and picked their pockets. Each time she took someone's wallet, she would bring it to Flarence, who would take the money out and morph all the bills into twenties, fifties, and hundreds. Then Claire would sneak the wallet back into the owner's pocket. She had nimble hands, and in a few hours, the two could afford a long stay in any hotel they wanted. They chose a place downtown which had class but wasn't too expensive. The rooms were comfortable and clean, and breakfast was served every day.

After reserving their room, Claire had spent her entire Tuesday in Tyrell's neighborhood. Because of the circulating picture, they had decided Flarence should stay away from the gang's territory unless it was absolutely necessary. Claire returned to the hotel late that night with plenty of information, specifically where the gang leader,

Jordan, lived, and that his younger cousin, who everyone called Rookie, was his right-hand man.

More importantly, she learned that Tyrell was not involved in the gang, but Darren had joined at a young age. Based on what Claire told him, Florence was beginning to think he had judged Soleil's new master too quickly. In spite of growing up in a rough neighborhood and not having a lot of money, Tyrell had managed to keep his record clean. Also, the people Claire had spoken with had portrayed Darren as someone who cared deeply for his family and wanted what was best for his wife and son. Needing something to focus on other than his brother, Florence continued to scan the newspaper for stories about robberies or murders.

He was reading through a column about a missing college student when the water in the bathroom stopped running. A few minutes later, he heard Claire walk into the main room and turn on the television. Florence put the paper on the chair and went back inside, where Claire sat on the armrest of the couch watching a morning weather report. She had a towel wrapped around her, even though she was dressed in her chain-decorated shirt and leggings. After all the years of fighting criminals with Florence, the Razor Punk outfit had become a second skin, which she took off only to bathe. Her wardrobe consisted entirely of baggy jeans and oversized shirts. Florence couldn't recall the last time she had left the house without being secretly draped in chains, even in the summer, when he knew she must have been overheated. Fortunately, the report said the day was going to be on the cooler side, with heavy wind.

"Breakfast is being served downstairs in ten minutes," Claire said as Florence entered.

He collapsed on the couch next to her with a hand on his stomach. "I hope they have waffles," he said. "Are you planning on going to Jordan's territory after you eat?"

"Yup. The issue here is Darren's affiliation with the gang, right? Well, I'm going to do what I can to keep the gang away from Darren."

There was a knock. The two of them sat up straight and balled their hands into fists in unison. Claire slowly turned her head to Flarence and whispered "room service?"

"I didn't call anyone," he responded as he stood up and turned off the television. "I'll get it. It's probably a maid or someone with a survey of how service in this place has been."

Claire went to her bedroom, and Flarence heard her shuffling through her clothes. She also had a collection of pocket knives and a switchblade mixed in with her luggage, and was probably grabbing one of them in case their uninvited guest turned out not to be friendly. Flarence opened the door and found a tall, thin man standing in the hallway. He was standing straight and trying very hard to maintain his posture, but his face was flushed and his knees were trembling. He was dressed nicely but was sweating profusely, and his tie was crooked. Although his hair was short, it was tangled and sticking up in places, and while he forced a smile, his eyes were darting around as though he was afraid something was going to pounce from around a corner any minute. In the stranger's hands was a piece of paper and a small bottle of dark fluid, which he handed to Flarence.

"Th-these are for you."

Flarence poked his head out and looked down the hallway to see if anyone was watching but saw nobody. The stranger took a small step forward. "Please take them. I don't want any more trouble."

"Who is it?" said Claire as she came back into the room.

"He's either an escaped lunatic or the world's worst door-to-door salesman," said Flarence. He tried to return the paper and bottle, but the man backed away until he almost hit the wall. "Sir," said Flarence, "whatever this is about, you have the wrong address."

The man reached into his pocket and pulled out a photograph, which he held up next to Flarence's face. "No, it's you. The man said you'd be here. He said if I gave you the paper, my nephew wouldn't be harmed further."

Flarence snatched the photograph out of the man's hand and looked at it. It showed him walking out of a local fast food restaurant he had visited the previous day.

The stranger started blubbering. "He said he was a student. That's all he said. He had his face covered up. He was in my house the other day and had a baby with him. I was going to run, but then I realized that the baby was my nephew. He's only two and a half years old, and he was crying." The man rubbed his eyes. "The student had a grip on my nephew's arm. He squeezed tighter, and my nephew kept crying louder. He said he'd break my nephew's arm and a few other things if I went to the cops."

Flarence stood silently in the doorway, but Claire pushed past him and put a hand on the man's shoulder. By now, he had given up on trying to control himself, and tears streamed down his face.

"We'll find him," said Claire.

"I asked him why he was doing it," the man managed to say between gasps. He looked directly at Flarence. "He said it had nothing to do with me. He said it was all about you. He said to go to this room of this hotel and give the paper and ink to the man in the picture. He said as soon as you spilled the ink on the paper, he would let my nephew go. The man's insane! Who is he? Who are you?"

"I'm a private investigator," said Flarence. "The man you described sounds a little more dangerous than the people I usually deal with, but I guarantee that my associate and I will track him down. For now, don't worry about your nephew. No further harm will come to him. I'll spill the ink."

Claire walked back into the room, and Flarence closed the door. They waited until they heard the man walk away. They then went into the kitchen and laid the paper and ink bottle on the counter. "Aren't you going to spill it on the paper?" said Claire.

"Not yet." He gripped the photograph of himself tighter and closed his eyes. "I want to know more about our spy."

He performed a psychometry spell and saw the same stranger, this time standing near an alley in the middle of the day. Around the corner of a building was the man Flarence assumed was the Student.

He wore an outfit that resembled a school uniform, complete with a white button-up shirt, navy blue dress pants, and black shoes. His head was covered with a beanie cap pulled down to almost cover his eyes, which were hidden by dark sunglasses. The collar of his shirt was popped up, and the front was held together with three safety pins. His shirt was covered with notes that looked as if they had been written with a permanent marker, and consisted of equations and famous quotations. In a shirt pocket were a mechanical pencil, a red pen, a blue pen, and a black sharpie. He had on thin, white cotton gloves with notes scribbled on them.

"Now," said the Student. On his command, the stranger took a picture. The Student looked over his shoulder as the gray screen was replaced by the image of a restaurant. "That's him," said the Student. "The guy in the gray suit. He's the one I want you to see. You know what he looks like now, so you can't make any mistakes.

The man spun around. "This has gone too far You need to let him go right now."

"In an hour, I'll either let him go or kill him It depends on whether or not the job is done by then."

"One hour?" said the cameraman.

"Did you think I was going to give you time to go to the police?" said the Student. "Don't get help, don't approach him in public, and don't make a scene. Go straight to the hotel, give him the items, and get out. Then I'll let your nephew go free."

Flarence had seen enough. He broke his focus on the picture and brought his consciousness back to the hotel room with Claire. "The Student never touched the picture. He knew I would be able to perform a psychometry spell and see the person who took it. He's keeping his distance from us, ensuring I won't be able to make a connection to him with my magic." He suddenly noticed the smell of smoke in the room. He looked at the counter and saw that in the spot where the paper had been there was a pile of ashes instead.

Claire stared wide-eyed at Florence and looked embarrassed. "Don't be upset, but I poured the bottle of ink on the paper while you were doing your psychometry spell. When I did it, the ink smeared on the page and formed a message. It said 'We're Not Pleased,' and then the paper burst into flames." She looked around the room, her muscles taut. "A genie used their magic to smear the ink," she said. "Somehow they knew exactly when I spilled it and gave us the message. Do you think someone's astral projection is in this room?"

Florence improved his hearing and stood as still as possible. He could hear Claire breathing, the sound of a fly buzzing around a window, and the wind blowing outside, but there was something else. In the corner of the room, near the television the two of them had been watching, Florence could hear a faint, rhythmic beat.

Florence summoned a coffee pot from the kitchen to his body. He caught it and hurled it across the room to the spot the sound was coming from. Though he threw it hard, the pot never hit the wall but stopped in midair and fell to the floor. There was a faint swooshing sound from the corner of the room and a blast of light, as if there was a moment where a section of the wall ceased to exist. It happened so fast it was barely noticeable. The only reason Florence saw it was because he knew what to look for, having done it many times himself. The wall had disintegrated and almost immediately been reconstructed. Someone had just summoned themselves out of the room.

"What just happened?" said Claire.

"The Student is a Genie," said Florence, not taking his eyes off the wall. "He knows about my powers because he has the same abilities. That's why he didn't touch the picture. Avoiding contact with objects makes him more difficult for me to track. He came into our hotel room, probably while you were in the shower and I was on the balcony, became invisible, and watched us from the corner. I wouldn't have noticed him if I hadn't improved my senses."

"You said it took a lot of focus to maintain invisibility."

"It does. I have trouble staying invisible for more than a minute. That's why I only do it when I'm summon-traveling. Whoever this guy is, his control over his magic is unreal."

"The message on the paper said '*we're* not pleased,' which means he's not acting alone. Mohinaux said the Council of Elders could use their powers in ways you and Soleil can't. Maybe this is what he meant. Maybe this is how the Council watches you."

"There's no evidence that the Student is part of the Council," said Florence. "For all we know, this is Soleil trying to get in my head and convince me to believe in the Council and get out of private detective work."

"Do you really think Soleil would kidnap and harm a child?" asked Claire. Florence didn't have to answer. They both knew that Soleil would never harm a helpless child. Additionally, even with the disguise, Florence was confident he would be able to recognize his own father or brother.

"There's still no proof that the Student is part of the Council," said Florence. "I never assumed that dad, Soleil, and I were the only Genies in the world. The Student might be a rogue Genie who snapped."

"And why would he be after us?" said Claire.

"Don't be too quick to jump to conclusions," said Florence. "We don't have a lot of information on this guy. We don't know why he's doing this or what his endgame is. There might be more to it than us." He held his hand out and summoned Claire's scarf. "I'm going to talk to that guy the Student went after. I'll be able to find the person who took this picture without too much trouble. You stay focused on Soleil's new masters."

Claire took off her baggy green shirt and looped a corner of the scarf through a length of chain before leaving to collect a few more things from her room.

Florence tugged on the door to make sure it was locked, grabbed the photograph, and summoned his body to a bank vault where he had bought a safe deposit box under a pseudonym. He didn't feel like wasting time getting the key, so once there, he deconstructed the door to his safe deposit box and removed a Colt revolver which had been customized to suit his style. The hammer had been removed, leaving a small hole in the back. Attached to the top of the gun was a small metal canister designed to hold compressed gas connected to the bullet chambers by a U-shaped metal tube that was fed through the spot where the hammer had been.

Flarence had modified the pistol so that when he pressed the cylinder release, the gas canister would disconnect from its position and pop up. This let him use his magic to force air into the canister, and then flip it back into position easily once it was full. The projectiles were atmospheric as well. Flarence could isolate and condense water vapor in the air, force it into the cylinders of the pistol, form the droplets into cones, and freeze them solid. Icicles did not do nearly as much damage as an ordinary bullet but were much more resourceful. As long as there was humidity in the air, the gun would never run out of ammo, and when he shot someone, the charge would melt away, so a ballistics expert couldn't track him down. Firing stakes made of ice is what inspired Flarence to call his weapon the Stakehail Colt. Alone, it would not be enough to kill a Genie, but being armed with both his weapons made him more comfortable. He pocketed the Stakehail Colt and summoned his body back to the hotel.

—4—

DARREN

It was quarter to six when Darren stood outside Jordan's apartment. He had arrived early to mentally prepare himself. The last time Darren was there, Atalissa had been pregnant, and he'd come to explain that for his family's sake, he didn't want to be involved with any gang activities that could get him in trouble with the law. Jordan eventually conceded, but he'd been upset and had roughed Darren up. With the memories of the beating fresh in his mind, he quietly knocked.

Rookie answered and brought Darren inside. Jordan's apartment was nicer than Darren's. It had three bedrooms and used to be shared with his mother and sister, but his mother had died a few years ago, and his sister had moved into her own place. Now, one of the bedrooms was filled with files of information on members of the gang. Jordan prided himself on his high level of organization. Every time a person joined, he made a file with their name and kept close track of them. The other bedroom was where Jordan questioned people. As Darren suspected, Rookie led him into the interrogation room. He felt a knot form in his stomach as he walked in. A chair facing the only window in the room was positioned below a light bulb that was activated by a pull chain. The walls and ceiling were painted solid black.

Jordan, tall and muscular, stood between the window and the chair with his arms folded. A file of papers was clenched tightly between two knuckles. Unlike the pants of other gang members, his didn't sag, and his belt buckle was a metal rectangle with a scorpion molded into it. He nodded to the chair, and as Darren sat, he heard the door close. He didn't need to turn to know two other people were in the room. Jordan never conducted these kinds of meetings alone. There was a rumor that years ago, an interrogation had ended with a man Jordan was trying to beat up fighting back and over-powering him. Darren didn't know if it was true, and at the moment didn't care. He sat under the spotlight, holding eye contact with Jordan and focusing on keeping his breathing even.

"Let's get right down to business," said Jordan as he opened the file and flipped through the pages. "We met twelve years ago. You got a family now. Atalissa. Tyrell. Hot girl. Weak kid."

Darren fought the urge to interrupt. Tyrell wasn't popular in the neighborhood, since he stayed away from the gang. Kids picked on him all the time. They called him a wimp and a nerd. Tyrell had come home a few times with a black eye or a bloody nose. Darren hated seeing his son treated that way just because he was different.

"You were a salesman once," Jordan continued. "Not no more. Ain't bring me a good lump o' cash since you knocked up Atalissa." Jordan snapped the file shut and dropped it to the floor. "That's why you here. I looked past you gettin' off the street for a while. Lately, though, bad shit's been goin' down."

"I know," said Darren. "I heard that J.J's brother died from his gunshot wound."

"We'll get to that," said Jordan as he snapped his fingers. The door opened and closed as someone left the room. Darren kept his eyes locked on Jordan, too nervous to turn around. He wondered what could distract Jordan from a gang member being shot. In a few seconds, the door opened again. One of the guards stood in front of Darren holding a cardboard box.

"Tried to deal recently, though, didn't ya?" Jordan continued. "There was a bag in a desk goin' to a buyer in the suburbs. But then you let the cops search the car."

"I didn't know about the bag," said Darren. "Josh didn't tell me he put drugs in the furniture."

Jordan cracked his knuckles. "Not knowin' ain't no excuse. You got any idea who the buyer was? He used to be like us. Grew up on these streets, in this neighborhood. Saved every penny he made to put himself through law school. Now he got a big house, wife and kids. Never shook his taste for the hard stuff, though. Outta loyalty to the gang, he used us as his supplier. Obviously, he needs to keep his addictions quiet, and he didn't get where he is lettin' accidents slide. School taught him how to survive in the courthouse, but we taught him how to survive on the streets. If he thinks you told the cops you were on your way to his house, he'll bring a world of hurt down on all us."

"I didn't tell the cops anything," said Darren. "I was out of that station so fast they barely had any time to question me."

"Thanks for bringing that up," said Jordan. "How'd you break out so fast?" Darren turned his eyes to the floor. He couldn't think of any reasonable explanation. "Don't be shy," Jordan said after Darren remained silent. "I think it's great when one of us breaks out. Makes me feel like we one step ahead o' the cops. I'm not mad you broke out. Don't get me wrong; I'm mad at you for a lot o' things, but breaking out ain't one. Just tell me what you did."

"I'm sorry," said Darren, "but I can't explain that part."

Jordan flung his arms out wide in frustration. "You can't explain it? What does that even mean? Don't know how you did it?"

Darren shook his head.

"What, then, did someone do it for you?"

Darren silently cursed himself for not thinking of that explanation on his own. "Yes, exactly, someone did it for me. Someone broke me out of jail. I didn't ask them to do it, and I don't know what they did, but one minute I was in a cell and the next I was out."

"Who was it?" said Jordan.

Darren shook his head again. "I can't tell you." He needed to be vague. The fewer question asked about Soleil, the better.

Jordan grabbed Darren by the collar and pulled their faces close, almost lifting him out of the chair. "I want a name," he growled.

"I don't know him personally. He's a friend of my son." Jordan gripped Darren's collar tighter.

"I swear it's true," Darren sputtered. "Tyrell has a friend who's good at this kind of stuff. He just showed up and dragged me out of the cell. I didn't even know what happened until I was already home."

Jordan pushed Darren backward. He felt the front two legs of the chair leave the ground as it tipped back, but he shifted weight to keep it from falling over.

"You honestly expect me to believe that?" Jordan shouted. "I know 'bout your son. He's smart, but he don't got no friends. He spends all day in his room reading and doing homework. No way he knows a guy who does jailbreaks."

Darren leaned forward and opened his mouth to swear that he was telling the truth but was interrupted as Jordan punched him in the mouth. There wasn't a lot in it, but it was enough to shut Darren up.

"Let's move on," said Jordan. "That shooting in the stairs. J.J. also went to the hospital 'cause his hand was hurt. The docs used a lot of technical terms, but what I understood was that his hand was exposed to extreme heat. There something you want to tell me about that?"

"I didn't know anything about that until Brodie came knocking on my door in the middle of the night. I had nothing to do with it," said Darren.

Jordan's hands curled into fists, and he took a step toward Darren. "The man who attacked the group in the stairs was seen leaving your apartment. Brodie, J.J., and all those guys spend all day in that stairwell drinking, smoking, and throwing dice. They get there early in the morning, and they don't usually leave until late at night. They're like living security cameras. They remember everyone they see entering and leaving the building. Nobody saw the guy coming in, but everyone saw him going out. That means in order for you not to know he was in the apartment, he woulda had to sneak in very early in the morning, before anyone was gathering in the stairs, hide in your apartment the entire day, and leave late at night when you were asleep."

"You said it yourself, those guys are usually smoking and drinking," said Darren. "They're not the most reliable resources."

"True," said Jordan, "they like to party, but there's never enough beer and pot to go around, so any moment of any day, there's usually at least one sober person. I got no problem taking their word."

"Right, their word," said Darren. "That's all this is, their word against mine. I'm telling you, that guy found a way to sneak into the apartment unnoticed. He tried to sneak out but wasn't so lucky. Believe me; I had no idea he was in the apartment and had nothing to do with anyone getting shot."

Jordan held out his hand and the man beside him handed him the box. Jordan opened it and dropped it in Darren's lap. Inside were scraps of metal. Darren mentally pieced the shards together and realized he was looking at the remains of a gun.

Jordan tapped the side of the box. "That's the gun J.J. used that night. The one that shot his brother. The guys in the stairs say it malfunctioned. I've heard of guns malfunctioning before, but it usually means the gun jammed. Look at that gun. The damn thing blew up. That ain't no malfunction I ever heard of. I'm betting it was sabotaged. Now, ain't there someone we know of who has a thing for machines? Ain't there been stories going 'round 'bout a man with a doorknob strapped to his arm?"

Darren put the box beside his feet. "I don't see what this has to do with me. An exploding gun isn't common, but this doesn't link me to any of the events on the stairwell."

"Don't J.J. live near you?"

"We live on the same floor," said Darren. "His room is at the end of the hall."

"And you been to his room before," said Jordan. "You know where he keeps his gun." It wasn't a question. Darren and J.J. had been friends for a long time. Darren also remembered when J.J. had bought his first gun. In hindsight, he probably was exposed to firearms too early and didn't understand the responsibilities that came with them. He didn't keep the gun hidden, or even in a locked container. There was a table by his bed where it lay while he slept. He never left his apartment without jamming the gun in the back of his pants, and was never shy about pulling it out during an argument.

"Okay," said Darren, "we live near each other, but that doesn't mean I sabotaged his gun."

"I'm not so sure about that," said Jordan. "It wouldn't be too difficult for you to mess with his gun, or even replace it with a bad one when he wasn't looking."

"I would never have risked the life of a gang member," said Darren. "We take care of our own. You taught me that."

"Are you still one of us?" said Jordan.

"I've been one of you for years," said Darren. "How can you accuse me of being disloyal?"

"I'm accusing you of being used," said Jordan. "Here's what I think's happening. The man who been attacking us upped his game. Now, instead of using that little gizmo of his, he's found a way to use our own weapons against us. I don't know what we ever did to him, but for that to work, he'd need a way to get into our territory. Lucky for him, there just so happens to be a member who's maybe a little too much of a family man for his own good. To stay close to your family, you avoided risky gang activities, but an even better option would be if the gang was taken out of the picture completely. I think this vigilante made you a deal. I think he promised that your family would be kept safe if you helped him."

"I would never do that," said Darren. "This gang has made me the man I am today. I have friends here. This neighborhood is my home. I like it here. I like the way things work."

"I want to believe you," said Jordan, "I really do, but I need more than your word on this." He turned to the two guards in the room. "Search his apartment. If his wife won't let you in, break down the door. Look under his couch, look in his pillowcases, see if there're any loose floorboards and tear 'em up if there are. I want to know how many dishes he has and what food's in his fridge. Then question Atalissa and Tyrell. Find out what they know 'bout the man who was seen leaving the apartment that night. Get every cell phone in the house and bring 'em to me so I can check the messages." He turned to Darren. "If they find anything suspicious, then as far as I'm concerned, you're working with an enemy, and I'll treat you like one."

"What do you think you're going to find?" said Darren.

"The man in question is resourceful and violent. If you're working with him, I have a hunch he'd be using your apartment to store supplies. If I was planning a series of attacks on a gang, I'd stash some of my arsenal on their turf." The door opened, and the two men left. Darren tried to follow them, but Jordan grabbed his shoulder and spun him back around. "You stay here," he said. He waited while Darren sat back down and then turned to Rookie. "Tell him about what happened earlier today."

Rookie had looked confident before, but now that he was put on the spot, he slouched and began scratching his wrist. "Someone got all up in my business. I didn't see her face, it was covered up, and she had a lot of knives on her. Said she was Razor Punk. Had her name written on her hands."

"Darren, you know 'bout 'er?" Jordan interrupted.

Darren stared blankly at Rookie, and then looked to Jordan. "I've never seen her before in my life."

"Well, apparently you've met," said Jordan. He looked at Rookie and moved his hand in a circular motion, giving him permission to continue his story.

"She had a message," said Rookie. "She said, 'Darren's off limits.' She had one of her knives against my neck when she said it. She didn't hurt me, though."

Jordan cracked his knuckles. "If you value your life, you'll tell me who she is and why she's using Rookie to tell me what I can and can't do."

"I swear," said Darren, "I've never met any girl who hides her face and calls herself Razor Punk."

Jordan moved behind the chair. Darren tensed, expecting a blow to the back of his head, but instead, he just heard footsteps, and soon Jordan was in front of the chair again, his fingers rubbing his chin.

"Here's the thing, Darren. In order to do what I do, I need to know details about people. Information, accurate information, is vital."

"I know," said Darren.

"Sure, you know," said Jordan, "but I don't think you get it. When I asked you how you could be so careless on a drug deal and get yourself arrested, you said you didn't know about the drugs. I asked you for the details on how you broke out of prison, and you told me you don't know how your son's friend did it. I asked you how the man responsible for the death of J.J.'s brother got into your apartment, and you told me you don't know." He walked close to the chair, his hands balled into fists and his elbows bent. "Nothing irritates me more than people using incompetence as an excuse for their screw-ups, and you've done it three times. Now I'm gonna to ask you again. Who's Razor Punk? And if you tell me you don't know, I'm gonna lose it."

Darren sat in silence for a moment while Jordan tapped his foot impatiently. His mind raced. Rookie had said he was approached by a woman who knew Darren by name. He thought back to the conversation at Soleil's Cafe when Flarence had walked in with a woman. He assumed she was Razor Punk. It was the only explanation he could think of, but he couldn't remember her name. His only option was to explain what he knew slowly and hope Jordan would be patient enough to hear him out. "You're right," said Darren, "my performance has been less than satisfactory lately, and I'm sorry about that."

"I asked you about Razor Punk," said Jordan.

"I know," said Darren, "and I'm sorry that I don't have an adequate amount of information on that particular subject."

"You telling me you don't know?" said Jordan.

"Well, I don't know ..." Darren started, but was cut off as Jordan kicked him hard enough to make the chair fall backward. Darren rolled across the room, clutching his chest with one hand and his head with the other. There was another surge of pain as Jordan delivered another kick to Darren's ribs, which made him flip over onto his back. "For sure," Darren called out as he rolled to his side. "I don't know for sure. I think I have an idea." He put his hand flat on the floor and pushed himself slowly to his feet. Jordan didn't attack again. Darren did his best to stand straight, but the pain made him hunch. "Look," he said slowly, "I met someone recently. I only saw her for a moment. We're not close friends or anything, but she's the only person who comes to mind."

"I want a name," said Jordan.

Damn, thought Darren. His mind flashed back to the cafe as he desperately tried to visualize the encounter. He was sure he had heard her name. It began with a K: Katy, Kirsten, Katherine. No, maybe it began with a C: Constance, Candice, Carrie … he felt like he was getting closer, but his mind wasn't working fast enough. Jordan grabbed him by the collar again.

"Don't know?" said Jordan.

"Um," said Darren. Jordan stepped sideways, dragging Darren across the room with him, and slammed him into the wall. Jordan pulled him back, stopped short, and then put all his weight forward. "You know now?" he said as he drove Darren into the wall again.

"It began with a C," Darren thought out loud. "I'm sure it began with a C." Jordan stopped his assault but held Darren firmly. "It was definitely a C name. Candy, Charity, Clarence, wait, Cl…that's it, it started with Cl. Clarity … Clar … Claire! That's it, it was Claire!"

Jordan released his grip but didn't move away from Darren. "I think we're getting somewhere," he said. "We have a first name. Now I want details. Give me a description."

"She's probably somewhere in her early 30s," said Darren as he rubbed his neck and collarbone. "She's about my height, with dark hair. She has a grunge look to her. When I saw her, she was wearing flannel and jeans."

"That's pretty general, but I'll take it," said Jordan. "It's something to look for, and it's the most I've gotten out o' you today. Don't stop now. Tell me where you two met."

Darren took a few deep breaths. He relaxed a little, feeling that Jordan was starting to calm down. "The first time I saw her was a few days ago at a place called Soleil's Cafe. It's not too far from here. I can take you there if you want, but I don't know how often she goes there. I know it's not much to go on, but the owner might have some information."

"Soleil's Cafe?" said Jordan. "Never heard o' it. Soleil. That the owner's name?" Darren nodded. He didn't feel right telling Jordan about him, but the worst that could happen was Jordan would send someone to ask questions about Claire, and as long as Soleil answered truthfully and didn't do anything stupid, he would be fine.

"Soleil. That's a weird name," continued Jordan. "I'll send some people out there right away to find out what he knows about Claire. What's her relation to the other guy?"

"Other guy?" said Darren. Jordan placed his palm on Darren's face and slammed his head against the wall. Darren staggered for a moment, momentarily dizzy from the impact, but stayed upright.

"Yeah, the other guy," said Jordan. "Two mysterious people show up out of nowhere and attack us. I'll bet my life that there's a connection between Claire and the guy in the picture."

"The other guy's name is Flarence," said Darren, "and yes, he's the man whose picture has been getting passed around the neighborhood."

"So you do know him," said Jordan.

"He was in the cafe with Claire," said Darren. "That was the only time I saw him. I don't have any personal connection with him, and I have no idea what he was doing in my apartment that night."

"So he was the person who was seen leaving your apartment," said Jordan.

Darren had assumed that Jordan had come to that conclusion on his own and was trying to get in Darren's head, making him feel that he had revealed something without realizing it. "Yeah, he's the one who was seen leaving my apartment, but he's no friend of mine. He never offered me anything. I'm not working with him, and I'm definitely not working against you. I'm sorry I didn't tell you about him earlier."

"I'm sorry this was what it took to get the information out of you," said Jordan.

Darren thought about Atalissa and Tyrell, and the two people who were on their way to search the apartment and interrogate them. "Am I free to go?"

Jordan walked to the door and opened it for him. "Sure, get outta here."

Darren hesitated. "Are we good now?"

"Not even close," said Jordan.

"I answered your questions," said Darren. "I told you about Flarence and that I'm not working with him."

"And I'd like to believe you," said Jordan, "but let's wait and see what the search of your apartment brings. Really, though, if you want to regain my trust, you'll bring Flarence here and let me question him myself. Either him or Razor Punk."

"I have no idea where they live. I just saw them by chance a few days ago. Jordan, I need my reputation restored. I don't like the way people have been looking at me lately."

"The people in this 'hood should be the least of your concerns," said Jordan. "I've been trying to get in touch with Martin, but haven't had any luck so far. That's not a good sign." Darren stared at Jordan for a moment, confused. "Martin was the one buying the crack you never delivered. When you never showed up, he called me. That was after you were caught. He knows what happened. Like I said earlier, that guy could be trouble. He got connections, money, and a lot to lose. I wouldn't put it past him to pay someone to come into our territory to shoot you down if he thinks you mentioned his name to the cops."

"But I didn't mention his name to the cops!" said Darren.

"Great," said Jordan, "but Martin don't know that, and I ain't been able to get in touch with him since you broke outta jail."

"You're going to give me protection, right?"

"If you want protection, you gotta help us protect ourselves. Find Flarence and Razor Punk. Bring 'em to me. Then we'll talk."

"I already told you I don't know where to find them."

"Then you'd better hope your luck picks up soon," said Jordan. He made a motion for Darren to leave.

Darren made his way back to the apartment as fast as he could. He was a block away when a stranger bumped into him hard, using his shoulder to knock Darren off balance.

"Hey, watch it," shouted Darren as he got up.

"Funny," said the pusher, "I was about to say the same thing to you."

Darren didn't recognize him at first because he was out of uniform but remembered him once he got a good look at the man's face and his calm but serious expression. It was Officer Tymbir. He stood with his hands on his hips, wearing a red cotton shirt and blue jeans. A pair of sunglasses hid his eyes, but Darren could still feel their intensity.

"I don't know how you did it," said Tymbir. "I'll admit you have talent. You manipulated the surveillance footage in a way I never thought possible. You destroyed the paperwork and got out of the police station without being seen. We didn't even find your finger-prints on the drugs."

"That's because I never touched those drugs," Darren blurted. "You arrested the wrong guy. That bag wasn't mine."

"Whatever," said Tymbir. "I'm willing to forget about the drug incident. There's nothing I can do with it anymore. But I'm keeping my eye on you. If you so much as jaywalk, I'm taking you in, and next time I have you in custody, I'm not leaving your side for a second. I'll even sit in the cell with you if I think you're acting suspicious. Whatever you pulled last time, you'll never pull it off again."

Tymbir turned on his heel and walked away, leaving Darren alone and speechless on the sidewalk. Someone had tried to kidnap his son, Martin was out to get him, Florence was out to get everybody, and now a cop was holding a grudge against him. He wondered if there was any possible way for the situation to get worse.

SOLEIL

Soleil walked down the vacant street toward the house where he had saved Tyrell two days ago. He was hesitant about returning to the house, worried he might get into another violent situation, but Tyrell had invoked his wish privileges and asked Soleil to investigate. On his way to the house, he had also been able to recover Tyrell's phone.

It was a bright afternoon with almost no clouds. October would arrive soon, and, on cue, the leaves were changing color and it was just chilly enough to require a light jacket. As he walked, he warmed the wind that blew against his exposed skin. He supposed it would have been easier to patch up his clothes, but warming air didn't take much effort, and he liked the holes-in-the-knees look.

He stopped walking half a block from the house and got a good look at it from a distance. It was near a set of railroad tracks on a dead-end street. The three houses on each side of the block looked abandoned. There were no cars outside, and all the lights were off. He guessed the residents had moved out when the passing trains became too loud to bear.

Soleil approached the house where Tyrell had been held. The front yard's small square of grass was brown and looked as if it hadn't been watered or mowed for a long time. The front windows were low with wooden shutters that swayed in the wind. The panes were filthy and cracked. The house was brick and looked like the kind a five-year-old would draw a picture of with crayons. It had two windows upstairs, two downstairs, and a wooden front door. The paint on the window sills had eroded until only small chips remained on the rotten wood. His projection had searched the house before he'd walked there and found it to be empty, but there was no telling if someone had arrived while he was on the way. He approached quietly, pulled back the shutter on one of the windows, and peered through the dirty glass.

He guessed that he was looking at what used to be a living room, but it was in the same condition as the front yard. There was no dust or cobwebs, but it didn't look like it had been taken care of very well. Like the windows, the walls had only remnants of paint clinging to them. The important thing was that the room was empty. He focused on the window and deconstructed the panes, followed by the wooden frame. He placed his hands on the window ledge and hoisted himself over it, landing gracefully on the wooden floor. He reconstructed the window as he took a closer look at the room and listened for signs of anyone else in the house. He didn't hear footsteps or creaking floorboards and decided he was alone. He looked at the window to make sure it was exactly as he had found it. He had reconstructed it perfectly, down to the grime and smudges that had been there before. Soleil also looked down and was relieved to find there was no dust for him to leave footprints. He started to walk out of the room but then paused.

There was absolutely no dust on the floor. As he looked around, he noticed that there were no paint chips on the floor either. Did someone live in this house or not? Someone had let the paint chip off the walls, weeds take over the yard, and the wooden window frames rot away, but had taken the time to sweep the floor. He improved his senses so that if people were in the house, he'd be able to hear their heartbeat and smell their sweat, but nobody was there but him. He let his senses return to normal and continued to explore.

The paint on the front door was also chipped and the wood looked old, but the three locks were new. Someone had been in the house recently, and wanted to keep it secure. Soleil wandered through the house and found the kitchen he had summoned his body to when he saved Tyrell. He approached the stove and tried to turn it on, but nothing happened. There was no hiss of gas or click of ignition. He tried all the burners; none of them worked. The refrigerator was silent and empty. When he opened the freezer, it was warm as well. There wasn't even any ice buildup in it. When Soleil tried to turn on the faucet at the kitchen sink on the opposite wall, there was a delay and a gurgling sound as water struggled to make its way through the pipes. When it finally flowed, it was a sickening dark brown. Who would triple lock the door to a house filled with inactive appliances and terrible plumbing?

Soleil continued exploring rooms. He knew where the basement stairs were but didn't want to go down there just yet. There wasn't much in the cellar other than the storage room. Fortunately, the house was small, and it didn't take long to find the stairs to the second floor. There he found a single narrow hallway, two bedrooms, and a bathroom. He walked into one of the bedrooms, which was empty except for a bed and wardrobe. The furniture in the other was the worst in the house, and a thin layer of dust covered the sheets and frame. Soleil knelt to one knee and placed a hand on the bottom of the bed, not wanting to leave a visible print in the dust for someone to find. He activated his psychometry and soon could see the last people to sleep in the bed: two teen-agers engaged in highly intimate activities. He pulled his hand away. If he had focused harder and longer, he could have gathered the names of the people he'd seen, as well as how old they were and what year they had used it, but he didn't want to look at that image again. He turned his attention to the wardrobe, and realized he should have examined it first. It was made of carved wood, with a curving wave pattern at the top. Unlike the bed, it was not covered with dust. In fact, Soleil thought it was the one piece of furniture in the house that had been taken care of. He deconstructed the doors, and took a step back after seeing what was inside.

It was full of guns, most of them attached to the back and side walls, hanging on racks. There were pistols, shotguns, and rifles. All of them were black and sleek and reflected the light coming in the window as if they had recently been cleaned, and possibly even recently used. Soleil reconstructed the wardrobe door and went to the other bedroom to find a single dusty bed and a clean wardrobe, which was also filled with firearms. Soleil walked to the bed and looked underneath to find a row of three pistols and three boxes of bullets attached to the springs with Velcro straps. He wandered through the house and found more weapons. He went back to the kitchen and opened the cupboards, which were full of more boxes of bullets and more pistols, all different sizes and models. He opened the cabinet at the bottom of the stove, removed the cookware, and found a sawed-off shotgun under the skillets. He went back to the living room and looked under the couch; a sniper rifle was there. In the basement, he took a closer look at the wine racks. He screwed off the top of one bottle and held it under his nose, waving his hand over the top to stir the vapors. It didn't smell like wine. Soleil had a guess about what was in the bottles, and went out the basement door to the back yard to confirm it.

After dealing with the door's many locks, he found the yard was empty. But as he looked around, he saw that it was combined with the yards of the other two houses on the block, with no fences between them. Together, they merged to form a long stretch of dead grass with a cluster of posts at the end opposite. When he went over to them, he saw that there were eight stainless steel posts arranged in a straight line. Behind them, a tall wooden board was covered with bullet holes. On the ground around the posts were shards of glass and aluminum beer cans with holes in them. It seemed the three yards had been combined to form a shooting range, and judging by the amount of garbage on the ground, it was used frequently. Soleil opened the wine bottle and poured some of its contents on the top of a post, then forced the temperature to rise. He didn't have to heat it much before the fluid burst into fire and burned quickly, its flames stretching high in the air. Soleil let it burn out, then put the bottle back where he'd found it in the cellar.

The other houses on the block were probably loaded with guns and wine bottles filled with flammable liquid as well. It seemed as if someone, or more likely a group of people, was preparing for a war. Soleil went back up to the wardrobes, placed a hand on each gun, and saw who had fired it last. A shotgun had been last fired by a man named Oliver Cash, one of the rifles was recently held by Barry Todd, and a pistol under the bed was used by Clark Greyson. Soleil could see all their faces but didn't know any of them, which was hardly surprising, considering he had been cooped up in his cafe so long. For once, he thought Flarence had it right about getting out and becoming acquainted with the criminal underground. Soleil decided there was nothing more he could learn at the house, and summoned his body to the bed in the upper level of his cafe where Tyrell had agreed to meet him.

The ground floor of the cafe was the restaurant, but above it were his living quarters. Other than the bed, his room had a dresser and a rack with his two coats: a thin one for fall and the thicker one stuffed with goose feathers. He didn't need the coats but wore them to fit in among other people when he went out in the winter. Soleil also had a variety of houseplants—three bonsai, an air plant, a cactus, a philodendron, and a shamrock—nourished by light from windows in all the walls and the ceiling. He took a deep breath to enjoy the fresh plant-filtered air before going downstairs to see if Tyrell was there yet. When he approached the door, he heard voices—Tyrell and Claire—and it sounded like they were arguing.

"What were you thinking?" said Tyrell.

"We're not used to second encounters," said Claire. "Florence and I usually attack quickly and then leave. This is the first time we've ever stuck around to witness how people react to our threats. We had no way of knowing what Jordan would do to Darren or how he would perceive our actions."

"What's going on?" said Soleil as he descended the stairs.

"I think I might have made a mistake," said Claire.

"You think you might have made a mistake?" repeated Tyrell. "You threatened Rookie and mentioned my dad's name! Did you really think he wouldn't tell Jordan about that? As far as Jordan's concerned, dad was involved with an attack on the gang."

"It was an error in judgment on our part, and Florence and I are both sorry," said Claire. "We'll be more careful in the future, and try to do what we can to make the situation better."

"If you want to make it better, you'll stay away from me and my family," said Tyrell. "We don't need or want your kind of help." He turned to Soleil, who was still standing on the stairs. "Did you find anything interesting at the house?"

"Interesting sums it up pretty nicely, although confusing and downright disturbing are the words I'd use. The place is an armory, and it's not just the one house. There are others on the block, and they're all packed with guns and explosives. Do you know anyone who would want to keep a secret emergency supply of firearms?"

"I live in the middle of a gang's territory," said Tyrell. "Everyone around there wants a gun."

"But you said most people can't afford them," said Soleil. "And I'm not just talking about Glocks. There's some really heavy-duty gear in there. It's the kind of stuff I've only seen in movies."

"Can you take me there?" said Claire. Tyrell shot her an annoyed look, but she kept her focus on Soleil. "I can probably help. I'm accustomed to dealing with weird, violent people."

Soleil shrugged. "I guess it couldn't hurt for you to take a look." He held his hands out, offering his left to Tyrell and his right to Claire. Tyrell grabbed on instantly, but Claire took a moment to put her gear on. She reached under her shirt and removed the scarf from the chains. "Nobody's going to walk in on us," said Soleil as she wrapped it around her face and adjusted it so the zigzag pattern of razor blades was centered. "I was just there. The place is empty."

"I always wear this when I'm working," said Claire as she slipped on leather gloves from the deep pockets of her jeans. Tyrell's jaw dropped when she pulled a needle from each sleeve and stuck them in her hair. She didn't take off her sweater to reveal the T-shirt with chains, but Soleil knew she was wearing it underneath.

"It's complicated," she said to Tyrell as she took Soleil's other hand.

In the upstairs bedroom of the house, Soleil didn't waste any time before turning the doors of the wardrobe to sawdust and giving his companions a clear look at the contents. Tyrell froze but Claire walked up get a closer look.

"You weren't lying," she said. "These are the kinds of things the police keep locked up in their stations. They only take them out in emergencies."

"There's more under the bed," said Soleil. Claire slid under the mattress. The sound of tearing Velcro filled the room, and Claire emerged holding one of the small, black pistols. She examined it and made sure it wasn't loaded, held it up, and pointed it at a wall to test its weight. The gun was an attractive addition to the rest of her outfit. It made her look ten times more dangerous, and for a moment, even Soleil felt unsafe being in the room with her. She pulled the grip back, held it for a moment, and let it slide back into place with a metallic ping. "Flarence and I have been dealing with criminals for years," she said as she put the gun back under the bed, "but I usually don't see people with things like these. Do you have any idea who owns them?"

"I got some names," said Soleil, "but none I recognize."

"Run through them," said Tyrell. "All of them. Maybe I'll know one."

Soleil pointed to the guns he'd felt. Tyrell didn't know the users. Then Soleil placed his hands on other guns and named the people who had fired them, but Tyrell kept shaking his head. Claire didn't recognize any of the names either. They had no success going through the guns in the other room either until Soleil touched a shotgun. "Kevin Tymbir?"

Tyrell started shaking his head again but then paused. "Wait, did you say Tymbir? My dad mentioned that name last night. He said the cop who arrested him was out to get him." Soleil took the shotgun out of the wardrobe and handed it to Claire. Like the pistol, she opened it to make sure it was unloaded before examining it more closely.

"Um, Claire," said Tyrell.

"Razor Punk," said Claire. "When I'm wearing the scarf and gloves, call me Razor Punk."

"Okay, well, could you put that back, Razor Punk? You're making me kind of nervous."

"I thought you grew up in gang territory," she said. "Don't be such a wimp. I'm not pointing it at you, and it's not even loaded. Anyway, this is a hunting gun and it's not difficult to get." She handed it back to Soleil. "What can you find out about Tymbir?"

Soleil gripped it tightly as the scene formed in his mind. He described what he was seeing out loud as it was happening.

"It's about two weeks ago. Kevin's in the back yard of this house, standing in front of the plank of wood behind the target posts where people position their beer cans. You haven't seen those yet. I'll show you them later. Tymbir is standing in front of that board with the sawed-off shotgun. The gun is loaded. He's not pointing it at the board. It looks like he's waiting for something. Some people are approaching him. They're hauling something large behind them. It's an animal . . . a deer . . . but it's dead. There are hooks in the deer, and chains bolted to the hooks. Tymbir's friends are using the chains to drag the dead deer to the wooden board. They're standing it upright. Four people are under the deer, holding it so it looks like its standing up. Someone else is holding the chains against the wooden board, and another person is using a drill to bolt the chains in place. There are hooks and chains in the deer's neck as well, and they're also being bolted to the board. From a distance, it makes the deer appear to be alive and well, even though its eyes are cloudy and blank. The group backs away from the deer. Tymbir cocks the shotgun and approaches it. The surrounding people are cheering him on. He points the shotgun at the deer's ribs and presses the barrel into its hair. He doesn't pull the trigger. He's waiting. His friends are chanting his name loudly. A train is approaching. When it's passing as close as possible to the house, Tymbir fires the gun. There's a bright flash but the train drowns out the sound. The shell blows off a huge chunk of the deer's body. It's nearly been blasted in half. Tymbir's friends are going nuts. They're shouting and drinking, cheering the carnage. Tymbir isn't done. He cocks the gun again. He's pointing it directly at the deer's skull . . ." Soleil broke his connection and brought himself back to the room with Tyrell and Claire. "I really don't want to see that," he said as he placed the gun back in the wardrobe rack. He reconstructed it and led them to the back yard to show them the shooting posts and wooden board.

"There's no blood on the board," said Tyrell.

"It was two weeks ago," said Soleil. "They probably replaced it."

He bent down and pushed the soil around with his fingers. He pulled up a small white fragment that at first appeared to be a rock but which they realized was too brittle. It was a piece of bone from the deer. They looked closer and noticed clumps of fur that had been left in the soil as well. "So Tymbir is a cop who has a fetish for guns and blood."

"And he's involved with the people who kidnapped me," said Tyrell. "He might even be the one in charge."

"You don't think everyone here is a cop, do you?" said Soleil. "Is it possible that this is a secret hangout for police officers who steal guns from their station and fire them at beer cans and dead animals to blow off steam?

"Police stations are more secure than that," said Claire. "Unless the entire force is in on this, there's no way a heavy duty firearm could disappear from storage and end up here, let alone enough to fill two wardrobes. But there are other ways for people to get their hands on those kinds of guns."

"That doesn't explain why three of these guys kidnapped me the other day," said Tyrell. "I'll talk to my dad tonight and see what he knows about Tymbir."

Soleil looked at Claire. "You should talk to Flarence about this as well. I'm sure he'll have an opinion about it."

"Flarence is a little preoccupied at the moment," said Claire. "Besides, I don't think Darren would be particularly thrilled to be working with him."

"Good point," said Soleil as he held his hand out to her. "Can I give you a lift anywhere?"

"Thanks, but I'd rather look around the houses a little more."

"You can't deconstruct the doors," said Soleil.

She walked past him toward the house. "There are other ways to get inside."

"Sorry," said Soleil. "I guess I'm accustomed to doing things my way." He held out his hand to Tyrell, who gripped it tightly.

"Bye, Razor Punk," Tyrell said as he and Soleil disappeared.

FLARENCE

It was Friday morning, and Flarence was alone in his hotel room, standing over the stove in his forest green cotton pajamas and scooping coffee grounds into a copper pot half full of water. As it simmered and turned black, he gathered his clothes for the day.

After receiving the note and finding out about the Student, he decided it would be best to give the victim time to calm down, so he spent Thursday gathering information about him. He used his psychometry on the picture and found that the man who'd delivered it was named Alex Hammerson and lived in Andersonville. Flarence had spent the previous day following him in the hope the Student would contact him again. But no such luck. Alex left his house seven thirty in the morning to work at an electronics store and went straight home afterward. Flarence had gone into the store and eavesdropped on some of his conversations with the customers. Alex seemed like a nice, normal guy who knew about computers and televisions and had good people skills. At least, Flarence felt, he'd have good people skills on a regular day. Yesterday, he had seemed distracted and nervous. He kept a brave face when talking to people but fidgeted when he thought no one was looking, which Flarence took as a sign that his nephew was still missing or had been returned in poor condition and was still recovering. That meant his meeting with Alex was going to be anything but pleasant. Getting through the day depended on his morning coffee.

Flarence slipped out of his pajamas and into his regular attire, concealing both the Wrist Cannon and the Stakehail Colt in different pockets of his suit jacket. He didn't anticipate using them when visiting Hammerson, but with the Student's location unknown, he felt more comfortable carrying his weapons at all times. He hoped Alex wouldn't freak out too much when they met.

Flarence decided to go to Andersonville the old-fashioned way and took a train there. When the two met, he wanted Alex to think he was just an ordinary person, and traveling in a non-magical manner helped him get into character. As he rode the train, he had to pay attention to the loaded Stakehail Colt in his pocket. With the extra heat radiated by the other people on the train, the icicles melted quickly, and Florence had to reform and refreeze them before they formed a damp spot on his clothes. It was annoying, but he felt better knowing that the gun was ready to be fired at a moment's notice. At half-past eleven, the train arrived at town; it would take him about fifteen minutes to walk to the store, which would coincide with Alex's lunch break. On his way there, he noticed that most people he passed were wearing thin jackets, which reminded him that it was October and the temperatures were starting to drop. The next time he went out, he would have to wear thicker clothes, but for now, he just gripped his collar and pulled his shirt tightly to his chest, pretending that the cold bothered him.

He could see the store sign in the distance and increased the length of his stride. The streets were busy, with plenty of cars on the road and kids who were either playing hooky or didn't go to school. Florence paused and took a moment to finalize how he planned to approach Alex. He decided that the first piece of information he would try to get was whether he had seen his nephew since he mailed the picture.

But he was later than he'd planned getting to the store. He was about three blocks away when a van rushed past him and stopped short at the corner. The side doors slid open, and five men jumped out. Two of them had copper pipes, and three had wooden baseball bats. The men immediately ran to Florence and surrounded him, poised to attack. They appeared to be middle-aged, wore shabby, ill-fitting clothes, and smelled as if they hadn't washed in days. They all stared at him as they fidgeted and twitched, as if each was visualizing his next move.

Florence heard one of the attacker's shoes moving against the pavement and the bloodthirsty shout as he lunged. Instinctively, Florence summoned his body to the brick wall of a nearby building. As he flew through the circle of attackers, he kicked out his leg and tripped one of them. The muggers stared at him confused as the man who had tried to attack him swung at air and stumbled. Flarence reached into his inside pocket and took out the Wrist Cannon as the man he had tripped regained his footing.

"You all look like you could use a night in a warm bed," he said, "but if you come at me again, that bed's going to be in a hospital."

One of the men approached Flarence and waved his copper pipe. "Mine's bigger than yours," he said. Gripping the pipe with both hands, he twisted his body to swing at Flarence's skull. But Flarence was quicker. He moved toward his attacker, extended a hand to stop the pipe, and struck with the Wrist Cannon. The man staggered back, out of attacking range.

"Last warning," said Flarence as he adopted a fighting stance. "I'm not in the mood for this."

All five men charged him at once. Just before the man at the front swung at his face, Flarence lunged to the right, rolling to regain his footing, a maneuver he had learned from Claire. Standing again, he pounced and struck one man in the kidney with his left hand while hitting another in the head with a right hook using the Wrist Cannon. As the man fell to the ground, Flarence threw his arm back, trying to elbow another man in the ribs, but the man caught his arm and twisted it, forcing Flarence to bend over. Another man hit him in his spine.

Flarence went down and felt a sharp kick in his side. He rolled away with the momentum and jumped back to his feet, the pain already gone thanks to a Genie's quick healing. The blow to his back had knocked the wind out of him, the kick to his chest might have left a bruise, but he was fine again now. If these men wanted to beat Flarence into submission, they'd need to hit him more and harder. But Flarence wasn't making much progress either. The man he'd hit in the head was still on the ground, but the other four were holding their weapons high, ready to strike again.

Tired of their advantage in numbers, Flarence drew the Stakehail Colt. The metal glistened in the light as he held it in front of him and moved it back and forth among the attackers, who froze at the sight of it.

Suddenly, curiosity got the better of him. The group hadn't attacked him until he was approaching the store. It seemed that someone didn't want him talking to Alex. "Who sent you?" he asked.

"What is that thing?" said one of the muggers. "A paint ball gun? Let me at this guy." He twirled his copper pipe as he approached, but Flarence pointed the gun at his leg and fired. There was a soft puff as the icicle burst out of the barrel and sank into the man's thigh. He collapsed and shouted, gripping his leg and staring in horror at the piece of ice that had impaled it.

Flarence aimed the Stakehail Colt at another mugger. "Tell me who sent you or the next one's going in someone's neck."

One man called his bluff. "Five hundred dollars. It's worth it," he said as he took three steps before Flarence pulled the trigger. The attacker fell to the ground with an icicle embedded deep in his throat.

"It's two-on-one now," said Flarence. "Your only advantage was outnumbering me. That's not going to last much longer. I don't really need to know who sent you, I'm just curious. You can tell me who paid you, or you can give me a reason to pull the trigger again." The remaining muggers turned around and ran back to the van. "Yeah," said Flarence as he slid the Stakehail Colt back in his pocket, "that's an option too." The mugger Flarence had punched in the head was back on his feet and followed the others, jumping in the van and sliding the door closed as it lurched and noisily sped away.

For a moment, Flarence thought about letting them get away, but he heard Soleil's voice in the back of his mind telling him he was all talk. Deep down, he feared what the Council would do to him if he broke the rules. If there was ever a time to break the rules, it was now. Claire had mentioned the possibility that the Student was a member of the Council, and if that was true, the quickest way to lure him into the open was to catch his attention, and that of other Council members as well. He was going to show Soleil that he wasn't afraid of being caught. He was going to use his abilities and chase down that truck in public in the middle of the day. He dropped to one knee, pushed off the ground, and ran after the van as it turned the corner.

The van was old, and its muffler was groaning violently as it quickly picked up speed. Summoning spells were difficult when an object was in motion. He might catch it, but summoned objects traveled in straight lines, and if the van turned while he was on his way, inertia would send him flying past it until his body could correct its trajectory. He might collide with another car and make the other driver crash. He might be breaking the rules but still didn't want innocent people to be injured. Accepting that he would have to go after the van the hard way, he pumped his legs harder. Flarence had centuries of speed training behind him, and it showed as he bolted down the street. Being a Genie also helped. On a chemical level, Flarence's muscle contraction process was no different than anyone else's, but he could reconstruct ATP as soon as they lost their phosphate group. Every molecule was immediately reformed and put through another reaction cycle, making Flarence's body a system that wasted no energy. He could run for miles without getting tired.

While his magic optimized his stamina, he still wasn't fast enough to catch the speeding van. As a taxi passed close, he leaped on the roof and gripped the sides of the car. The driver slammed on the brakes, and Flarence kicked off, using his momentum to increase the jump. It brought him closer to the van but not close enough to catch it. He needed something more drastic, and was glad when the van cut off a U-Haul truck and the driver had to slam on the brakes to avoid a collision.

He darted across the lanes and leaped at the back of the metal storage crate the truck was transporting. In the air, he generated an electric current through the wire on his Wrist Cannon, which caused the doorknob to pivot, but it was the magnetism Flarence was interested in. The crate had only a small ledge to use as a foothold, and there wasn't anything to grasp except the metal bar at the bottom that latched the crate's sliding door closed. The Wrist Cannon's magnetism wasn't strong enough to hold his body to the crate on its own, but it could help him keep his balance. The truck lurched forward as Flarence positioned himself on the crate. He had both feet on the ledge, which was only large enough for his toes. His left hand was stretched across the sliding door, with his fingernails digging into one of the grooves; his right hand was draped around the corner with the magnetized Wrist Cannon stuck to the side. He had his head around the corner as well to see the road ahead and keep an eye on the van.

The driver and Flarence eyed each other in the passenger side mirror. The man at the wheel gestured wildly and shouted insults that Flarence couldn't hear, but he didn't slow down. Flarence focused on the road. The truck was picking up speed and would soon catch up. A traffic light turned red, but the muggers kept going, nearly colliding with a turning car. There was a scream of tires as the van's driver slammed on the brakes and came to a stop halfway into the intersection. Other drivers screeched to a stop too, causing major congestion at the intersection.

For a moment, the attackers were pinned in the road. Drivers honked their horns as the van moved back and forth a few inches at a time trying to straighten out in the little space available and get back in the right lane. As the truck Flarence was riding on approached the light and slowed down, he deactivated the Wrist Cannon and jumped up on top of the crate, then sprinted across it and leaped across the intersection. Soaring over the moving cars with his hands extended, he grabbed the metal bar of the traffic light, swung back and forth twice, and pushed off from it onto the roof of the van. *Let's see Claire do that*, he thought as the van jerked forward.

The driver panicked at the sound of Flarence landing on the roof and tried to move forward but clipped a car in the oncoming lane. The impact threw Flarence onto the front of the van. He grasped the hood just below the windshield wipers as the driver spun the wheel trying to shake him off; it wasn't going to happen. Flarence's magic not only gave him infinite stamina but also sustained his muscle contractions to freeze his fingers in place. It would take more than a little swerving to knock him away.

Florence pulled himself toward the windshield and brought his right hand down on the glass as he activated the Wrist Cannon. He pulled out the Stakehail Colt, pointed it into the hole he had made, and fired the remaining four shots. Genie or not, aiming was tough on the hood of a moving van, and none of the icicles he fired hit any of the muggers, but he wasn't trying to. He jammed his elbow in the window hole, focused on the icicles, and increased their temperature, surrounding the driver with a cloud of steam. The man choked on the vapor, and his eyes teared up. Coughing, with Florence blocking his view, he struggled to avoid crashes. The driver hit the brakes, sending Florence sprawling across the hood, then ran out as fast as he could, not caring about the keys still in the ignition of the idling van. The other attackers quickly ran off too.

Florence broke his death grip and slid off the van. His left hand felt numb, as though it had been asleep for a week, but that was normal after holding a contraction for so long. Feeling would return soon. He put the empty Stakehail Colt back into his pocket and chased after his prey.

The muggers were slow, and Florence didn't need powers to catch them. He grabbed one in mid-stride and pushed him into a lamppost. The mugger's head hit the metal, and he went down. Florence grabbed him by the ankles and dragged him into an alley. He raised his Wrist Cannon and pointed it at the man. "I want to know about the man who paid you," he said.

"You didn't have to kill Joey, man," the mugger said, holding his head and writhing on the ground. "We weren't going to kill you; we were just supposed to scare you off."

Florence heard a siren in the distance. A police car was on its way, and an ambulance had probably found the man on the sidewalk with an icicle in his neck. "I don't care what you and your friends were supposed to be doing. I just want to know about the man who hired you."

"Sorry man, I got nothing. I never even saw his face."

"Because he had it covered up, right? He wore his hat low and his collar high. His shirt was covered with writing, wasn't it?" The man nodded, and Florence continued. "The man who hired you forces others to do his dirty work for him. He's not afraid to torture innocent people in order to push them into performing assignments. I want to stop him, but I'm having trouble finding him. You can make my job a lot easier by helping me get in touch with him."

"Tough break. I don't have his number."

The siren was close now, and Florence knew he was running out of time. "I don't need anything that specific. If you could just give me something he might have touched, I'd be able to track him down."

"I've got nothing on me that he touched."

"He paid you, didn't he?" said Florence. "As long as he held that money at some point I have a chance at finding him."

The man became enraged and moved closer to Florence. "You can't have that money—it's mine!"

Florence shoved him away. "This is very important. If you don't give it to me, I'll take it by force."

The man laughed. "You think I have it with me? Want to know what I do with every penny I get my hands on? I guard it with my life until I can hide it. If I'm that careful with a handful of quarters, what do you think I do with a few hundred dollars? That's my money, and nobody but me is ever going to lay a finger on it. You'll never find it. Nobody will."

Florence had been so caught up in defending himself he hadn't considered the significance of the man's shabby clothes. "Who are you?"

"Who am I? I'm a freaking bum. At least that's what most people call me. I hate that word. It implies I'm lazy and useless. I'm just as hard-working as you. I'm just as useful as anyone else in this city. The only difference is I'm down on my luck. We're all down on our luck. You shot Joey with your fancy gun without hesitating because you thought he was just an old, worthless, worn-out bum. He was a good guy who had a lot going for him, but you don't care about that, do you?"

Flarence pushed the man against a brick wall. "I'm not the bad guy here. The Student is powerful and dangerous. He didn't give you money to be nice; he did it because that was the easiest way to make you obey him. He would have killed Joey himself if he thought it would be an effective way to manipulate you. I need to find him so the people he's hurt can have closure. I need to find him before he hurts anyone else, and believe me, he will. For all I know, he already has."

"Hands in the air!"

Flarence turned to the end of the alley to see a police officer pointing a Taser at him. The cop fired as Flarence ran toward him and rolled to avoid the shot. The officer dropped the gun and pulled out his nightstick to attack, but Flarence had no intention of getting in a fight. He vaulted over the officer and sprinted back to the van. Three other officers talking to witnesses at the intersection heard the pursuing officer call out and fired their Tasers at him, but Flarence made it to the van unharmed and slammed the door shut.

The damaged windshield made it hard to see, so he stuck his head out the side window. He hit a police car as the other officers began chasing him, and he knew the old, clunky van couldn't outrun them. But Flarence had a head start and didn't need to drive far.

Two blocks away, he turned hard into a parking garage, plowing through the ticket machine. He raced up to the third level and purposefully crashed into a parked car. The sirens were close, and Flarence heard the screeching tires of a police car. He summoned his body to the wall of his hotel room and was gone before the officer got there, not bothering to become invisible as he moved. When he arrived, he leaned against the wall and closed his eyes, mentally reviewing what had happened. The stunts he'd pulled on the street would probably be on the news later and would have people talking. He was bound to be seeing some very interesting stories in the coming days. But, more important, he wasn't any closer to finding the Student than he had been that morning.

The cell phone in his pocket vibrated. He didn't recognize the number. Flarence flipped the phone open and held it to his ear.

"Hello?" said a voice on the other end of the line after a moment of silence. Flarence didn't respond but breathed heavily so the caller would know he was there. "Hello," the man said again, "listen, my name's Alex."

"Alex Hammerson?" Flarence asked.

"Who are you people? How do you know my name? Where's Nick? I just want to know he's safe. You don't have to tell me where he is. Just give me some proof he's alive."

Flarence guessed that Nick was Alex's nephew, and it didn't sound like the Student had let him free. "I don't know where your nephew is, Alex, but I'm trying to find his kidnapper. I need you to give me any information you might have on the Student based on your previous encounters."

"All right, I have something you might be interested in. He had a message for you. He said you were right and that it's unfair for him to attack people weaker than him. He says that after that stunt you pulled, it's clear that more drastic actions need to be taken, and that from now on, he'll go after people you have stronger feelings for. He said that once I delivered that message, he'd let Nick go. I hope he was telling the truth this time."

There was a click as Alex hung up. Flarence stood still for a moment and thought about what Alex said, before he slowly slipped the phone into his pocket. The Student must have been watching him chase the van down the street and heard what he'd said to the homeless man. On the one hand, he had been right about breaking the rules being an easy way to lure the Student closer to him, but in doing so, it sounded like he might have made things personal. The part about going after people he had strong feelings for was especially troubling. The Student didn't seem to target other Genies, so Soleil and Mohinaux were probably safe.

That left Claire.

—5—

DARREN

Darren had been spending most of his time inside since meeting with Jordan. After Tyrell told him about the guns, he spent Friday wondering what to do about Officer Tymbir. He thought about telling the police but couldn't make an accusation on the basis of Soleil's psychometry spell. And he doubted the police would take the word of a gangster seriously.

When Saturday arrived, he couldn't take being a shut-in anymore and decided to treat Atalissa and Tyrell to breakfast. When he went to the kitchen area with a towel around his waist, Tyrell was pouring what Darren assumed was his second cup of coffee. Tyrell went through tons of the stuff and was buying a new bag every month. Darren didn't complain. He figured the addiction would come in handy when Tyrell was pulling all-nighters in college.

Darren went to the couch cushion where he stashed his money. There was never anything substantial there, but by the end of the month, it was usually enough to treat Tyrell and Atalissa to something special.

"You can take a study break for a few hours," he said as he undid the zipper. "I'm taking you and your mom out for breakfast." He slipped his hand under the fabric—and felt nothing. He reached in deeper until his entire arm was inside but still felt no money

"Jordan's goons found your stash," said Tyrell. "They took it and said it helped make up for your low profits. I'm sorry I forgot to tell you. Things have been happening kind of fast lately."

Darren rezipped and replaced the cushion before slumping down on the couch. He couldn't even take his family out for a day of fun anymore.

"I'm sure Soleil can pull some kind of magical stunt to replace the money," said Tyrell as he blew on his coffee.

"Yeah, you talk to him about that," said Darren. "He owes us that much. And a whole lot more."

"He's only trying to help."

"I'm starting to think his breaking me out of prison was the reason for you being kidnapped. Maybe if I had stayed in prison, Tymbir wouldn't be so interested in me. Being locked away would be better than knowing a secret society of gun nuts is after my family."

"That's not how I see it," said Tyrell. "I was really relieved when I found out your arrest was a mistake. I'm glad you didn't do too much time for it."

Darren selected a pair of jeans and a plain black long-sleeved shirt. Atalissa stirred as he dressed but didn't wake up. He found one of his shoes by the door and another under the couch.

"Where are you going?" asked Tyrell.

"I've been sulking around the house for the past two days. I need to get out. If you need me, I'll be at Danny's."

Darren put on a brave face and walked out of the apartment. As he wove his way through the stair dwellers, some of them gave him the stink eye and rubbed their palms with their fists but didn't try to harm him. Jordan had put the word out that there wasn't enough information to consider Darren a threat or claim he was fully responsible for the death of J.J.'s brother.

Things were not very busy at the gas station where Danny worked, which was really more of a neighborhood supermarket, selling junk food, milk, water, fruit, and beer. Three cars were filling with gas while the drivers were inside, probably talking to Ashlee, Danny's sister. She was a major reason business was so good, young and pretty with smooth skin and curly hair. Lots of guys in the neighborhood bought gas and food there just for a chance to talk to her.

Darren always thought she wore too much makeup, which for him was a turnoff. Every time he saw her, she had on bright red lipstick, sparkling nail polish, and fake eye lashes that she had a habit of batting every time someone told a joke. She liked the attention the customers gave her and flirted with most of them but wasn't the kind of girl who slept around. Some guys in the neighborhood said that she was a tease, and Darren agreed with them, but he knew better than to talk about one of his best friend's sisters that way.

Inside, sure enough, the customers were at Ashlee's register, leaning close with their elbows on the counter. Ashlee smiled wide, showing her bright, flawless teeth, while her hands were linked behind her back and her body turned left and right as she spoke. Two of the customers were courteous enough to look her in the eye, but one stared directly at her chest. Danny was pretending to be focused on a crossword puzzle, but Darren knew he was listening to the conversation and would jump in if one of the guys started coming on to his sister too strongly. He had asked people to leave before when they tried to get Ashlee to go home with them. One time, when a customer grabbed Ashlee and tried to kiss her, Danny beat him up and threw him out. By now, everyone who went to the gas station for Ashlee knew that talking to her was fine but getting close required Danny's approval, which was not given often.

Danny put his pencil down and slid the puzzle across the counter. "Hey, Darren. Been a while. We've all been worried about you. Josh feels really bad about what happened, by the way."

Darren peeked at the puzzle and noticed that not a single box had been filled in. "When you see Josh, tell him it's fine. I'm not mad at him." He actually was a little upset with Josh for not telling him about the drugs in the truck, but considering the nosedive in his neighborhood popularity, he needed to hold onto as many friends as he could. "Listen, I know I haven't asked you for a favor in a while, but I'm sure by now you know that Jordan's a little upset with me. He found my stash of cash. Could you give me some merchandise on the house?" It wasn't an unusual request. When Danny first started working at the gas station, he would let his friends take free cases of beer once.

Danny looked at a digital clock above the glass doors, which showed it was only ten o'clock in the morning. "Little early, ain't it?"

"I've been locked in my house replaying everything that's been happening in my head," said Darren. "I need something to get my mind off of things."

Danny waved his hand toward the back of the store. "Help yourself, man. You know what—I'll tell Josh to pay for it. I'm sure he will if he knows it's for you."

Darren walked to the refrigerated section, and Danny continued to eavesdrop on the customers talking to Ashlee. After selecting a thirty-pack of cans, he made his way to the door, but Danny stopped him. "What you up to now?" he asked as he opened the cash register.

Darren placed the case of beer on the counter and shrugged. "I don't have anything going on. I'll probably just go to the park."

Danny walked around the counter with a handful of quarters. "Let me call the guys. We'll all go there together." Darren smiled while Danny approached a pay phone. He took the receiver off the hook and put it to his ear. Before inserting the money, he turned to Darren and pointed to the three customers, nonverbally asking Darren to keep an eye on them in case they started taking things too far. Darren nodded and leaned against the counter with his head down but tilted toward Ashlee so he could hear what they were saying. As far as he could tell, Ashlee didn't appear to be uncomfortable, and the conversations seemed to be innocent enough. A few minutes later, Danny came back to the counter. "Mike's stuck at work, but everyone else is in," he said. "They'll meet us at the park as soon as they can. If you want to wait a few minutes, I'll walk there with you. Ashlee can watch the shop until I get back. We'll go . . ." he raised his voice so the three customers could hear him, ". . . as soon as those guys pay for the gas that stopped pumping ten minutes ago."

"Relax, man," said one of the customers, "we're just being friendly, trying to make the pretty girl feel appreciated."

"The pretty girl has a name," said Danny, "and you can make her feel appreciated by treating her like a professional business woman. Your cars are all filled. Pay her and go."

The three customers reluctantly pulled money out of their pockets as Ashlee looked up what each of them owed. When they paid, they all winked and smiled at her as they left. "The one on the right was nice," said Ashlee when they were all out the door.

"That's great," said Danny. "Tell him that next time he comes in. I'm stepping out for a little bit. Think you can keep an eye on the place?"

"Are you sure you're all right leaving her alone?" said Darren.

"I've watched the store on my own before," said Ashlee. "I'm a big girl. Danny's just overprotective."

Darren and Danny made their way to their usual park bench. They were the first to arrive and, not feeling like waiting, Darren took out two cans of beer. Danny only sipped while Darren gulped his greedily. He belched and opened another. It was beginning to look as if they'd drink all of it in silence until Danny waved and Darren turned to see Juan and Josh approaching. By the time they arrived, Darren had three empty cans at his feet while Danny was just finishing his first.

Josh shuffled his feet and bit his lower lip. "Listen, Darren, about the delivery, sorry I didn't tell you 'bout the package. I didn't know my dad would go to you for help. Guess I shoulda told you 'bout the shop's other activities."

"It's all right," said Darren. "I don't blame you for anything that happened. I blame the jerk that ran through the stop sign. I blame the cop for looking in the cabinet. It's not your fault you got sick. We're good."

Darren pulled out two more cans and gave them to Juan and Josh. Juan pulled out a deck of cards, and the four of them started a game of Texas hold 'em. They played and talked for a long time as Darren out-drank the others. As the alcohol took effect, he opened up about what had been happening the last few days. He described the events out of order, beginning with Tyrell's being kidnapped before jumping to the car crash that had resulted in his arrest and then describing his meeting with Jordan.

Darren paused to take another long gulp. He finished off another can as Josh flipped over the last card. "How'd you get outta jail so fast?" he asked, "and who got Tyrell back home after being kidnapped?"

Darren crushed his empty beer can and tossed it over his shoulder. With his elbows on the table and his hands raised he snapped his fingers. "Do you believe in magic?"

"No," said Juan.

Darren slowly turned to Juan. "Do you believe I'm nuts?" he asked. They all laughed at that. Darren leaned back, slammed his palm on his cards, and flipped them over. "Pair of kings."

Juan flipped his cards over next, showing the four and Jack of spades. "I've got nothing," he said, "and yeah, I believe you're nuts."

"Me too," said Danny as he flipped over his cards. "And it looks like I got you beat."

"Don't celebrate yet," said Josh with a grin. "Straight."

Darren was the next dealer. Because it was only a friendly game, there was no money on the line. The only reward was being able to gloat for a moment.

"Seriously," said Josh as Darren shuffled, "I really want to know how you broke out, and don't tell me you just made a mad dash for the door when nobody was looking and got lucky. I know a guy who tried that once. It didn't end well for him."

Darren chuckled and shook his head as he cut the deck. "I didn't tell Jordan everything, and he was beating me up at the time. What makes you think I'm going to tell you? Look, I want to tell someone about what's been going on, and if I could I would, but honestly, I don't fully understand it myself. If I ever think of a sensible way to explain it, you'll be the first people to know, but not yet." He tried to shuffle the deck again but his hand slipped, and a third of the cards flew across the table.

Danny looked at his watch and noticed they had been in the park almost an hour and a half. "One more round," he said as he helped Darren pick up the loose cards, "then I gotta go."

Darren gave the collected cards another shuffle. Before dealing, he leaned over the box. "Still three cans left," he said.

"Give 'em here," said Juan, "you've had enough." Darren gave each of them a can and laid out the cards. In the end, Danny won the hand and the four of them collected the empty beer cans and put them back in the box. Josh carried them to the garbage can as Darren and Danny walked back to the gas station together.

Darren's masculinity kept him from saying how much it meant to have spent time just relaxing and playing cards with the three of them, but inside it felt really good to be able to say he still had friends.

There were no cars at the gas station when Darren and Danny got there, and they could see that Ashlee was alone. "Business is pretty slow right now," said Danny. "I'll walk you back to your place if you want."

"I'll be fine," said Darren. "I walked here without running into any trouble. It's not that far."

The two shook hands and slapped each other's backs before going their separate ways. Suddenly a car pulled into the gas station close to Darren. The back passenger window rolled down and a gun emerged. Darren wanted to move but was too drunk to act. His mind told his body to run, but his muscles weren't listening. The man with the gun was wearing a yellow baseball cap and black T-shirt. Darren had just enough time to realize that black and yellow were the colors of a rival gang, and Jordan's warning had come true. The man Darren had failed to deliver the drugs to, worried about police learning of his addiction, had put a price on his head, and these two were on a mission to collect. Three bullets tore into Darren. He stumbled a few steps back and fell.

In the distance, he thought he heard screaming, but for all he knew, it could have been cheering. Was his reputation so bad that the gang members would rejoice when they saw someone take him out? His thoughts drifted to Tyrell. From the day his son was born, all he'd wanted was to see Tyrell get out of this slum of a neighborhood, go to college, and be successful. Now he would never see his son studying in college, or even getting his high school diploma. Then he thought about Atalissa. When Tyrell left for school, she'd be alone. How long would it be before she found someone else? Just how much had he meant to her anyway? Had he been a lousy husband? Atalissa brought home a bimonthly paycheck, and Tyrell had a part-time job after school, but Darren just spent his days doing grunt work and brought home a handful of change every night. He should have tried to find a normal job to contribute more. He hadn't been able to step up to the responsibilities of having a family, nor had he been able to live with the risks that came with his lifestyle. He had been a lousy gangster, an unsupportive husband, and a sorry excuse of a father.

Darren's vision was blurry, and his eyes stared blankly at the sky. Danny's face came into view, but he wasn't looking Darren in the eye. "Hold on," he said, his gaze focused on Darren's torso, probably looking at his wounds. "Ashlee's calling 911." The pain made Darren want to scream, but all he could do was groan as his vision faded to black. He was losing consciousness and didn't hear the siren approaching. He gave up and allowed his body to go limp despite Danny's pleas for him to stay awake.

SOLEIL

The radio clipped to his jeans was playing Bruce Springsteen's "Dancing in the Dark" as Soleil filled a one-gallon plastic milk jug with water at the kitchen sink. As he walked up the stairs, Springsteen sang, "Baby I just want a kiss," and he tried to pull off a dance move that involved crossing his ankles and spinning, but he misjudged the width of the steps and lost his balance. He pinwheeled his arms until he found the railing and gripped it before he fell down.

Soleil took a moment to collect himself and was glad nobody was in the cafe to see him. Some of the water had spilled, so he evaporated the puddles and directed the resulting cloud back into the jug. In his room, he started watering the plants. There weren't many clouds in the sky, and the sun coming in the windows kept the room warm. "Can't start a fire," he sang, "can't start a fire without a spark . . ."

There was a crash from the floor below, and Soleil almost dropped the jug. He turned off the radio, unclipped it from his pants, and tossed on his bed.

"Soleil!" he heard. It was Tyrell. He put the jug on the floor and ran down to the cafe, where he found Tyrell bent over the counter, gripping the edge and panting heavily. Lucy was with him, and had her hand on his shoulder. Tyrell turned to Soleil, his eyes red and damp. "It's my dad," he said through short breaths. He looked away and dropped his head back to the counter. "My dad . . ." he said again, unable to get the words out.

"His dad's been shot," said Lucy. "He's at a hospital right now, but we don't know how bad his condition is. I was driving Tyrell to the hospital, and he said we should pick you up on the way."

"Sure, let's go," said Soleil as he rushed to the door.

"It's chilly out," said Tyrell, "you'll want a jacket."

Soleil looked down and realized he was still wearing a thin cotton T-shirt and old, tattered jeans. "Sure thing. Just give me a second. Lucy, can we meet you in the car?"

Lucy backed toward the door looking from Tyrell to Soleil. "Um, sure. Whatever."

He rushed upstairs to his room and threw on something warmer. When he went back downstairs, Tyrell was standing by the door and Lucy was waiting in the car.

"You can do something, right?" said Tyrell. "I'm wishing for you to make this better. Tell me you can do something."

"I'll do what I can," said Soleil, "but I should tell you right now that magic has limits. If your dad is already dead, I can't revive him."

Tyrell didn't say anything. They all were silent for most of the ride. When they were stuck at a red light, Lucy tried to comfort Tyrell, telling him his dad would make it and that she'd get her parents to help with the hospital bills. It made Tyrell smile, but he didn't say anything in response. At the hospital, Lucy dropped Tyrell and Soleil off and looked for a place to park. They walked in and saw Atalissa sitting on a chair with her elbows on her knees and her head in her hands. Tyrell walked to her silently and placed his hand on her shoulder. She jumped at his touch, then pulled him close and hugged him.

Tyrell broke away from her. "It's going to be all right. I brought help." Atalissa looked behind Tyrell, and when she noticed Soleil, she stood up and wiped her eyes with her sleeve.

"He's in surgery right now," she said, "but I don't know what room he's in,"

Soleil stared at them. Tyrell had a frustrated look on his face. The three were silent while Soleil just moved his head back and forth stupidly, looking at Tyrell and then Atalissa.

Tyrell threw his arms out to his sides. "Well?" he said.

Lucy came into the hospital and rushed to them. "I got here as fast as I could," she said to Atalissa. "Has there been any news?" Atalissa shook her head, and Lucy held her hand comfortingly as they sat down. Tyrell looked at Soleil and mouthed a silent "Get to work" before sitting beside them.

Soleil looked around the room and spotted a vending machine in the corner. "Can I get you a bottle of water or something?" he asked.

"Yeah," Tyrell said, sounding annoyed, "that sounds good."

Soleil walked past the vending machine to a bathroom down the hall. He locked himself in a stall, and performed an astral projection, floating through the floors and walls until he was looking down at Darren on an operating table, surrounded by doctors desperately trying to remove the bullets. It looked as if Darren had lost a lot of blood, but the beeping of a nearby machine confirmed that his heart was still active.

Soleil's projection returned to his body. He flushed the toilet and ran water over his hands before returning to the lobby. "Sorry," he said to Tyrell, Atalissa, and Lucy, "I don't have enough change for the vending machine. I was walking around looking for coins some-one might have dropped, but I didn't have any luck."

"That's all right," said Lucy. "I'll get it. Be right back." She pulled a small change purse out of her large leather purse. When she was gone, Tyrell stood up and looked eagerly at Soleil. Atalissa stayed seated but had the same look on her face.

"He's alive," said Soleil. "I saw him in the operating room. His heart is still pumping, and the doctors have been able to remove one of the bullets." He tried to rest his hand on Tyrell's shoulder and tell him everything was going to be fine, but Tyrell slapped it away.

"And?" said Tyrell. His look of frustration had turned to anger. "What are you going to *do* about it?"

Soleil stared back blankly. "That's all I can do for the moment. If you want, I'll wait here with you and keep checking in on him."

"That's it?" Tyrell said, a little too loudly. He remembered they were in public and took a deep breath to calm himself down. "That's all you're going to do?" he said a little more quietly. "Why do you think I brought you here? You're supposed to make everything bet-ter." Soleil was becoming frustrated.

"What exactly did you expect me to do? It's not like I can just walk into a room full of doctors and magically heal a gunshot wound."

"Are you kidding me?" said Tyrell, still struggling to keep his voice low. "You can control light! Figure something out."

Lucy returned with four bottles of water. "Is everything okay?"

Soleil tried to sit down, but Atalissa grabbed his wrist. She put the bottles under her chair and stood up. "Everything's fine, Lucy. I'm going to talk to Soleil outside for a minute." Soleil followed Atalissa out of the lobby. Once they got to a brick wall where they could stand alone, she said, "Tyrell isn't mad. He's just scared. Don't take anything he says too personally."

Soleil looked at the ground and put his hands in his pockets. "He's right, I can do a lot of things with my magic, but there are limits. Sure, I can help him when he's attacked or kidnapped, and I can break his friends and family out of prison when they're arrested, but bringing a man back from the verge of death? That's a little much."

"Is there anything you can do?" said Atalissa. Soleil didn't answer right away. She put a finger under his chin and made him look up. "Soleil, if this is reversible, you need to tell me now."

She dropped her hand, and he sighed. "If I was there when he was shot, I could have stopped the bullets from hitting him, but now that the damage has been done, I don't have many options. The only way to help him would be to magically heal his wounds."

"Then do it," said Atalissa.

"I can't. It would Enchant him. There are rules about passing on magical powers to other people."

"This is an extreme situation. His life is on the line."

"That isn't a good enough reason. If I Enchanted someone every time their life was in danger, the world would be full of Genies. I can only pass my powers on to one person in my life, and we both have to agree to the transfer."

"Your brother said there's no proof the people making the rules even exist."

Now it was Soleil's turn to have trouble keeping his voice low. "That's no reason to ignore them. I believe that the Council of Elders exists. I believe the rules were made for a reason. I believe I have too much power not to have restrictions put on what I can and can't do. I take the rules seriously, and I won't break them, not even to help Darren." He paused and looked at Atalissa apologetically. He meant what he'd said but regretted how he had said it. "Look, I know Darren means a lot to both you and Tyrell. I've never lost a family member before, and I'm not going to pretend I understand what you're going through."

"But Tyrell understands what you're going through," said Atalissa. "You said it yourself; we're asking too much of you. Darren and I have been doing that to Tyrell from the day he was born. All his life, the world has been trying to knock him down, and for years, Darren and I have been telling him to suck it up. We told him to excel in school even though Darren and I never went ourselves and knew perfectly well we wouldn't be able to help him with his homework. We told him to stay away from the gang, even though most of the kids in the neighborhood join the Slugs at a young age, and most kids he goes to school with are afraid of him because they think he's some scary badass from a rough neighborhood. I don't know what Lucy sees in him, but I thank God every day that she's around. Darren, Lucy, and I are all Tyrell has ever had. Everything he does is to make his parents proud and impress Lucy. He's all too familiar with putting his own comfort aside for the sake of others."

"I'm in a different situation than he's ever been in," said Soleil.

"But the request is the same," said Atalissa. "I know you don't like breaking the rules, but there are more important things going on right now. Darren is more than important to us; he's critical. I can't tell you what to do, but if there was ever a time to step outside your comfort zone, this is it. If the Council does exist and they come after you, tell them why you did it. Tell them about us. Feel free to blame everything on me if you want. I'll plead my case to them."

Soleil walked away from Atalissa. "Give me a minute," he called over his shoulder. Alone in the parking lot, he leaned against a car and thought about what she'd said, and how scared Tyrell had looked at the cafe. When he considered the situation, it did seem selfish letting Darren die to avoid getting in trouble with the Council. But it wasn't just about getting in trouble. The rules were made for a reason. The power of a Genie in the wrong hands could have disastrous consequences. He had seen people become consumed with greed and destroy their friends to reach a higher position in a corporation. He had been around to witness dictators come to power and later fall, and he didn't want to imagine what might have happened if any of those people had been able to use magic.

Images of corruption were replaced by hundreds of violent scenes in his mind. He remembered people suffering during wars and riots.

He had done nothing to help them because of the rules that emphasized the importance of keeping his abilities secret. It was no wonder that Flarence had finally lost his faith in the Council and gone rogue; he was tired of watching the pain and wanted to do something about it. Maybe it was time for Soleil to rebel a little. It wasn't as if he was going to expose his magic to the world. He was just going to save one person. Besides, he knew Darren was a good man who loved and cared for his family. He couldn't imagine Darren becoming a power-corrupted monster. Atalissa and Tyrell would make sure he stayed a good person.

Soleil tried to imagine a worst-case scenario. Suppose he Enchanted Darren, saved his life, and the Council disapproved of his actions. It might remove Darren's powers, but by then, it wouldn't matter. Darren would be healed from his wounds and be just a regular person again. But the Council would likely remove Soleil's powers as well. Was he willing to risk losing his magic? Atalissa's words echoed in his mind, and he forced the thought away. This wasn't about him. Tyrell was a good kid who was about to lose his dad, and Soleil could stop it from happening. As Tyrell's friend, it was his responsibility to save Darren's life.

He went back into the hospital and got as close as he could to the operating room his projection had found earlier. He improved his hearing and tried to listen to the events inside through the chaos of the doctors and nurses. Darren's heart was racing, desperately pumping what blood he had left through his system. Soleil focused on Darren's bone marrow and willed blood cells to be released more quickly to replenish what was lost. There was a moment where he could feel the biological reactions in Darren's body, but soon the sensation was gone. Soleil wasn't losing focus on what he was doing but he was losing control. Not only was Darren producing more blood cells but his skin also was closing and his heart rate slowed. The chaos in the room subsided as the doctors stared at their patient in amazement. The lead surgeon ordered them back to work, but they found nothing left to do.

Outside the room, Soleil felt a shudder run down his spine as the reality of what he had done sank in. It was over—Darren was now a Genie. Soleil walked back to the waiting room, where he found Tyrell, Atalissa, and Lucy. "I provided the spark," he said. "Now all we have to do is control the fire." Tyrell looked confused, and Soleil couldn't help chuckling. "Never mind, I guess that's before your time."

Soleil sat next to Atalissa. Before too long, a doctor approached them. "Excuse me, Atalissa Raleigh? I have news about your husband."

Atalissa stood up immediately. "Is he all right?"

"He's alive, but there were some complications with his operation. We'd like to run some more tests."

"What do you mean complications?" said Tyrell.

"We honestly don't know," said the doctor. "He's unconscious, but he appears to be stable. We're going to keep him here for a while and observe him closely. We'll inform you if there are any changes in his condition."

"But he's alive?" said Atalissa. "Is he better?" The doctor nodded but didn't say anything else. "Thank you," said Atalissa as he turned and left.

After the doctor was gone, Tyrell motioned for Soleil to step outside with him. They stood in the same spot where Soleil and Atalissa had spoken earlier. "I'm curious, what exactly did you do?"

"The only thing I could do to save his life," said Soleil. "The doctors aren't the only ones who are going to be observing Darren's progress. He's one of us now, and we're all going to have to do our part to help him through the change."

"One of us?" repeated Tyrell.

"There was no way of saving Darren without Enchanting him. Your father's a Genie."

Tyrell's face was blank for a moment. "Cool," he said.

Atalissa drove Tyrell back to their apartment, while Lucy drove home alone. Despite Lucy's offer to drive Soleil to his cafe, he said he preferred to walk and clear his head. When the three of them were gone, he quickly turned down a street, hid between two houses, and summoned-traveled to Tyrell's apartment. He sat on the couch and waited, expecting that Darren would be conscious soon and would return to the apartment before the sun set.

Soleil heard the apartment door open, but when he turned around, it was Atalissa and Tyrell in the doorway. "We would have given you a ride," said Tyrell.

"I really thought Darren would be back before you," said Soleil. "I've never Enchanted anyone before, and I'm not sure how long it takes before the powers take full effect, but magic is amazing, and I thought he would be awake by now."

"I haven't gotten any calls from the doctors," said Atalissa. "If we hear anything, the first thing we'll do is go to your cafe. Seriously, Soleil, you've done enough for one day. Go home and get some rest."

Soleil was about to summon his body out of the apartment when he heard footsteps in the hallway.

"Tyrell?" Darren's voice called. "Atalissa? Something weird happened. I feel . . . well . . . I feel fine, but that's the weird thing. Atalissa?" The door was still open, and Darren came in, wearing a hospital gown that left his arms and legs bare. "I ran here," he said. "I ran here from the hospital, and I'm not even out of breath."

"Your new abilities kicked in instinctively," said Soleil. "You subconsciously improved your stamina. I'll teach you how to summon your body places later so you can move around unnoticed."

"My abilities?" said Darren. "The last thing I remember was being shot. The next thing I knew, I woke up without so much as a scar anywhere."

"The only way to save you was to give you powers," said Soleil. "You have Atalissa and Tyrell to thank for convincing me to do it. You don't have any scars because your new abilities include rapid healing. In fact, if I remember correctly, the doctors didn't even remove all the bullets before you healed. Let me get it for you." Soleil extended his hand, catching the metal fragments that erupted from Darren's body and flew across the room to him. Darren staggered back and looked for holes in his torso, but the wounds had healed before his blood had a chance to stain the hospital gown. "We should all get some rest," said Soleil. "I'll be back soon to show you how to use your powers." He left the three of them in the apartment as he summoned his body back to his cafe.

FLARENCE

Saturday came to a close as dusk fell. Flarence and Claire sat across from one another in the hotel room. "What happened with Nick, Alex's nephew?" she asked.

"We'll know in a few days," said Flarence. "Once I knew his name, I was able to find him and get help. I checked on him while he was in the hospital, and he wasn't in good condition. The poor kid was dehydrated and didn't even have the energy to lift his head. The Student didn't even bother cleaning up when he shit himself. By the time I got to him, he was filthy and his skin was covered in rashes. Alex is glad he's alive, but he's going to have a rough recovery."

"Did you find anything to do a psychometry spell on? He must have had something on him that would have let you see the Student when he had him captive."

"I used a shred of his clothes. It didn't help. The Student always had his disguise on, and I'm pretty sure he uses magic to disguise his voice."

"Sorry to hear that. Believe it or not, there's been even crazier stuff going on around here." She told Flarence about the guns they had found in the house by the tracks, and that a police officer was involved with Tyrell's kidnappers.

"There weren't any phone calls made to Tyrell's parents after he was kidnapped?" asked Flarence.

"None that I'm aware of. Soleil and Tyrell didn't mention anything about that."

"Tyrell might have been kidnapped to lure Soleil to the house. If that's the case, it follows the Student's methods. A group of non-magical people was used to manipulate a Genie."

Claire left the room and came back with a stack of papers. "I don't think the Student is in cahoots with the gun nuts. I think Tymbir is the center of it and had his own reasons for kidnapping Tyrell." Florence looked at the papers. They were copies of articles involving seemingly random crimes. Some involved drug arrests, others drunk drivers, and a few were about domestic disturbances. When Florence skimmed through them, he noticed that each article involved an officer named Kevin Tymbir. He read through them carefully, looking for any details that might be important, but couldn't find anything particular.

"Where are you going with this?" asked Florence. "He seems like an ordinary cop."

"On paper, there's nothing that stands out," said Claire, "but the testimony of the people he's arrested tells a different story. I was able to track down some of the people Tymbir arrested in those articles, and there was a pattern in their stories. Some of the drug dealers said Tymbir got rough without provocation. He knocked them to the ground before handcuffing them even though they were surrendering. I talked to one man arrested for drunk driving who said Tymbir broke his finger while leading him to his police car. Tymbir claimed his hand had slipped because the driver was so drunk it was impossible to keep a firm grip and help him walk to the car without hurting him."

"Those aren't serious crimes," said Florence. "All it means is that Tymbir is a little rough."

"I know it doesn't seem like a big deal," said Claire, "but it says a lot about this guy's character. It sounds to me like Tymbir enjoys hurting people and uses his job as an excuse to do it. So far, he's always gotten away with it. Somehow, he's gotten his hands on heavy-duty guns, and he looks for an excuse, any excuse, to use them. He usually just shoots dead animals, but what if he's found a reason to go further? He arrested Darren, and right after Soleil broke him out,

Tyrell was kidnapped. I think Tyrell's kidnapping was about getting to Darren, not Soleil. That's not all that's been going on either. Look at the last article."

Flarence turned to a story about a drive-by shooting that day. He skimmed it looking for a mention of Tymbir but didn't find one. It was only the third time he read it that he noticed the name of the victim. "Darren?" he said, not taking his eyes off the paper.

"Yeah," said Claire. "I saw that story online just before you got back, and I thought it was particularly strange considering I saw Darren earlier today. He was dressed in nothing but a hospital gown and was running down the street as fast as he could. I swear, it looked like he had lost his mind. I followed him for a few blocks, and I noticed that he wasn't getting tired. For someone who was shot, he didn't seem to be in any pain and had a ton of energy. I'd go as far as to say he had an inhuman amount of energy. I tried to catch up with him, but I lost him. You know me, Flarence; I don't lose people when I'm in chase mode. You're the only person I can't keep up with. We need to talk to Soleil."

Flarence put the article down. "There's got to be another explanation. Soleil wouldn't Enchant someone like Darren. He's a low-life drug-dealing gangster. Putting our power in that kind of person could only lead to problems. Soleil can be emotional, but he isn't that stupid. At least I hope he isn't that stupid."

"I'm sorry Flarence, but you didn't see Darren today. Ordinary people don't run that fast for that long. Soleil did something. I'll keep an eye on Darren tomorrow, and I'll call you if I see anything else suspicious that might suggest he's been Enchanted. You can go to Soleil's Cafe and ask your brother yourself. I'm going to get some sleep." She stood up but stopped and snapped her fingers. "Oh, one more thing—you were in the news too." She went to the kitchen area and returned with another article. "Chaos in the Street Leaves Residents Speechless," she read aloud. "It says a mysterious man chased down a car, beat up the people inside, trashed the car, and then disappeared without a trace. I'm guessing that was you."

"Soleil called me a coward," Flarence said defensively. "I showed him."

"I'm not judging you," said Claire as she put the page back on the counter. "I'm just letting you know you were noticed." She started walking back to her room.

"Wait," said Flarence, "there's one more thing you need to know. The Student gave me a message. He said he was going to start focusing on people I care about. He saw us in this hotel together that day we got the letter, so he knows we work together. He's going to try to get to me through you."

Claire pulled one of her needles out of her sleeve. "He was invisible last time. Do you think he's here now?"

"He isn't here. I noticed him last time because I improved my senses and heard his heart beating. Since then I've made a habit of improving my hearing periodically to make sure we're alone. I did it the second I walked into this room, and I didn't hear the heartbeats other than ours. I just want you to keep your wits about you tomorrow.

"Don't worry, I'll be careful."

"Not when your eyes are shut," said Flarence. "I think we should sleep in shifts tonight. He could summon-travel here while you're asleep."

Claire replaced the needle in her sleeve, and as she brushed her teeth, Flarence moved a chair into her bedroom. When her head hit the pillow, she fell asleep almost immediately, and Flarence decided to let his shift last the entire night. Genies did need sleep but not nearly as much as humans, and staying up one night wouldn't hurt. Besides, he didn't think he could sleep even if he tried. He kept thinking about Soleil and what could have possibly possessed him to Enchant Darren.

—6—

DARREN

Darren slept well for a man who had just returned from the brink of death. He and Atalissa fell asleep holding each other close and didn't let go all night. When he woke up Sunday morning, she had her arm draped over his side and her face buried in his neck. He had thrown his hospital gown in the garbage before going to bed and replaced it with a pair of gray sweatpants and a plain white T-shirt. He walked into the kitchen, took a bowl from a cabinet, and filled it with cereal. He was about to go to the refrigerator for milk when he heard a voice say, "Oh good—you're awake."

Darren spun around to find Soleil sitting on the couch. "What the hell, man?" Darren shouted, "don't you knock?"

"That's one of the benefits of being a Genie. I don't have to knock, or even use a door."

Darren pointed to his bedroom. "Okay, we need some ground rules. See that room? That's my room. You do not enter my room without my permission, and you do not enter that room at all when Atalissa and I are alone in there."

"Fair enough," said Soleil. "Anything else?"

Darren turned back to the refrigerator and took the milk out. "I'll think of more as we go. What are you doing here anyway? Don't you have customers to serve?"

Soleil rose from the couch. "I left the cafe closed today. I just came by to see you. I've never Enchanted anyone before, and I wanted to know how you're feeling. Besides, it's not like anyone ever goes to my cafe anyway."

"How do you keep that place running?" asked Darren as he poured milk. "Don't you have bills to pay? Taxes?"

"Another benefit of magic is that it makes stealing easier. I swipe what I need without people noticing."

"You're a thief?" said Atalissa, who entered the room and also made herself a bowl of cereal. "And you say you're uncomfortable breaking rules?"

"Stealing isn't against the rules of sorcery," said Soleil, "and I don't steal in large quantities. I walk around the city, summoning a few dollars out of people's pockets here and there. I'm sure they notice it's gone eventually, but I doubt they make a fuss about it."

"There's no need to be defensive," said Atalissa. "I'm not judging you. I also didn't get a chance to thank you for saving Darren." She put her hand on his shoulder and gave him a quick hug. "You'll never know how much it means to us." She shoveled down a few spoonfuls of cereal. "Has there been any backlash yet? About passing your powers on to Darren without his consent?"

"Not yet," said Soleil, "but it hasn't even been a day. I'm sure the Council is discussing it."

"Morning," said Tyrell as he walked into the room. He made himself a bowl of cereal too, and the three of them slurped milk and scooped the flakes into their mouths as they stood around the refrigerator.

"Do you feel any different since getting powers?" Tyrell asked between bites.

"Soleil asked me that too," said Darren. "I really don't feel anything new. I didn't feel any different last night when I ran home from the hospital either. I just ran."

"Some spells are instinctive," said Soleil. "Flarence and I both had experiences where we ran away from trouble and didn't get exhausted. Improved stamina can be helpful at times, but just wait until you master summoning."

"How do you know I have all your abilities?" Darren asked as he put his empty bowl in the sink. "I told you I don't feel any different. Maybe you only gave me healing powers."

"There's no middle ground," said Soleil. "If you have one ability, you have them all. You just need to learn how to use them. It's all a matter of focus." He looked around the apartment and set his eyes on a remote on the table between the couch and the television. "That remote," he said. "Try looking at it."

Darren shrugged and stared at the remote. There was silence as he kept focusing on it, but he didn't see anything different.

"Concentrate on it," said Soleil. "Forget everything else in the room, and focus on that one object."

Darren folded his arms and closed his eyes. He imagined holding the remote in his hand, but it didn't help. He opened his eyes and stared hard. He couldn't explain exactly how it happened, but suddenly a feeling overcame him. "I think I feel it moving," he said. He suddenly wasn't observing the remote as a single object anymore but could feel each individual component of the plastic. He felt the atoms spinning, vibrating, and emitting a noise like trillions of strings being plucked at once.

"Genies have control over energy and forces," said Soleil. "You can control gravity, sound, and even light. Your powers are limited only by your concentration."

Darren willed the remote to counteract gravity, and was surprised when it did, becoming lighter than air and floating up. When he stopped concentrating, it fell back onto the table.

"You can also make objects gravitate toward each other," Soleil continued. "You already levitated the remote, but now try bonding with it."

Darren followed Soleil's instructions, and the remote flew across the room to him. It traveled fast, and Darren didn't have time to catch it before it struck his chest and clung to him like a magnet on a refrigerator. He gripped the remote, broke focus, and set it gently next to the sink.

Darren decided to move on to bigger challenges, and focused on the couch. As with the remote, he manipulated gravity and made it hover. He walked around the counter until he was standing in the middle of the room a few feet from the floating couch and tried to make it move toward him. He expected the couch to drift to him, and that he would be able to lift it easily now that it was light enough to float. Instead, his body flew through the air and collided with it. The surprise caused him to lose focus, and both Darren and the couch crashed to the floor. Atalissa, Tyrell, and Soleil rushed to him.

"There's the healing power at work again," said Soleil, who noticed a scrape on Darren's arm heal instantaneously. "I'm sorry, I should have mentioned that when summoning, the object of smaller mass travels to the larger one."

"But I changed its mass," said Darren. "I was heavier than it. It was floating on air ,and I wasn't."

"There's a difference between weight and mass," said Tyrell. "Weight is a function of gravity, but mass is based on how much space an object occupies."

"So there are limits other than focus," said Darren. "I'll never be able to summon a car to my body."

"No," said Soleil, "but feel free to summon your body to as many cars as you want. Word of warning, though—try not to summon your body to objects that are in motion. You can't control your direction while traveling, and you just keep moving until you hit whatever you're summoning to. Also, I would advise not summoning long distances until you master invisibility. I explained how that trick works to Tyrell, so he can walk you through it. However, the main purpose of my visit is to give you this." He pulled a folded piece of paper out of his pocket. Darren reached his hand out to take it, but then backed up a few steps and summoned the paper to his body, catching it before it hit his chest like the remote. "Those are the rules," said Soleil as Darren unfolded the paper.

"Number one," Darren read aloud, "I'm supposed to keep magic a secret. I knew that one already. Number two, I can't use magic directly on another living thing unless I intend to Enchant it. I knew that one too. Number three, I'm supposed to keep an inventory of magically acquired personal gains. Personal gains?"

"It goes back to the stealing thing," said Soleil. "We're supposed to use magic to get what we need but no more. Keep track of what you steal, and don't take anything unless you can explain why you need it."

"Number four," Darren continued, "I'm not to use my powers violently unless it is requested by my master."

"Doesn't Flarence break that rule?" asked Tyrell.

"Bending maybe but not exactly breaking He considers himself to be a private detective," said Soleil. "Being hired could be equivalent to a master's request. So far, the Council hasn't come after him, so I assume they agree."

"Number five," said Darren, "I can only have one master at a time. Number six, I have to provide a talisman to mark a person as my master."

"I gave Tyrell a key," said Soleil, "but you can use any object you want, as long as the person you give it to knows what it represents."

"Number seven, I'm supposed to maintain surveillance over my master after I discontinue my services to them."

"Wait—I'm your master," said Tyrell to Soleil. "What do you mean you have to maintain surveillance on me?"

"It goes along with keeping magic a secret," said Soleil. "I have to watch you to make sure you don't tell other people about me and what kind of services I provided. If I'm worried that you're about to tell someone about me, I can step in and take whatever steps are necessary to stop you."

"How long are you required to stalk me?" asked Tyrell.

"Until you can't talk anymore," said Soleil. "Genies live a long time. I'll be watching you until you're dead, to make sure my secret is kept safe."

"What about me?" said Darren. "You Enchanted me. What happens to my life span?"

"You have all my powers, including my long life. You'll outlive all your current friends as well as Tyrell and Atalissa." There was an uncomfortable silence as the three of them let the impact of Darren's long life sink in.

"Number eight," Darren continued, "mutual agreement between me and my master is required before performing any magical services."

"That rule is the basis behind the extinction of monsters," said Soleil. "An animal can't verbally give consent to be Enchanted, so they're off limits."

"Number nine, I can choose to terminate my services to my master at any time with or without reason, and my master can do the same. Number ten, I am not to interfere with free will."

"That last one is critical," said Soleil. "Agreement is necessary between a Genie and their master, but if a Genie intimidates the master into agreeing to a request, it doesn't count and is against the rules. If you try to force someone to make a wish, you'll be in serious trouble."

"I'll keep that in mind," said Darren. He flipped the paper over. "Is that all?"

"That's it," said Soleil. "Those are the ten rules that have to be followed. Anyway, that's the main reason I came by. I'm going to get back to my cafe. You stick around here and practice your new abilities. Remember: Don't summon anywhere until you're more comfortable with invisibility."

With a slight wave, Soleil summoned his body out of the room.

SOLEIL

The cafe was just as he'd left it when Soleil got there. The lights were off, the blinds were drawn, and the chairs were tucked under the tables. He turned on the lights and summoned the radio to his body, and was about to turn it on when he noticed Flarence in one of the chairs with his arms crossed tightly over his chest.

"Is there something you want to tell me?" asked Flarence as Soleil walked to the long counter. Flarence followed him. He placed both hands on the wood and stared at Soleil. "I said, is there something you want to tell me?"

"Actually, there is," said Soleil. "I don't just use the radio for music. I get news stations on it too. There was a report last Friday of an incident. The details are sketchy, but people described seeing a man with a gun and a strange machine on his wrist. Is there something you want to tell *me*?"

He pulled a small piece of paper out of his pocket and slammed it hard on the counter. "Don't you dare lecture me about responsible use of powers," said Flarence. "That's a story Claire found yesterday. It says Darren was shot in a drive-by."

"He was," said Soleil, not looking at the article. "Tyrell was really broken up about it."

Flarence put the paper back in his pocket. "I'm sure Tyrell will get over it, especially since Claire tells me she saw Darren running down the street last night like a bat out of Hell. Tell me, Soleil, how could a person recover so quickly from a gunshot wound? And why is it that when I tried to perform an astral projection earlier, I was able to lock on to Atalissa just fine, I was able to lock on to Tyrell just fine, but somehow I couldn't lock on to Darren? It almost felt like he was resisting it, which is impossible unless he was recently Enchanted."

"You're right," said Soleil. "Darren's been Enchanted. I did it to save his life. I don't expect you to understand why, but I do expect you to shut up and let me handle this on my own. Now please get out of my house."

Flarence's hands curled into fists, and his face turned red. "Damn it, Soleil," he shouted as he pounded on the wood. The counter instantly turned into a pile of sawdust, sending the cash register, radio, and salt shakers on it falling to the ground. Flarence summoned his body to the wall behind Soleil. He grabbed his brother's shoulders as he flew, and slammed Soleil into the wall back first. Not releasing his grip, he spun to his right and summoned his body to another wall. Flying across the room had caused the pile of sawdust to be kicked up. Flarence spun his brother around and kicked him in the chest, sending him sprawling backward into the cloud. The blow knocked the wind out of him, and he instinctively took a breath, drawing in a large amount of sawdust. His eyes watered, and he fell to his hands and knees as a fit of coughing overtook him. Even with his powers, he still needed to breathe. Ignoring the pain in his throat, he used all his mental powers to focus on the dust in his airway and a floor tile below his face. He summoned the dust to the tile, and the wood powder flew out of his body into a neat pile on the floor. Flarence just watched. He had no desire to hurt his brother; he was just letting off steam.

"I get that you like Tyrell, but how could you have been stupid enough to Enchant Darren?" said Flarence. "This is beyond reckless."

Soleil focused on the air in the room and altered its temperature to create small pockets that were warmer than others. The rapidly changing temperature caused it to move, and the changes occurred so suddenly that a small cyclone formed which sucked up the pile of sawdust. He moved the twister toward Flarence, who raised his arm in front of his mouth to avoid the dust. As the dust spun, Soleil forced the grains to come together and solidify into a multitude of small wooden blocks, which he summoned to the tiles on the floor around Flarence. When Flarence was fully encased, Soleil solidified the entire structure, enclosing Flarence in a wooden casket, and increased the temperature of the wood until it burst into flames.

A moment later, Flarence manipulated the air so the box was surrounded by carbon dioxide rather than oxygen, and the fire died. There were a series of pounding noises as Flarence punched his way out of the casket, his Wrist Cannon strapped to his arm. Soleil was ready for him, and leaped forward and struck him with a chair. As Flarence stumbled back, Soleil picked up a pepper shaker from a table and hurled it at Flarence's face, deconstructing the glass while it was airborne. Flarence put his hands up a moment too late and took a face full of pepper in his eyes and nose.

"None of what's been happening was Tyrell's fault," Soleil shouted over Florence's groaning. "I chose Tyrell as my master because I wanted to make his life easier, but so far, all I've done is screw everything up. Saving Darren wasn't a stupid mistake; it was the only thing I've done right so far."

Florence's moans subsided, and he stood up. The pepper was piled neatly on the floor by his feet, and he was completely healed, his eyes not the slightest bit bloodshot. He lunged at Soleil, grabbed his arm, and twisted it to pin Soleil to a table. "Darren is a gangster. He's dangerous, and he can't be trusted."

Soleil jerked his body clumsily against the hold, and his shoulder disconnected from its socket. He cried out, but he wasn't pinned to the table anymore. He kicked his foot into Florence's knee, knocking him down as Soleil's arm popped back into place.

Soleil backed away from Florence. "Darren has a history of gang activity, but that's no reason for him to be taken away from his son. I was trying to save Tyrell from the pain of losing his family. I didn't want him to end up like Claire."

Florence held his hand in front of him, and the Stakehail Colt flew out of his pocket into his palm. "Don't you dare bring Claire into this," he shouted as he clicked the cylinder release with his thumb and loaded the gun with gas and ice.

Before Soleil could apologize, Florence set the canister and the cylinder back in place and fired all six rounds. Soleil focused on the ice as it flew at him, and melted the charges before they struck his body. Florence pressed the cylinder release again and drew the mist back into the gun.

"I'm sorry," said Soleil, "I shouldn't have said that."

"No, you shouldn't," said Florence as he fired again.

"What I meant," said Soleil as he melted the second round of icicles, "was that Claire went through the pain of losing a loved one, and she was never the same again."

Florence drew the mist back into his gun and prepared to fire again. He knew Soleil could just keep melting the bullets, but that was all right. Every time Flarence pulled the trigger, he felt a little better. "You're right," he said as he emptied his gun again, still failing to hit Soleil, "Claire had a hard time getting over her dad's death, but the experience made her a stronger person. She went from being a troubled kid to a valuable partner."

"Were her troubles worth you gaining a partner? If you could go back, knowing what you know now, would you save her dad, or let him die so she could be your sidekick?"

Flarence stood still with his gun aimed at Soleil but didn't reload it. The two stared at each other as the mist dispersed through the cafe. "I'd save him," said Flarence as he slipped the Stakehail Colt back into his pocket. "What happened to Claire wasn't fair. I helped her get revenge because I wanted her to be happy. That's the same reason I let her stay with me and help me with my work."

Soleil relaxed and turned away from Flarence. He deconstructed what was left of the once-burning wooden cage and remolded it into a solid counter again.

"But this is different," Flarence said when Soleil turned back around. "Enchanting someone without their consent or approval of the Council is probably going to get you in a lot of trouble."

"You don't even believe in the Council," said Soleil, "and if a Council member doesn't approve of what I did, they can come find me. I'm prepared to defend my actions."

"You won't get the chance," said Flarence. "The Council doesn't work that way. You don't get a warning. They don't even punish you directly. One day, everything is normal, and the next thing you know, people are suffering at the hands of one of the Council's henchmen."

"That's ridiculous," said Soleil, "and how would you even know that?"

Flarence dropped his gaze to the floor. "Because it's happening to me," he admitted. "A Genie has been hurting innocent people specifically to get to me. Claire thinks he's from the Council. I haven't found a lot of evidence supporting that, but I haven't found evidence against it either."

Soleil approached Flarence. "How long has this been going on?"
"A few days."

Soleil threw a right hook that temporarily broke Flarence's nose. The moment it was healed, he swung with his left and broke it again. Flarence didn't flinch either time.

"You've had contact with the Council for a few *days*, and you didn't tell me?" Soleil threw another punch, but this time Flarence blocked it.

"No, that's what I'm trying to tell you. I haven't had any direct contact with the Student at all. He's been torturing me by tormenting innocent people. He's also been very careful about not leaving evidence behind. I haven't been able to track him down. My only leads on him are what I've been able to see through his victims' eyes."

"He calls himself the Student?"

"No, that's the nickname Claire and I gave him. That's how little we know about him. We don't have a name or even a decent description other than what he wears. It's a white shirt, if you're interested. He wears a white shirt with notes scribbled all over it in black marker."

Soleil's brow furrowed, and he looked around the cafe. "Where is Claire anyway?"

"She's outside Tyrell's apartment with a pair of binoculars. She saw everything Darren did and relayed it to me over her cell phone before you arrived. She even told me the part where Darren threw himself into a couch. The man's not only dangerous, he's a moron."

"Flarence, stop spying on my master and his family, stay out of Darren's business, and get out of my cafe. I have the situation under control. I don't know what's going on between you and the Student, but it's your problem."

Flarence opened his mouth to say something, but Soleil pointed to the door, and Flarence held his tongue. Defeated, he summoned his body out of the cafe.

FLARENCE

Landing gracefully on the bed of his hotel room, Flarence took a moment to improve his hearing and listen for signs of others in the room but heard only his own heart and lungs. He thought about what Soleil had said, especially about Darren's being a good person, but he was worried that his brother wasn't seeing the whole picture. Flarence had dealt with the gang often enough to know that anyone involved with it was bad news. If the Slugs ever found out that one of their own was Enchanted, they would exploit it without hesitation. There was no way he was going to stop surveillance of Darren.

Thoughts of the Student and Darren were giving him a headache, and he tried to push them out of his mind. He performed an astral projection and focused on Claire. She was on the roof, hiding behind a brick chimney wearing her scarf and gloves with her hair tied back and the two needles stuck in it. He brought his projection back to his body and summon-traveled to the chimney.

"You were just supposed to be keeping an eye on Darren," he said when he appeared in front of Claire. "Why are you in your Razor Punk gear?"

"Because I'm not the only one watching him," said Claire. She slipped the binoculars off her neck and handed them to Flarence. "He's two buildings over. I don't think he's looked in my direction, but if he does, I'd feel more comfortable if he doesn't see my face."

Flarence looked through the binoculars, and sure enough, someone two buildings over was perched near the edge of the roof looking across the street. He wore a white baseball cap, gray polo shirt, and jeans. "I don't recognize him."

"I do," said Claire as Flarence handed back the binoculars. "I spent hours the other day researching him. That's Officer Tymbir."

"Are you sure he's watching Darren? He might just be a peeping tom, watching a woman who lives in the apartment."

Claire lifted the binoculars to her face and looked at Tymbir. "I've been sneaking glances in his direction. He looked surprised when

Darren summoned the remote and levitated the couch. Darren's been practicing his magic ever since we hung up, and Tymbir's had a look of shock on his face the whole time. Either he's watching Darren or a woman in the apartment is giving him one helluva show."

"I'll see what I can find out," said Flarence. He walked to the edge of the building and looked down into the alley. When it was deserted, he stepped off the roof and floated gracefully to the pavement, then walked down the alley to the base of the building Tymbir was on, bent into a low crouch, and with one last glance to make sure no one was watching launched himself upward, restoring his weight to normal as he approached the top and gripped the edge of the roof. He pulled his head above the ledge and found Tymbir still watching Darren's apartment. Flarence pulled the rest of his body up and approached the oblivious officer. "Can I ask what you're doing?" he asked.

Tymbir turned quickly and cocked his arm as if ready to throw a punch. Flarence put his hands up in an I-mean-you-no-harm gesture and Tymbir relaxed.

"It's a police matter. We're monitoring an individual on this block."

"I'm sorry to interrupt you," said Flarence. "You're not wearing a uniform. I didn't know you were an officer."

"I'm undercover," said Tymbir. He reached into a pocket and pulled out a badge.

Flarence walked toward Tymbir, stood next to him, and looked across the street at Darren's apartment. "Can I ask who's being watched?"

"I can't reveal that information."

"Can I ask what the person you're watching did? We don't have a killer on our street, do we?"

"Did you just move here?" said Tymbir. "Do you know what neighborhood you're in? That building is full of bad people."

"I'm well aware of the dangers of this neighborhood. I heard a man was shot recently. Have you been looking into that?"

Tymbir rubbed his temples and sighed deeply. "Sir, this is a police matter. It's a very important police matter, and you're interfering. If you care about the well-being of your community, you'll leave me alone so I can get back to my surveillance."

"I care about my community more than most," said Flarence. "That's why I get concerned when I find a police officer spying on a resident from a roof."

"I understand your concern, but your actions aren't helping. I'm busy. Leave."

"If you could just give me any information at all about the person you're watching, I would appreciate it. I'm not asking for a name. Just tell me what they are suspected of. Is there anything you can tell me?"

"I said back off," Tymbir shouted as he swung his elbow, which caught Flarence in the chin. Flarence staggered back and pretended to be in more pain than he was.

"I'm just a concerned citizen," said Flarence. He tried to sound as if his lip was swollen, and kept his hand over his face to hide that he was unharmed.

"You want another one?" said Tymbir, his hand in a fist.

Tymbir turned back to Darren's apartment and put the binoculars to his eyes. Flarence went in the stairway door, but as soon as it closed behind him, he summoned his body to the chimney where Claire was waiting. She gripped Flarence's forearm, and he summoned the two of them back to their hotel room. When they arrived, Flarence held up a finger, telling Claire to be quiet while he improved his senses and listened for heartbeats, then gave her a thumbs-up when he determined they were alone. "You were right," he said as Claire slipped her gloves off, "that cop's a real jerk."

"A jerk who knows about magic," said Claire as she took the needles out of her hair and slipped them under her sleeves. "You should have roughed him up a little, told him to stay away from Darren."

"We already have our hands full with the Student. I didn't want to have a cop on our backs as well."

Claire untied the scarf and looped it through her chains. "After we hung up, Darren learned how to make objects spontaneously combust. Tymbir saw him set fire to a door in his apartment and put it out without an extinguisher. If I were him, I'd be freaking out right now. What if Tymbir goes to Darren's place and brings a bunch of cops? Darren won't just surrender and let them take him. He might not have as strong a grasp on his powers as you and Soleil, but he'll be able to fight off the cops without too much trouble." She untied the shirt around her waist and put it on, adjusting it until there were no visible lumps from the scarf or the chains underneath.

"That's assuming Tymbir even brings more cops into this," said Flarence. "When I talked to him, he said he was undercover, but I'm not sure I buy that. We know he's involved with the people who kidnapped Tyrell, and might have been the one who set it all up. If he wants to take action against Darren, I'll bet he won't bring other officers into it."

"Even if he doesn't, it's going to be bad," said Claire. "You didn't see what was in that house Soleil found."

"No matter what he does, Darren can heal quickly now. Tymbir can bring his whole artillery right to Darren's door, and it still wouldn't be enough to kill him. Whatever happens in that apartment, the only way it can end is with Darren standing over a pile of bodies."

"It's not Darren I'm scared for," said Claire. "I don't want Tyrell getting caught in the crossfire. He's a good kid."

"I'm getting sick of hearing that," said Flarence. "Tyrell's a good kid. I get it. Apparently, he's a sweet boy who deserves nothing but the best. You can go keep an eye on him if he means that much to you. Personally, I'd rather focus on the Student."

"That sounds good to me," said Claire. "I'll get closer to Tyrell and let him know Tymbir is spying on his dad. Keep me updated on what you find out about the Student." She pulled her cell phone out of her pocket. "I'm going to order out for lunch. What are you in the mood for?"

The two decided on a pizza, and spent the rest of the day discussing their next moves.

-7-

DARREN

Darren was alone in his apartment while Monday afternoon seemed to fly by. Tyrell was at school, Atalissa was at work, and he had the whole day to become more comfortable with his new abilities. He'd spent an hour on his bed with a knife, cutting himself in various places just to watch the wounds heal. No matter how deep he drove the knife or how serious the cut was the wound closed before any blood dripped onto the floor. He stopped after he'd slashed his wrist, and decided he was taking things too far. Atalissa would have freaked out.

He filled a glass with water and spent another hour playing with the temperature. He willed the water to a rolling boil, then instantly decreased the temperature to zero. The change was so fast the bubbles formed when the water was boiling froze in place. He altered the temperature more to make the water lukewarm, then chilled it, then froze it again. After his fun with water, he followed Soleil's advice and practiced making objects invisible. He picked up a metal spoon from a drawer and pushed the light reflecting off it to a wavelength outside the visible spectrum.

He also experimented with deconstruction, manipulating the spoon to create a series of small, strategically placed dents in the handle that caused it to weaken and the spoon to bend. Then he reversed the technique, slowly restoring its original shape. He did the same with a scoop, making it resemble a spearhead that flew across the room.

He became bored with practicing by himself. He needed to show off what he had learned, but there weren't many people he could show off to. The rules said he had to keep his powers a secret, which meant the only people he could talk to were the those who already knew about magic. With Tyrell and Atalissa unavailable, he was stuck with Soleil.

He ate a quick bowl of cereal took a shower. Keeping the water on its coldest setting, he warmed the droplets to a comfortable temperature before they hit his body. He thought about how handy temperature control was going to be during the winter months. Instead of toweling off, he heated the water on his skin and hair until it evaporated, and summoned a set of clothes as he walked by his room. Once he was dressed, he stood before an open window. He looked around and summoned his body to a distant place. Soon he was standing in Soleil's Cafe with his hands on the wooden counter.

Soleil jumped when Darren appeared. He was wearing black jeans and a Dark Side of the Moon T-shirt, and had a joint hanging from his mouth. The miniature radio was playing a guitar solo from a classic rock tune that Darren didn't recognize.

"That's a filthy habit," Darren said.

Soleil tore the joint from his mouth and rubbed the tip with his thumb and index finger. "What are you doing here? You shouldn't be using your powers in public this soon. There's no way you're ready yet."

"I just summoned my body to your cafe," said Darren. "I think that goes to show I'm getting the hang of it."

"You were slow. You disintegrated the wall as you traveled to it, but you were already at the counter before you had it completely reconstructed. You need to be able to break things down and put them back together so fast it's unnoticeable."

Darren sat in a chair by the counter. "Well, I'm already here, so you might as well give me some pointers." Soleil slipped the joint into his back pocket and nodded in agreement. "I never took you for a smoker," Darren said.

"I bought these years ago," Soleil answered. "I kicked the habit for a while but kept my stash around. It's been a stressful week, so I got back on the horse. It's not like it has a lasting effect on me. Thanks to my healing powers, the buzz lasts only a second. But it still tastes good going down."

"Can I get a hit?" said Darren. Soleil looked hesitant. "We both had a stressful week," he urged.

Soleil lit the joint again and the two passed it back and forth while the radio continued to play old songs. When all that remained was a stub of paper, Darren incinerated it, and Soleil taught him the tricks he hadn't figured out for himself yet, like how to control electricity to make light bulbs burn out. Darren also continued practicing the process of deconstructing and reconstructing objects, but no matter how fast he did it, Soleil said it wasn't quick enough, and Darren had to stop from frustration. He also had trouble performing astral projections, but Soleil said that was one of the more difficult things to do. Remembering running home from the hospital after being shot, Darren decided to explore his physical abilities. Soleil didn't have any exercise equipment in his cafe, so the two of them did simple exercises, and Darren was shocked at how many pushups he could do without breaking a sweat.

"Don't get any ideas about becoming a body builder," said Soleil when Darren stood up. "You're not feeling any discomfort because your abilities are lessening the toll physical activity takes on your muscles, but it's the burn that adds mass." Soleil went to the refrigerator and pulled out two water bottles. "You've made some serious progress," he said.

"I can't believe how easy it is," said Darren. "I just think about it and it happens." He froze the water and then warmed it to liquid again. They heard the door open and turned around to see Tyrell and Lucy walk in. "Shouldn't you be in school?" said Darren.

"School's over for the day," said Tyrell as he held the door open for Lucy. "We thought we'd stop by." Behind him, Claire appeared in the doorway. Darren looked surprised, but Tyrell cut in before he could say anything. "Soleil, this is Claire. She's an old friend."

Soleil played along. "Hi, Claire, I'm Soleil. This is my place. Make yourself at home. Can I get you anything?"

"In a minute," said Lucy. "See, Claire, I told you this place was old-school. You've got to see the roof. Soleil keeps a sundial up there, and he paints his own calendars too."

"You two go right ahead," said Soleil. "The ladder is resting on the wall. Don't mess with the string-and-nail art."

Claire and Lucy left, but Tyrell stayed in the doorway. "Aren't you coming?" asked Lucy.

"I've seen it," said Tyrell. "I'll order you some food while you're gone."

The two left, and Tyrell let the door swing shut as he approached the counter. "Do you know what this is about?"

"Flarence came here last night," said Soleil. "He said he's been watching you, but I told him to knock it off."

"Well, you should have told Claire. I was leaving school, and she just walked up to me like we're old friends."

"Tell her to leave you alone," said Darren. "She works with Flarence, and I don't trust her."

"I'd like to tell her to leave," said Tyrell, "but her and Lucy are really hitting it off. If I tell Claire to go home, Lucy is going to ask me why I'm being rude, and I don't have a good explanation."

Soleil took a carton of eggs out of the refrigerator. "This can't be Flarence's idea. I told him to back off, and he said he would. I'm sure Claire has her own reason for showing up."

"I don't care what her reasons are," said Tyrell. "I don't trust her either. She's the one who tried to intimidate Rookie and got dad beat up by Jordan."

Soleil two eggs in a bowl and stirred them with a fork before pouring them in a skillet. He didn't bother turning on the stove and used his magic to cook them. Claire and Lucy came back in as Soleil finished serving the food.

Lucy started asking how Tyrell and Claire knew each other. Tyrell ordered a milkshake and stayed quiet while Claire made up a story about how she used to live in the same apartment and had been good friends with Darren before moving to Indiana for work. Soon the conversation between Claire and Lucy shifted to movies and music. It turned out they had similar interests and Darren could see why they were becoming friends so quickly. "It's getting late," said Darren when everyone was done eating. "I'd better get going."

"I'll give you a ride," said Lucy. "I was going to drop Claire back at your place later anyway."

Darren looked at Tyrell. "Claire is coming to our place?"

Tyrell nodded sheepishly.

"Since I'm back in town, I thought it might be fun to catch up," said Claire. When they arrived, the apartment was empty, since Atalissa had not gotten home from work yet.

"All right, what the hell?" said Darren when they were all inside.

"That's no way to greet a guest," said Claire, "especially an old friend back from Indiana you haven't seen in years."

"I'd prefer it if you really would move to Indiana, and we really didn't see you for a few years," said Darren. "I don't want anything to do with you or Flarence."

"He doesn't want anything to do with you either," said Claire. "He has his own problems to worry about. I'm here because I think you're in trouble."

"We've been in trouble for a while now," said Tyrell. "Our reputation has been going downhill. Jordan sent people to search our house. I've been kidnapped, and dad was shot. The time to warn us is long past."

"It's about the man who kidnapped you," said Claire. "Officer Tymbir was by your apartment yesterday. I'm pretty sure he was watching you."

"How did you see him?" said Darren.

"I was standing on a different rooftop with my own pair of binoculars. I was watching you too. I saw you running down the street the night you were supposed to be in the hospital, and I noticed something wasn't right. I was worried that you might have been Enchanted."

"You were right," said Darren. "Soleil Enchanted me, and with my new powers, I'm perfectly capable of looking after myself. I'm curious, can you use magic yourself?"

"No," said Claire. "Florence and I have talked about it, but I told him I don't want to be Enchanted."

"Then you're the one at a disadvantage here," said Darren. "You're the one who needs to be warned when she's in trouble. Stop worrying about me and start watching your own back."

Claire put her hands on her hips. "I'm not helpless."

"I'm sorry about that," said Tyrell. "What dad meant to say was that we appreciate you warning us, but we both saw Tymbir's secret house. If he wants to start trouble, he's going to come here with firearms. Dad's magic can give us more of an advantage than your needles and razors. Again, thank you for caring, but there's nothing more you can do here. You should go back to helping Florence. We'll be fine."

Darren heard a thud behind him. Before he could turn, a sharp pain in his back made him fall down. He rolled over and saw another man where he had been standing. It was just like what had happened the night he was in jail: Soleil entered the cell to break Darren out by falling through the ceiling.

The man was taller than Soleil. His collar was up and held closed with safety pins. His hat was pulled almost to his sunglasses.

"I'm not sure I even want to ask who you are," said Darren.

Claire took on a fighting stance. "That's the Student," she said. "He's the one Florence and I have been looking for. He maimed a helpless child. He bribed a group of homeless people into jumping into a fight he knew they couldn't win."

Claire took a step forward and delivered a series of kicks. The Student moved back to avoid them and grabbed an arm of the couch, which he made light enough to swing like a baseball bat. Claire fell onto her back to narrowly avoid the blow. When she regained her footing, the Student was holding a leg of the couch raised above his head like an ax. He swung it at Claire, who caught it before it hit her face. The Student increased the weight of the couch, and

Claire's knees buckled. She pushed as hard as she could and then leaped out of the way. The Student lost his balance and fell to one knee as the couch crashed to the floor. Claire dove and kneed him in the face. The Student stumbled back. She tried to punch him, but he countered and threw her to the floor, driving a knee into her back and twisting her arm. He reached into her sleeve and pulled out one of the needles.

Darren couldn't just sit and watch someone be murdered in his apartment. The spoon he had been experimenting with was still resting by the sink. He summoned it to his body, sharpened the tip into a spear, and entered the fray. The Student heard him charge noisily across the room and let go of Claire's arm before summoning his body to a wall of the apartment, stiff-arming Darren in the throat as he traveled. The air was forced out of Darren, and he fell to the floor, but two deep breaths later, the air came back easily. The Student stared at him, confused at the fast recovery, and Darren tried to take advantage of his dropped guard. He approached the Student and raised the hand that held the spoon but stopped when he saw it was no longer in his hand. He turned and saw a pile of metal flakes on the floor where he'd been standing.

"He's a Genie, you idiot," said Claire, who was back on her feet and standing next to Darren. "He can do everything you can do, including deconstruct objects." Tyrell cowered in a corner, trying to stay as far from the fight as possible. Claire had once again adopted her fighting stance, but the arm the Student had twisted was lower than the other. He circled them, threateningly waving Claire's needle.

She quickly knelt and picked up a handful of metal shavings that had once been the spoon, then charged at the Student. He stabbed at her with the needle, but she dropped to the floor and slid past him. The Student turned to stab at her again, but she avoided that strike as well. Darren rushed the Student and tried to punch him in the face, but he bobbed aside and stabbed Darren in the chest. The needle punctured his lung, and the Student threw him across the room to the corner where Tyrell was trembling. Tyrell tried to examine the wound, but Darren pushed him away and got back on his feet. Though his wound had healed, getting stabbed still hurt, and he had no intention of letting it happen again.

The Student continued attacking Claire, who kept ducking and weaving to avoid his blows. Frustrated, he lashed out with wide, sloppy swings. With a grunt, the Student held the needle high over his head and swung it directly at Claire's neck. She leaped back as the Student charged at her and quickly tossed the metal shavings on the floor so he slipped and fell forward. As he lay on his stomach in front of her, Claire brought her foot down on the Student's hand, and he let go of the needle. He tried to grab it with his other hand, but Claire kicked it away and reached for her other needle. But before she could remove it, she was flung across the room into a wall. Instead of letting her collapse to the floor, though, the Student, now back on his feet, made her body fly toward him.

Tyrell had told Darren about Claire's attire, and he realized the Student was performing summoning spells on her chains, jerking her around like a dog on a leash. Claire flew helplessly across the room toward the Student, who grabbed her by the shirt with one hand and the waist of her jeans with the other. He lifted her above his head and threw her to the ground. She hit the floor hard, and when she tried to get up, he kicked her in the ribs. She stayed down with her knees tucked into her chest as she tried to breathe. The Student extended his hand again, and the needle Claire had kicked away flew to him. He stood over her, prepared to deliver the final blow—but Darren grabbed his arm. The Student threw a punch with his other hand, but Darren grabbed his wrist, and the two stood grappling together over Claire as she struggled for air.

The Student gripped Darren tightly and tried to make him lose his balance. But Darren wasn't trying to overpower the Student; he was positioning him. Darren took a quick step back and to the right so the Student was between him and the television. Old and bulky as it was, it was still smaller than a person. He summoned the television to his body—making it crash into the back of the Student's head. The Student fell forward into Darren, who seized him in a bear hug and summoned his body to a wall so that the Student was driven into it. Darren did it again and again, summoning to different walls and the ceiling while holding the Student.

The two of them bounced back and forth until the Student finally broke Darren's grip in mid-summon and sprawled to the floor while Darren continued to the wall. The Student rose to his feet, but Claire was ready for him with the other needle in her hand. Now it was her turn to give in to frustration. With a shout of anger, she ran at him and drove her knee into his chest. Darren seized the Student from behind and held him while Claire prepared to drive the needle into his eye. Her hand moved, but stopped before she made contact. Claire stood in front of them with the needle in her hand and looked around the apartment as if distracted.

"You freaking wuss!" she yelled. "Where are you?"

The Student thrashed about and broke Darren's hold. He started throwing wild punches, which Darren easily avoided. Claire was acting wildly as well. She ran around the apartment, waving the needle and making random strikes as if trying to stab a ghost. Ignoring the Student, she ran to a window, threw it open, and stuck her head out. A moment later, she pounded her fists on the windowsill. "I see you, you bastard. Get over here!" The Student threw one final sloppy punch and then collapsed at Darren's feet. Claire pounded her fists on the windowsill again. "Damn it," she screamed.

She stood by the window gasping, the needle still clenched tightly in her hand. Darren's gaze switched from her to the Student lying still at his feet. Claire pulled her head back into the room and rushed to Darren. "Look into his past," she shouted. "Now."

"Look into his what?" said Darren. At that moment, the Student vanished.

"Great," said Claire. "He's just summoned the body away." She sat on the floor, leaning against the couch with its partially shattered frame and two broken legs. "You can learn about an object's history when you make physical contact with it," she said while she tapped her needle on the ground. "I guess Soleil hasn't taught you that yet. You can also improve your senses. If you improved your hearing, you would have been able to hear heartbeats, and you would have noticed he didn't have one. He probably hasn't had one for a while. It's called the Corpse Puppet spell. At least that's what Flarence calls it. You can't perform magic on a living thing without Enchanting it, but dead people can't be Genies, so you can do all the spells you want on them without giving them powers. The Student we've been chasing has been a dead body this whole time. A dead body being controlled by another Genie."

"How did you know it wasn't really him?" said Darren.

Claire slowly rose to her feet and placed the needle in her sleeve. "I should have realized it earlier. The first clue was when he threw me. He touched my skin when he grabbed my pants, and his fingers felt cold. Too cold. The second clue was when I kneed him. Usually I can feel the air pushed out of someone's lungs, but that didn't happen with him. He didn't have any air to get pushed out." She collected her other needle from the floor.

"So where's the real Student?" said Darren.

"I saw him across the street. He was standing on the same rooftop I was watching you from last night. I don't think he had his disguise on, but he summoned off somewhere when he saw me staring at him, not wanting me to get too good a look. Not that it mattered. He was too far away for me to see his face."

Tyrell finally found the courage to emerge from the corner. "We need to tell Soleil."

Claire shook her head. "We need to tell Flarence. He's been looking into the Student. He's been talking to the victims and trying to track him down. He has more information than Soleil."

"They both should know," said Darren. "This guy is too much for one person to handle."

"I say we meet at Soleil's Cafe as soon as possible," said Claire as she walked to the door. "I'll call Flarence and tell him to meet us there. I'm taking the bus. You two get there any way you want."

"We can all go together," said Tyrell. "It would probably be safer to travel in groups."

"Thanks," said Claire," but I think I'd rather go alone."

"Claire," said Darren, "I'm sorry about what I said before. That was out of line. I didn't expect you to be able to land a hit against someone with powers."

Claire turned around and looked coldly at Darren. "I've been living with Flarence for years. In that time, he's told me everything Genies are capable of. He's taught me how to hold my ground even when I'm at a disadvantage."

"Again, I'm sorry," said Darren, "but the Student might come back, and you can't take him by yourself. He almost stabbed you earlier. You can't be alone right now."

Claire didn't say anything, but nodded in agreement and stayed in the apartment as she dialed Flarence's number.

SOLEIL

It was a little after six in the afternoon, and everyone was at Soleil's Cafe. Soleil gave Claire a few ice cubes wrapped in a napkin to place against her sore ribs. She was sitting at his counter, with Flarence on her right next to Darren and Tyrell as they described their encounter with the Student.

"Wait, you think he was controlling the corpse from across the street?" said Flarence. "The Student must have been drastically improving his eyesight, controlling the corpse's skeletal muscles, and summoning objects to the dead body. How could anyone have that much control over their powers? Soleil and I have been practicing for centuries, and even we can't perform that many spells simultaneously."

"Claire," Tyrell interrupted, "I know this isn't the best time, but I have to ask how you got into all this. Being around Flarence only puts you in danger, and it doesn't seem like he's forcing you to stay with him. I don't mean to sound offensive, but why are you helping him?"

"That's a story for another time," said Claire. "We have more important things to worry about right now."

"That's right," said Darren. "We have to focus on this Student business. By the way, Soleil, why didn't you tell me we could make dead people walk?"

"I never imagined a time when you would have to use it," said Soleil, "and I was going to tell you how to improve your senses tomorrow."

"Why does he hate Claire so much anyway?" asked Tyrell.

"He doesn't hate Claire," said Flarence. "He's been trying to get to me for days, but he's never come to me directly. He's been attacking other people to get to me. Claire and I have been exploring the possibility that he's part of the Council. I didn't believe it at first, but Dad always said those Genies could use their powers in strange ways. I'm sorry, Soleil. For years, you and Dad have been warning me that the Elders wouldn't allow my behavior to slide forever. Now it's starting to look like they're actually stepping in."

Soleil thought about what it would mean if the Student was in fact a member of the Council. He had wanted a sign of the Council's existence for a long time, but if hurting innocent people to make a point was how they operated, he wondered if he really did want to meet them. "Did you find out anything when visiting the Student's victims?"

"Nothing particularly useful," said Flarence. "None of the people he's gone after have had any enemies or troubling pasts. It seems he's only interested in going after innocent people. Weak people. People he can overpower easily."

"He broke that pattern with us," said Darren. "We weren't so easy to overpower."

"He didn't know you were Enchanted," said Claire. "When you healed, he looked surprised, or at least the corpse paused. He was caught off guard. If he goes after you again, he'll know what to expect."

"If he comes after me again, I won't hesitate," said Darren. "He caught me off guard too. I've never fought anyone with powers before, but next time, I'll be ready."

"That's if you're the one he goes after next," said Tyrell, who suddenly looked scared. "Flarence, you said the Student likes going after people weaker than him. He knows Darren has powers now, so he's probably safe."

Soleil realized why Tyrell was so frightened. "Flarence, you said the Student wanted to focus on people you care about. It's possible that he believes you're in some way connected to Tyrell and his family, since Claire was with them tonight. He knows now that Claire can hold her ground in a fight with a Genie, especially when she's working with Darren. Tyrell will probably be safe as long as one of us stays close to him. Who's left?"

"Atalissa," said Darren. "She's the next weakest link. She doesn't have powers, she's never had any experience fighting Genies, and right now she's alone!" Claire pulled her phone out and handed it to him. Everyone was silent, and the room was quiet enough for Soleil to hear the phone ringing.

"Nothing," said Darren as the phone went to voicemail. "We have to get home."

"Wait," said Flarence as he turned to Claire. "Can you walk?"

Claire took the ice from her chest, got up, and stretched. "It's just a bruise. I've had worse."

"I think you should go with Darren," said Flarence. "No offense, Darren, but you haven't had powers for long and may need backup."

"Claire just had the wind knocked out of her and almost died," said Darren. "She needs to take a break."

"I don't want a break," said Claire. "I want a rematch."

Darren looked back and forth from Tyrell to Claire.

"Dad," said Tyrell, "we need to move. Mom might be in trouble. Just grab her and let's go." Darren sighed, took Tyrell's arm with one hand and Claire's with the other, and summoned them all away from the cafe.

When they were gone, Flarence stood up and started pacing. "I'll be honest, I didn't ask Claire to leave just to give Darren backup. I have a hunch, but I need to run it by you first."

"A hunch about what?" said Soleil. "Do you have an idea where the Student is?"

"I have a hunch about who he is." He turned to face Soleil. "Think about what the Student does. He threatens other people to make them do his dirty work. He sends me messages, but they never come directly from him. He always makes someone else deliver the paper."

"It's to cover his tracks," said Soleil.

"But that's just it, why is he bothering to cover his tracks so well? Why bother hiding his face?"

Soleil shrugged. "He probably used the disguise to make the corpse appear less dead. Besides, if he's a member of the Council, he probably would need to keep his identity a secret."

"That's what I thought at first, but I'm starting to think there's more to it. I don't think he's hiding his identity from everybody, just me specifically. You heard Claire's description of the fight. The Student knew she had chains under her shirt and used them against her. He also knew she kept needles in her sleeves."

"You said he was watching you. He probably knows that Claire is Razor Punk. This is all an interesting profile, but it doesn't tell anything useful. It just means he's familiar with your personal life and he wants to teach you a lesson without hurting you directly … " he trailed off as he realized what Flarence was suggesting. The kidnappings, fights, and threats were the actions of a monster, but familiarity with Flarence's life, disapproval of his activities, and using tough love to teach him a lesson were characteristic of a parent. "Flarence, no. Tell me you don't think Dad is behind this."

"I'm not comfortable admitting it either, but it's time we considered him a suspect. Dad has had more time to practice control over his powers than both of us combined, which makes him the only person I can think of who's capable of doing the things we've seen the Student do. I'm going to pay him a visit, and I need you to come with me. I hope I'm wrong, Soleil. I really do." He summoned out of the café, and Soleil disappeared right after him.

FLARENCE

Flarence reached the rock he had summoned his body to and stepped aside so he wouldn't get in the way when Soleil arrived. He was in the cave in the Rocky Mountains where he had grown up. Mohinaux had carved the structure into the mountain long ago, and had kept it hidden. There was no way in or out other than magic or explosives. Once Mohinaux carved the cave, he placed stones in the entrance, which became hidden over the years by moss and trees.

The room was a perfect dome but was too small for three people to live in comfortably. It peaked at about twenty feet high, had a thirty-foot diameter, and took some getting used to when Flarence and Soleil were growing up. The closest thing to furniture was the scattered boulders, and the only light came from torches in the walls and floor. Each held a glass orb filled with neon gas. Flarence magically excited the atoms to make the gas glow, filling the cave with an eerie radiance. Mohinaux was even more serious about living in secret than Soleil, and blocked out any connection with the outside world. He didn't even make holes for sunlight or ventilation, and maintained the air quality by magically breaking down exhaled carbon dioxide to generate fresh oxygen.

Flarence knelt down and felt the ground. He let a handful of dirt fall through his fingers as memories of childhood came back. "Dad says I don't visit often enough," he said to Soleil. "It's been almost fifty years since I've been here. I just never had a strong connection to this place. It's so small and empty. I need to move around."

"I still visit once every few years or so," Soleil answered, "but then again, it means more to me. It's how I got my name, remember?"

Flarence nodded and stood up. "Dad said that when he became a father, he had no reason to see the sun anymore because we were the light in his life. Of course, you were the one who got the sun-based name. Even then, you were the favorite."

Soleil paced around while Flarence sat silently on the ground. In his heart, he refused to believe that his father had attacked Claire, but his gut told him he was right. His mind told his gut and his heart to shut up. The silence became unbearable, and he punched a wall. "Where is he? The man lives in a freaking cave! He doesn't have any friends, we're his only family, it's not like he has a job. What could he possibly be doing right now?"

"He's probably out walking around," Soleil said calmly. "It's a cramped room, and even he needs to go out for some fresh air once in a while."

"He'd better get here soon. If he isn't the Student, then Claire is still in danger. I can't wait around much longer."

There was another breeze, and Flarence turned around to see Mohinaux standing at the boulder. His face lit up when he saw them, and he gave each son a hug. "Flarence, what brings you here? I hardly remember the last time you visited me."

Flarence pulled away from Mohinaux's embrace. "Where were you just now?"

"I was just walking around the mountains, enjoying the day."

"You weren't reburying a dead body you were controlling earlier?" said Soleil.

"Does that question have meaning?" said Mohinaux. "I like it when the two of you come by, but I'm a little uncomfortable with you visiting just to ask me if I'm exhuming people."

"This is serious, Dad," said Flarence. "Claire was attacked earlier. Someone tried to kill her using the Corpse Puppet spell."

"I'm sorry to hear that, but what makes you think it was me?"

Flarence noticed Mohinaux's eyes darting back and forth between him and Soleil.

"The attack on Claire wasn't entirely unexpected," said Flarence. "Someone's been following me for a few days, and I have reason to believe he's a member of the Council. Claire and I have been calling him the Student because we don't know his real name."

"I always thought I'd be happy to meet a member of the Council," said Soleil, "but based on what Flarence has been telling me, it seems they aren't what I was expecting. Flarence is the one they're upset with, but he's the only one the Student isn't punishing."

"The Council always has a reason for their actions," said Mohinaux.

"The reason for their actions was to get my attention," said Flarence. "They have it. Innocent people have been hurt because of me. Claire was nearly killed earlier. The Council owes me an explanation. I'm ready to listen."

"You're ready when the Council says you're ready," said Mohinaux. "They come to you, you don't go to them."

"If there's one thing the Council should know by now, it's that I'm not much for following the rules," said Flarence.

"And that's exactly what got you in trouble in the first place," said Mohinaux. "Searching for the Council is only going to make things worse."

"What if I look for them?" said Soleil. "I've been following the rules for years, but I'm worried that I've made a mistake. Flarence doesn't trust my new master's family, and I can see his point. If the Council shares Flarence's perspective, I'd like to know what they plan on doing should they decide to get involved."

"I'm sure everything will be fine," said Mohinaux.

"I'm not," said Soleil. "When the Council decided to take action against Flarence, they sent the Student without warning."

"If it makes you more comfortable, I'll help keep an eye on Darren," said Mohinaux. "I'll watch him from a distance, and if he gets out of line, I'll let you know, but there shouldn't be anything to worry about as long as he follows the rules. Have you walked him through those yet?"

"Soleil just said I didn't trust his new master," said Flarence. "He didn't say anything about Darren being Enchanted."

Mohinaux glanced back and forth between Flarence and Soleil. "I just assumed it. Why else would he be so worried?"

Flarence walked to the boulder that the three of them had used as a summoning object. He made it levitate, kicked it across the room, and examined the spot it had been resting on. "You didn't assume it, you knew it. You knew because you invaded Darren's home and fought him. You went there to kill Claire, but Darren was familiar enough with his powers to put up a fight, and you weren't a match for both of them. I have a feeling your outfit is in this room somewhere." He walked to a smaller boulder, kicked it across the room, and once again examined the dirt, but there was nothing there.

"Flarence, stop. I promise you there is nothing under any of the rocks."

Flarence was about to kick another one but stopped. He walked up to Mohinaux until their faces were inches apart. "Say that again."

"There is nothing under the rocks, I promise." Mohinaux's face stayed straight.

"Tell me there are no clothes hidden in this room," said Flarence.

"There aren't," said Mohinaux. Flarence held his gaze, and noticed Mohinaux's eyes drift.

"There is something here," said Flarence, "but it isn't under the rocks, is it?" He approached the boulder the three of them had summoned themselves to and turned it into a pile of gravel. He plunged his hands into it and felt something soft. He stood up with his right fist extended in front. "I can feel it, Dad. Show us what it is." Mohinaux sighed, and several strands of white strings materialized in Flarence's hand.

"Reconstruct it," said Flarence. More strands emerged from the gravel and weaved themselves together to form a white collared shirt stained with writing. Flarence opened his hand, and the shirt fell in a heap on the ground.

"It's true," said Mohinaux. "I'm the Student, and I ...."

"Attacked Claire," said Flarence.

"That's what you're concerned about right now?" said Soleil.

Flarence's hands curled into fists, and he approached Mohinaux. "Yeah, it is. You tried to kill Claire!"

Soleil rushed in between them to hold Flarence back. "There are more important things to worry about." He turned to Mohinaux.

"Dad, you can introduce us to the Council. You can arrange for us to have a meeting with them."

"No, I can't," said Mohinaux.

"The Council used you to send Flarence a message," said Soleil. "You're the Student. Can't you give us their location? That's all we're asking."

"You're asking too much," said Mohinaux. "I can't give you any information on the Council. I'm sorry."

Soleil dropped his hand from Flarence's chest and stepped closer to Mohinaux. "Please, Dad, just give us one detail to confirm the Elders' existence, and we can finally stop arguing. Introduce us to the Council, let us meet them face to face, and prove Flarence wrong once and for all."

"I can't prove him wrong," said Mohinaux.

"Why not?" asked Soleil.

"Because he's right," said Mohinaux. Behind him, a chunk of wall fell to the ground. A book with a leather cover flew from the cavity. "I kept secrets from you boys to keep you and the people around you safe," said Mohinaux as he caught the book, "but lately, it's been causing both of you nothing but pain. The truth isn't going to be easy for you to hear, but it's time you knew what really made us what we are today. You two better sit down."

−8−

DARREN

"I still can't get it," said Darren as he attempted an astral projection to find Atalissa. He had been trying since leaving the cafe. Every few minutes, he took a break, and Tyrell tried calling Atalissa's cell phone. "Soleil says using magic is all about focus, but I'm thinking about her and I still can't see her."

"This spell is different," said Claire, "at least Flarence describes it as being different. To perform an astral projection, you actually have to lose focus first. You have to surrender your senses and break your connection with the world around you. You might be having trouble with it because you're so stressed about Atalissa being missing. You're expecting her to walk through the door at any minute and so you're listening for the door to open. I know this isn't the time to be negative, but try assuming that Atalissa isn't going to walk through the door. Assume she's in trouble and needs to be found."

"Maybe I should just summon myself to where she works," said Darren. "I'll ask around and see if she's there, and if she's not, I'll ask if they know where she went."

"I'll try calling her again first," said Tyrell. He started dialing, but before he could hit the call button, the door opened and Atalissa rushed into the room.

"Darren!" Atalissa ran to him and threw her arms around him. Then she broke away and hugged Tyrell. "I'm so glad you're all right." She turned to Claire.

"Hi, I'm Claire, Flarence's sidekick. You can call me Razor Punk. You're Atalissa, Darren's wife and Tyrell's mom. Now that the introductions are out of the way, let's get back on track. Where have you been? We've been trying to call you."

Atalissa turned to Darren. "I wanted to call you too, but my phone died. I wanted to come home right after work, but I felt like something was wrong. There was a car behind me, and when I was halfway home, I noticed it was still there. I thought it was following me."

"You might just be nervous," said Claire.

"No, the car was definitely following me. I'm home late because it took me so long to lose them. When I first noticed the car, I turned and went a few blocks in the opposite direction, and they were behind me the whole way. After weaving through the city, I finally got on the highway and drove like a maniac. I was going over the speed limit and switching lanes every second and swerving around cars, but the people following me were able to keep up. I finally drove off an exit too quick for them to follow and came home as fast as I could. Darren, someone is after us. We need to leave."

"Do you think it's the Student?" said Darren.

"The Student can summon places and become invisible," said Tyrell. "Why would he follow Mom in a car?"

"He wouldn't," said Claire as she walked to the window. "It isn't the Student. Atalissa, can you describe the car that was following you?"

"It was a black SUV with tinted windows," said Atalissa.

"Did it look like that?" asked Claire. Atalissa approached the window and nodded as she saw the black SUV parking outside their apartment. "They knew where you lived," said Claire, thinking out loud. "Why would they follow you if they knew where to find you?"

"I was followed once too," said Tyrell. "When it happened, I woke up in a strange house tied to a chair."

Claire pulled her shirt over her head and tied it around her waist.

"What are you doing?" asked Tyrell, as Claire tied her hair in a bun.

"It's Tymbir," she said as she inserted the needles into her hair.

"That doesn't answer my question," said Tyrell.

Claire tied the scarf around her face. "I think Tymbir became a cop just because he likes being in a position of authority. He does it so he can wear a uniform and have an excuse to push people around. He's looking for trouble. Stay close. I'll help keep you safe."

Darren looked down at the SUV.

"You need more time to recover from your fight with the Student," said Tyrell. "Dad, you should just get us out of here. Summon us back to the cafe."

"No I shouldn't," said Darren. "Take a look." Everyone approached the window. The SUV's lights were off, and seven people got out.

"They're coming in," said Atalissa. "Darren, we need to leave. Get us out of here."

"Why aren't they wearing police uniforms?" said Darren. "Whatever Tymbir has planned, the Police Department isn't involved. The guy's gone rogue." He walked to the door. "We're not going anywhere. I'm going to talk to them."

Tyrell grabbed Darren by the sleeve. "You heard Razor Punk, these people have guns. You can't even do all the spells Soleil can do yet."

"I can't perform astral projections very well," said Darren, "but I'm very good at deconstructing things. I'm capable of surviving a bullet shower."

"What about the rules?" asked Tyrell. "You have to keep your powers a secret. If you dissolve a bunch of guns in front of these people, they might not jump to the conclusion that you're a Genie but they'll know something supernatural is happening. You'll be in trouble with Tymbir, the Slugs, and the Council."

"I already stood up to the Council," said Darren. "The Student was sent to kill Razor Punk, and I stopped him. I'm probably already in trouble with them."

"Then why would you want to make it worse?" said Tyrell.

"Look, Tyrell, I'm just going to talk to them. Stay here. I'll be back before you know it." He took the stairs to the lobby, noticing that the group usually hanging out in the stairwell wasn't there, and he also became aware of voices from the ground floor. He rushed down and found the stair dwellers standing by the elevator. Darren knew nobody in the building liked it when strangers visited; the situation could quickly become violent.

"Why are you being so defensive?" one of the men from the SUV asked. "We're just here looking for a guy who lives in the building. Do you know someone named Darren Raleigh or not?"

J.J. stepped up to the stranger who had spoken. "We 'getting defensive' 'cause Darren been causing trouble lately. You wanna know where he is? You gotta tell us who you are and what you want him for."

"I'm right here," said Darren. He was standing at the foot of the stairs, the seven men from the SUV were in front of the broken elevator, and the stair dwellers were in between them.

"You're Darren?" said one of the men by the elevator. "Tymbir sent us to give you something." He reached into his jeans, pulled out a phone, and tossed it in a high arc. Darren caught it. "There's only one number in the contacts list. Call it when you're alone."

"Thanks," said Darren. He turned to leave, but J.J.'s voice stopped him.

"Who's Tymbir?"

"None of your business," said one of the strangers.

"Darren, tell me Tymbir isn't the guy who was in the apartment the night my gun went weird." J.J. reached behind his back and drew a pistol. "I've got a new one, and I've been keeping my eye on it. No way this one's goin' bad on me. If this got anything to do with my brother's death, I'm pulling the trigger again, and this time I'm going to hit what I'm aiming at."

"Put it down, punk," said one of the men by the elevator. J.J. kept his gun pointed in Darren's direction but turned his head to the strangers. They all were holding pistols of their own, as were two more stair dwellers.

"Okay, let's all just take it easy," said Darren. "There are a lot of guns out right now, and if someone makes a move, there are going to be losses on both sides. Why don't we all put them away, everyone who doesn't live here goes home, and everyone else goes back to the stairs and keeps having fun. Nobody gets hurt."

"We gave him the phone," said one of the strangers. "The ball's in his court now." Slowly the men lowered their guns and made their way out of the building. When they were gone, J.J. approached Darren. "You owe us all an explanation for that."

"And I would explain if I could," said Darren, "but I don't know any more about this Tymbir guy than you do."

"Call the number," said J.J.

"I'll call it when I'm alone," said Darren. "I know you're upset right now, but this is a personal matter."

He turned around and started walking up the stairs but stopped when he felt a hand on his shoulder. As he turned, J.J. swung the butt of his gun into Darren's forehead. "That's for … I don't know… everything."

Darren kept his hand up to his face to hide the healing bruise. "All right, I'll admit you had a right to do that, but you only get to do it once. If it happens again, I'm taking you down. Gun or no gun, I can do it." He continued up to his apartment, passing Claire crouched by a railing in her Razor Punk gear.

"Way to go," she said. "I was expecting a firefight for a minute."

"I hope I never see another gun again," said Darren.

Back at the apartment, Darren pulled up the contact list on the phone. He called the only number there and put the phone on speaker.

After two rings, there was a click and deep breathing on the other end of the line. "*This better be Darren.*"

"Tymbir?" said Darren. "Yeah, this is me."

"*You've been causing me some trouble lately.*"

"I've been causing you trouble? You just sent seven armed men to my apartment."

"*That's the least of your problems.*"

"Yeah, I know. You've also been going after my wife and son. Just tell me what you want."

"I might not have your wife or son, but I do have somebody." There
was a soft panting on the other end of the line.

"Tyrell?" said a female voice.

"Lucy!" said Tyrell.

SOLEIL

The boulders had been reconstructed and placed in a triangle in
the cave. Mohinaux sat cross-legged on one with the book in his lap.

"Not everything I told you was a lie. I truly have walked the earth
for centuries—millennia, actually. I was born during the seventeenth
century B.C. in Egypt. My home by the Delta was destroyed in an
invasion by what historians call the Hyksos, but the truth is much
more bizarre." He tossed the book to Soleil. "Open it. First page."

Soleil leaned close to Flarence and flipped back the leather cover.
The pages were yellowed with age, but Mohinaux had kept them
readable. On the first page was a hand-drawn sketch of a monstrous
figure. Its torso looked like a human's, with powerful abdominal
muscles. Its right arm looked like a bear's, large and strong and almost reaching the knees, covered with fur and ending in a set of
thick claws. The left arm was completely different—scaled, much
longer than the right, and rolled into a coil at the creature's feet. A
stinger extended from its end. The creature's legs were equal in
length and also covered in fur, with paws like a rat's. The head was
furry with pointed ears and a snout like a wolf, but above its dark
nose there appeared to be a fleshy straw. The teeth were razor sharp.
On its back was a pair of thin wings like an insect's.

"What is it?" said Soleil.

"Different groups called it different names," said Mohinaux. "The
closest translation of the word my people used is the Cannibal. We
saw it as a monster that was composed of all animals and feasted on
all animals. No matter what it consumed, it was eating its own
species. It had the arm of a snake, and it ate snakes. It had the chest

of a human, and it ate humans. It had the wings of an insect, and it ate insects."

"Why hasn't anyone seen it?" said Soleil.

"It's dead," said Mohinaux. "It died a long time ago."

"Then why should we care?" said Flarence. "Why are you showing us this?"

"My people cared because the Cannibal brought terror everywhere it went. You boys should care because that was the first Enchanted creature to walk the Earth."

"You made this thing?" said Soleil.

"No," said Mohinaux, "it made me. This creature traveled long distances for the sole purpose of finding food. As it traveled, people saw it, and its legend spread. Everyone had a different idea of where it came from, but one thing all people who saw it agreed on was that it was an effective predator. Nobody knew where it was going to strike next, and it traveled quickly, which made it difficult to track. It couldn't fly like a bird, but the wings let it travel long distances without leaving a trail to follow. As its legend grew, entire tribes lived in terror of it. It came to my homeland and killed dozens. It attacked Memphis and Heliopolis, tearing through houses and devouring men, women, and children as it pleased. We tried to kill it, but my people weren't strong enough on our own.

"Then a group of foreign people appeared with advanced armaments—metal weapons, compound bows, chariots. This was no random leap of technology. They had seen the Cannibal and devoted all their time and energy to producing weapons that could destroy it, and, like the Cannibal, they roamed the land ceaselessly looking for their prey. Some of the Cannibal's victims were my closest friends, and I wanted revenge. I joined the newcomers, and we looked for the monster together."

"Could the Cannibal perform spells?" said Soleil.

"I believe it could, but it didn't have control over its powers. We pierced its flesh with our arrows and spears, but it healed instantly. It also had infinite stamina like we do. But while it was fighting us, it didn't use tricks like disintegrating weapons or summoning objects."

"But it must have been able to use magic," said Flarence. "Otherwise it wouldn't have been able to Enchant you."

A pained look came over Mohinaux's face, and he hesitated before continuing. "We fought several battles with the Cannibal, and each time, we lost more of our army. We persevered, though, convinced we were wearing it down just as it was wearing us down. Then one day came the deciding confrontation. The battle was looking grim. The Cannibal was slaughtering us like we were flies, but we had injured it. One of my comrades had impaled it in the back with a spear, and the rest of us kept attacking to keep the creature too busy to remove the spear."

He put a hand to his chest. "It leaped at me and got me with its talons. I was bleeding out, but by willpower alone, I was able to keep my eyes open. The monster thought I was done for and turned its back, preparing to kill the remaining soldiers. But when it turned around, I grabbed the spear and drove it as deep into the beast as I could, then I pulled it out and stabbed again and again. In my near-death state, the blow wasn't as strong as it could have been, but it did enough. I drove the spear deep into the Cannibal's skull. I must have activated some kind of reflex because the next thing I knew, the creature was screaming, and I was flung away from it with burns all over my body. In its last efforts, the Cannibal decreased my weight so it could throw me farther and had increased the temperature of my flesh. I truly believed my life was over.

"But then I noticed that the immense pain I was feeling had begun to subside. I thought it was because I was losing consciousness until I saw that my wounds were disappearing. The gashes where the Cannibal scratched me were closing, and my burns were fading. The wound I inflicted on the Cannibal didn't kill it, but it injured the beast enough to allow the remaining soldiers to finish the job. While the Cannibal was twitching on the ground, trying to wrap its snake hand around the spear in its head and pull it out, my comrades picked up their weapons and hacked away at the creature. It took a while, but they disassembled it piece by piece. They beheaded it, tore the protrusion off its nose, amputated all its limbs, and separated the talons from its legs. Even an Enchanted beast can't come back from that."

Mohinaux rubbed his eyes. He looked like he was going to start tearing up.

"Go on," said Flarence.

Mohinaux took a few deep breaths and collected himself. "I'm sorry, but I can still see that image in my mind, even after all these years. I can still feel the pain from the gashes and burns that monster inflicted on me, and I still remember the shock when I saw my wounds healing before my eyes. I also remember the look on my friends' faces when they saw me stand up as if I had never been cut. The survivors and I collected the Cannibal's body parts, burned them to ashes, and became heroes.

"The surviving soldiers said they would keep the city safe in case another Cannibal terrorized their home. Most people did not think there was another Cannibal, believing it had risen out of the waters of Nu and was the only one of its kind, but that idea was shattered when word of what had happened to me spread. It was believed that the Cannibal had placed a curse on me, and that one day, I would become like it. The story of my impossible healing from a near-death state sparked fear among the people of the city, and soon I was kicked out of my home with no food or even a horse or chariot for travel. Messengers were sent to surrounding cities warning others not to let me into their homes. No matter where I went, I was treated like a potential monster, so I wandered the desert alone.

"Like the Cannibal, I wasn't aware of my powers, but I discovered what I could do through experience. I could walk for days without becoming tired. Sometimes when an animal I was hunting for food fought back, I would be injured, but my wounds always healed quickly. Once I dropped a rock I was using as a weapon in a hunt and summoned it back to my body to deliver the death blow. I didn't know how I did any of it; it was instinctive. Magic affects all creatures in different ways, but the common effect is that an animal's ability to survive is increased, whether or not that animal is aware of how it works. As time passed, I tried to use my magic in productive ways. I noticed that I had the ability to break down and reconstruct rocks with my mind, which I used to create better tools for hunting."

Soleil flipped through the book and found more pictures of monsters. "What are all these?"

"My creations. Sometimes while I was hunting, I would accidentally Enchant my prey. That's how I discovered the contagious property of magic. An animal would evade me, try to run away, and I would snap its neck with a thought. The animal would go down for a moment, but just like me, it would heal and rise stronger than before. At first it was all accidental, but a part of me became curious about what different Enchanted animals would be able to do. I'm not proud of this, but I created monsters just for the thrill of hunting and killing them."

"I'm sorry for what you went through," said Flarence, "but why didn't you tell us this earlier?"

"Because my people were right to shun me. I also was unsure of what I was becoming. I was devastated, lonely, and frightened. I wandered the world alone for a while, confining myself to a life of solitude. I was so insecure that I tried to kill myself several times. I jumped off cliffs and tried to hang myself, but spells cast on instinct kept me alive. When I jumped off a cliff, I created an updraft and used the wind to cushion my fall. When I tried to hang myself, I deconstructed the rope. Concluding that I couldn't be killed through injuries, I decided to try starving myself. I wandered until I finally collapsed, which was no easy feat. But even that wasn't enough. I was so tired I began losing consciousness, and in that weakened state, I discovered how to perform astral projections. When I was on the verge of passing out, my senses left me, my spirit separated from my body, and it found a herd of camels not far away. My pro-

jection returned to my body, and I controlled the wind to create a
sandstorm that blew into them. As it did, I turned the sand into
glass which tore them to shreds, and when they had bled out, I summoned my body to one of the corpses and ate it.

"I was still nearly passed out. Killing them and eating their flesh
felt like a dream, but it really happened. It seemed impossible for
me to be killed by my own hand. Not being able to die but being
too afraid to live was driving me mad. Out of sheer boredom, I created and killed monsters, sometimes able to stop them before they
could attack innocent bystanders. Each fight made me more familiar with my powers, and the more I fought, the more curious I became about my limits. I wanted to know everything I was capable
of, and to do that, I needed to keep fighting and let my instincts
guide me."

"What does any of this have to do with the made-up stories you
told us?" said Flarence, "and what about our mom? Was she a
Genie, too?"

"Don't interrupt an old man in the middle of his story," said
Mohinaux. "I'm getting to your mother, and the purpose of the
lies, but in order for you to understand why I did what I did, I need
to tell you everything. As I was saying, I wanted to strengthen my
control, and I did so by putting myself in situations where I had
to rely on magic to survive. Eventually, I succeeded in finding and
killing the monsters I had created, but I wanted more experience,
so I sought variety. I became interested in places outside Egypt
and traveled to new countries, watching the world grow from different vantage points.

"I wandered to different parts of the Middle East, Asia, and Eu-
rope, as areas became populated and land that was once vacant became villages. There I found new animals to Enchant. I let them run
free for a while so they could become accustomed to their new powers, and then I would hunt them down and kill them. This process
went on for years. The world grew, civilizations rose, cities were built,
but all I was concerned about was becoming stronger. When villages

were attacked by monsters, I would show up and save them from the evil that they didn't realize I was responsible for. I became a legendary warrior.

"So it seemed that my life was turning around. The people who had once shunned me were long dead, and the battles I fought made people welcome me wherever I went. I was not only growing more comfortable with my magic but was becoming socially accepted as well. Everywhere I went, I learned the language of the land, immersed myself in its culture, and, most important, became familiar with its technological advances. I witnessed the progress of metal work and later the discovery of magnetism.

"I heard of chemists who were discovering properties of atoms, and biologists who discovered cells and bacteria and learned how organs worked. I took particular interest in biologists, and spent a considerable amount of time sneaking into scientists' labs and reading their notes. I traveled to universities and sat in on lectures. In the beginning, I tried to improve my magical abilities by being a fighter, but I found that being a student was much more effective. Each discovery provided ideas of new ways to use my powers. With the discovery of electrons, I got the idea of controlling and even generating electricity. Meteorological discoveries gave me ideas of controlling weather."

"Our mom," said Florence. "How did you meet her?"

"Your mother was also an experiment. I had sworn off creating monsters, but I became lonely and decided it was time to find a companion. I met your mother in France in the mid-sixteen hundreds. Like me, she didn't have a family. Her parents were deceased, and her siblings had traveled to faraway places. She did have friends, as well as a lover, although I didn't know about him when I met her. Before I Enchanted her, I charmed her. I promised her eternal life and told her anything she wanted would be hers for the asking, and then used magic directly on her. I still remember the day. There was a scar on her face that I healed, and then told her to go home, and that she would soon experience many wonderful things. Then one day, I went to her house and found her lying dead on the floor."

"What happened?" asked Soleil.

"There's still much I don't know about how magic works. I also didn't know she was pregnant with you two. When I Enchanted her, you two experienced the effects as well. Once you became Enchanted in in her womb, you matured at a supernaturally fast rate and tore your way out of her. Your rapid change along with the internal and external physical damage was too much for your mother. I found her on the floor of her house covered in blood with you two next to her."

"We killed our mother?" said Flarence.

"It wasn't your fault," said Mohinaux. "You were just acting out of instinct, the same way I was. It was very interesting watching you grow. Like me, you slowly became aware of your capabilities. I fed you for the first year of your lives, but then you started summoning food to yourselves. For five years, you grew normally, but then you seemed to subconsciously learn how to use your magic to speed up the aging process and started to mature incredibly quickly. Now, like me, you use your magic to slow down your aging so you can maintain your young appearance forever."

"What was our mother's name?" asked Flarence.

"Jocelyn. Jocelyn Roux. I wish I had a picture of her."

Soleil brought the story back on track. "Where did the story of the Council come from?" said Soleil.

"When I offered to Enchant your mother, it was with the intention of gaining a partner, but when I found you two, that didn't seem like a possibility, at least not immediately. Your mother was a gentle, kind, and understanding person. She was also wise for her age. You were children born with incredible powers. I didn't trust you to be able to use magic responsibly."

"So you made up the story about the Council of Elders," said Soleil. "You scared us into using our powers responsibly by convincing us there was a group of superior beings who would punish us if we misbehaved."

"It worked for a very long time," said Mohinaux. "Flarence, even you were not always such a skeptic. You believed in the Council and followed the rules for years before becoming a vigilante."

"I'm not a vigilante," said Flarence, "I'm an investigator. I've devoted years of my life to sticking my nose where it doesn't belong. I've seen plenty of disgusting people. I've seen children sexually assaulted, I've found innocent people shot and left for dead because some robber needed a getaway car, I've tracked down drug addicts who ran away from a rehab facility and were nearly dead from overdosing when I found them. If there's one thing I've learned from those cases, it's that everyone has an explanation for their actions, which is why Claire and I try to keep our minds open and free of judgment. I never looked down on the child-molesters, or became angry with the trigger-happy criminals, or pitied the drug addicts who couldn't seem to stop their self-destructive tendencies. But for you, I'm making an exception. There's no way of justifying what you did."

"I told you," said Mohinaux, "I couldn't let you kids run free without some kind of motivation to be responsible."

"I'm not just talking about us," said Flarence. "If that story you just told is true, you spent years wandering the world as a pathetic loner, trying to commit suicide because you felt sorry for yourself. After that, you slaughtered innocent people by infesting villages with monsters, and you didn't even respect the creatures you created. You gave new life to animals just so you could take it away. After that, you killed our mother and covered it up by feeding us that cock-and-bull story that we both swallowed like idiots. Then, worst of all, you tried to kill Claire. I might be able to forgive everything else in time, but I'll never be able to move past what you tried to do to her."

"I know I made questionable decisions," said Mohinaux, "but try to understand that I was thrown into a very unusual situation. I didn't ask to be given these powers, but everything I did was an attempt to take responsibility for what happened. I'll admit that you and Soleil being born and being Enchanted was an accident, but I tried to make up for it. From the day I found you, I've cared for you like sons."

"And I love Claire like a daughter," said Flarence. He hopped off the boulder and turned his back on Mohinaux. "As a wanderer, you killed my mother; as the Student, you made my life hell; as our father, your stories of the Council turned Soleil and I against each other; and to top it all off, you just tried to kill my daughter."

"If it helps, I was only trying to scare her," said Mohinaux. "I was never actually going to kill her."

"It doesn't," said Flarence. "It doesn't help at all." With that, he summoned his body out of the cave.

Once he was gone, Mohinaux turned to Soleil. "Are you angry with me as well?"

"No, but it's because I think I understand what you went through and why you did it. I Enchanted Darren, and I trust him, but what if Flarence is right? If Darren does become dangerous some day, there's no one who can step in and discipline him."

"Then keep up the story. Make him believe the Council exists. I know you feel betrayed by finding out it was never true, but you have to admit that it did keep you and Flarence in line for a long time."

"That's the problem, dad. A long time isn't good enough. You said yourself that once someone becomes Enchanted, they get pretty close to immortal. Eventually everyone starts asking questions. You think of Flarence as a rebel because he started bending the rules, but the truth is he isn't defiant. He just lost patience faster than I did. It was only a matter of time before I started following in his footsteps, and Darren will as well. I'm going to tell him the truth, or at least anything he has the right to know. I won't tell him about you creating monsters or what happened between you and Mom."

"Good luck with him," said Mohinaux. "And talk to Flarence. Try to make him understand that I'm not a bad person. I just worry about you two."

Soleil nodded and summoned his body out of the cave.

FLARENCE

He was sitting in a chair in the cafe, and stood up when Soleil arrived. "What do we do about this?" Flarence asked. "We can't just let everything slide."

"Yes, we can," said Soleil. "He's not the man we thought he was, but he's still our dad. We can forgive him."

"I'm not talking about forgiveness," said Flarence. "This new story doesn't clear anything up. I don't know about you, but for as long as I can remember, I've wanted to know where my powers came from and what their purpose was. Dad created us, and the Cannibal created Dad, but what created the Cannibal? If the picture is accurate, that thing was way too bizarre to be natural, which means somebody made it. We're missing a key piece of information."

Flarence felt his phone vibrate. When the caller ID said it was Claire, Flarence flipped it open and asked his usual opening question: "Are you hurt?"

"It's sweet that you care so much," said Claire. "I was wondering if you were on your way back to the hotel."

It wasn't her usual response—"I'm fine"—which meant something was wrong. Flarence moved the phone away from his face and silently mouthed, "find Claire" to Soleil, who slumped into a nearby chair and performed an astral projection. Flarence made small talk on the phone. "I'm going to head back in a minute. I'm just taking care of some business first. Where are you?"

"I'm back at the hotel already, and I'm bored," said Claire. "Seriously, where are you? I want to go out. I'll meet you wherever you are."

Soleil rose from the chair and indicated that Flarence should wrap up the conversation. "I'm with my brother. I'll be back later." He clicked the phone shut and slid it back in his pocket.

"She's cornered in Darren's apartment," said Soleil. "She's wearing her Razor Punk gear, and there's a bunch of guys with guns pointed at her."

"How many?"

"Four were still on their feet. Three were on the floor." Florence drew the Wrist Cannon and Stakehail Colt. "Tyrell and Atalissa might be in there too," said Soleil. "This isn't the time for rash actions, just wait a minute and . . . ," but Florence was gone before he could finish.

He landed by the refrigerator and saw that Soleil was right. Four men were aiming their guns at Claire, who was wearing her scarf and gloves with one of her needles in her right hand and her cell phone in her left. Three men were lying on the floor; only one of them was unconscious, while the other two were groaning and having trouble standing up. They all had cuts on their faces, and one had an arm that was bending in an improper direction. Claire was standing in the corner of the apartment and looked ready to lash out the second anyone moved.

Luckily, by summoning himself to the refrigerator, Florence had placed the gunmen between himself and Claire, so all the attackers had their backs to him and didn't hear him enter. Florence extended his index finger, twirled it around, pointed to his left, and held up three fingers. Claire adjusted her grip on the needle in her right hand, which Florence took as a signal that she understood: He was going to count down from three, and when he hit zero, Claire was going to dive away.

"Call him again," one of the men said as Florence lowered his ring finger.

"If he doesn't want to come, then you can't make him," said Claire. Behind the attackers, Florence lowered his middle finger.

"She's knows she's dead and is just stalling for time," said another man. "I don't know what Tymbir thinks he saw, but these things don't exist. Lunatics, however, do, and we're looking right at one. I joined this group to bring down people like her, not hunt for wizards."

Florence was just about to lower his index finger when suddenly Soleil appeared at the wall next to Claire, threw his arms around her, and the two of them disappeared as the gunmen opened fire. They looked around in confusion, and it didn't take long to notice Florence standing by the refrigerator.

"I'm going to tear you all a new one as soon as I talk to my brother," he said and summoned his body back to Soleil's Cafe to find Claire shouting. She had Soleil pinned to a wall with both her hands gripping his neck.

"I was only trying to help," Soleil rasped. "I was watching you with my astral projection, and it looked like you were in trouble."

"Flarence and I had it covered," said Claire. "We have our own way of doing things, and it does not involve appearing in a room and grabbing me. Don't ever do that again." She let go of him and turned to Flarence. "I tried calling you but your phone wasn't working."

"I was out of signal range," he said. "The good news is we don't have to worry about the Student anymore."

Claire paused a moment when he said it. "That's great, but you can tell me about it later. Right now, Lucy's been kidnapped and Darren's on his own trying to save her."

"Who's Lucy?" said Flarence.

"She's Tyrell's friend," said Soleil. "Is Tyrell going after her too? Do you have any idea where she is?"

"Atalissa showed up shortly after we got back to Darren's apartment. She was worried about a car that she thought was following her. It turned out her concerns were right, and a group of people showed up at the building. They delivered a phone to Darren, who was ordered to use it to contact Tymbir. He's holding Lucy captive. He said he was holding her in the same place he took Tyrell, and told Darren to go there unless he wanted Lucy's blood on his hands.

"Tymbir hung up quickly, but Tyrell and I were able to describe the location of the house. I tried to talk Darren into taking me with him. I told him that I would hide and listen and only appear if it sounded like he needed me, but he was in too much of a hurry. A few minutes after he summoned out of the apartment, all hell broke loose. I'm guessing kidnapping Lucy was just a distraction. There must have been someone watching the apartment from across the street, and as soon as Darren left, they told the group in the van to return. We heard guns going off, which could only have been the stair dwellers trying to defend their ground. I don't know if any of them are still alive, but all seven of Tymbir's goons made it to the apartment.

"I asked Tyrell if there was another way out, and he said there was a fire escape, so I told them I would distract Tymbir's men while they made a break for it. I tried to fight off the goons as best I could, but there were too many of them. Fortunately, one of them wanted information before pulling his trigger. He asked me who I was, and I told them I worked for another one of the magical people, which caught their attention and bought me some time. They told me to bring my boss to them, which was when I called you."

"I'll use an astral projection to find Lucy and make sure she's still alive," said Flarence. "If Darren hasn't completely messed up his rescue mission, we'll help him out. Soleil, you use your projection to find Atalissa and Tyrell."

"No, I'm going with you," said Soleil. "Lucy's my friend too. Tymbir's caused Tyrell and his family enough trouble, and threatening her life is going too far."

"Soleil, you saw the inside of the house where Tyrell was kidnapped," said Claire. "There were guns everywhere, and all the people who attacked Darren's apartment tonight had hand guns. Going there means walking into a bloodbath. You're not psychologically ready to handle that."

A square section of the wall behind Soleil turned to dust to reveal a small metal safe with a combination lock. He opened it and pulled out what appeared to be a folded-up wool blanket. Soleil held two corners and let the fabric fall, revealing a hole in the top. Flarence realized that it wasn't a blanket but a poncho covered with dozens of leather pouches. Each contained a glass vial stoppered with a cork. A string attached each cork to its vial. "I guess it's a night for revealing secrets," said Soleil, as he slipped his head through the hole.

"What the hell is that?" said Claire.

Soleil patted the fabric once he had it on. "This is my weapon," he said. "I know you're accustomed to Flarence and his machines, but I've always found plants much more interesting. Years ago, I Enchanted a tree to see what would happen but didn't tell anyone, not even dad. When a human is Enchanted, it strengthens our minds and gives us mental control over the world around us, and when an animal is Enchanted, it improves their physical strength and makes them a deadlier predator. Trees have neither mind nor muscle, but they're still living creatures, and magic affects them. At first when I Enchanted the tree, I didn't think there was any change, but when I returned the next day, I found a pile of dead bugs around it. As the tree grew, I noticed each branch producing leaves of a different shape, and every day, there were more dead bugs around the trunk. Everything that ate a leaf died, because each one contained a different poison. I consulted several botanists about extraction techniques, which I used to isolate the toxins the tree was providing."

"Have you used those toxins in a fight before?" said Flarence.

"Not very often, and not on a person," admitted Soleil. "I was worried about the Council being upset for using magic in violence, but I couldn't pretend the tree didn't exist. I've gone hunting with these poisons, and I've killed a variety of game, including a grizzly bear."

"But wouldn't the poisons Enchant the animals you hunted?" asked Claire.

"There's nothing supernatural about the chemicals," said Soleil. He pointed to a vial near his shoulder. "For instance, this is similar to curare." He pointed to a lower vial, "and if this gets on skin, it acts like poison ivy. Enchanting the tree altered its genome, giving it the ability to create effective poisons, but the compounds themselves have no magic associated with them."

Flarence took a moment to absorb the scene. There he was, in a cafe with an electromagnet strapped to one arm and holding a revolver that shot icicles in the other. His partner was next to him wearing a shirt adorned in chains and a scarf decorated with razor blades. His brother was now wearing enough poison to supposedly take down a grizzly bear. He pulled up two chairs and placed them in front of him. "All right, I guess we're all . . . I don't know, geared up? Let's get back to the task at hand." He was about to sit down but then paused and handed the Stakehail Colt to Claire. "If we're going up against firearms, I'd feel more comfortable if you were able to attack from a distance."

"How is she going to use that thing?" said Soleil.

"Razor Punk and I have been doing this for a long time," said Flarence. "She's used it before. We have a system worked out. Well, it's kind of a system. Just shut up and project."

—9—

DARREN

He collapsed onto his back with bullets embedded in his arms, legs, and chest. He took a deep breath and summoned the bullets to the ceiling above him. When all the metal had exited his body, he rolled to his right and broke his focus and the bullets fell to the floor. He paused a moment, waited for his wounds to heal, and then stood up. He was in the living room of one of the houses on the block Claire and Tyrell had told him about, and was surrounded by the bodies of strangers, some which he had killed and others which had fallen victim to friendly fire.

When Tymbir called, Darren faced a challenge. Lucy was being held in of one of the six houses. Each one was filled with armed men ready to ambush Darren the moment he set foot in any of them he would be ambushed and would have to fight his way out. If he was able to find the house which Lucy was being held in, he would have a chance to set her free. There were six houses on the block and he had already been in two of them, and hadn't found Lucy. Wishing astral projections weren't so hard, he waited for his wounds to heal, then walked out and into another house at random.

He opened and closed the door slowly to make as little noise as possible as he entered. A staircase near the door led upstairs, and he decided to try it first. On the second floor were three closed doors. Darren tiptoed to the middle one and gently placed his hand on the doorknob. He stood to the side, turned it until he heard the latch click, and pushed gently. Then he slowly leaned over and peeked inside.

A man in a ski mask was holding a shotgun and pulled the trigger. His shot smashed into the doorframe below Darren's face. He could feel the wood splinter as the other doors opened and two men came out. The one on his left had a pistol and the one on his right a crossbow. A bolt from the bow hit him in the shoulder, making him spin enough that the other man's shot missed. The arrow hurt, but he pulled it out of his shoulder and summoned it to the wall behind the man with the bow. To get there, it traveled through him, piercing his eye as it passed through his skull.

The man fell, and Darren summoned the arrow back to his body. He caught it and advanced on the man with the pistol. Three bullets struck him, but he ignored the pain as he grabbed the shooter by the collar and stabbed him in the throat. Then he turned his attention to the man with the shotgun, who was more cautious than the other two and slower to rush out. Darren waited as well, removing the bullets from his body and giving his wounds time to heal. Then he took the gun off the man he'd stabbed in the throat and went into the room next to the shotgun wielder's. Disintegrating the wall between the rooms gave him a clear view of the man with the shotgun, whom he shot in the head.

He disintegrated the floor and landed in the kitchen near a man with a carving knife, clearly waiting to surprise Darren when he came down the stairs. The man heard Darren land, spun around, and lunged, but Darren was quicker and fired four times. Darren waited tensely in case anyone else in the house attacked. Everything was quiet for a moment, then suddenly Darren thought he heard a creak from another room.

"Darren," said a voice from outside the kitchen, "it's Soleil."

"It's about time you showed up," said Darren as Soleil came in. "Where have you been? Claire tried calling …" he stopped when he saw that Soleil, wearing his poncho covered with vials, was dragging a man by the ankles. Darren wasn't sure if the man was alive or dead; his face was covered with rashes, and blood was dripping from his eyes.

"I learned the truth," said Soleil, as he dropped the man, "and it set me free. Free to fight, free to kill, and free to help you. I'll fill you in on the details later, but right now, you just have to know that there's no need to worry about getting in trouble with the Council for improper use of your powers. It turns out the Council doesn't even exist. None of us have to hold back."

Flarence and Claire followed him into the room. "We took care of the rest of the people in the house," said Flarence. "Soleil and I surveyed the block with our astral projections, and we know where Lucy is."

"Great," said Darren, "let's go get her."

"She's in the basement alone with Tymbir, who has a walkie-talkie and has been in contact with the other houses," said Soleil. "They've been keeping track of which ones you've been in so far. If you make it to Lucy, he can easily call reinforcements to that basement. You'll be surrounded in a confined space. It's the best advantage he has on you."

"There are three more houses to go," said Flarence. "Razor Punk and I will take one, Soleil will take another, and you take the one with Lucy. There are three people in the attic. Two are armed with 22-mm pistols, and one has a knife. Tymbir has a Desert Eagle. Think you can handle it?"

"I've made it this far," said Darren.

"Lucy is being held next door," said Soleil. "Good luck." He pulled a vial out of a poncho pocket and disappeared.

SOLEIL

Soleil knew there was an enemy in each room on the second floor, and he planned to take them out first. He traveled to a wall in one of the rooms and landed silently behind the guard there. The vial Soleil slipped out of his pocket was filled with a liquid similar to capsaicin. The fluid from Soleil's tree, however, was much stronger than any pepper, and the volume in the vial would be fatal for anyone who drank the whole thing.

Like all the other guards, this one wore a ski mask over everything except his eyes and mouth. Splashing the capsaicin in his eyes would blind him but would also cause him to scream. Soleil snuck up behind the man, wrapped an arm around his neck, and drove the vial into his mouth while forcefully tilting his head back. The man gasped and swallowed as the solution poured down his throat. He collapsed in a fit of heaves, madly rubbing his eyes, as some of the liquid spilled onto his lips and burned his skin.

Worried that the man's coughing would be heard, Soleil wasted no time in moving to the next room. He disintegrated the wall while removing a vial of powder from his poncho which he threw at the guard's feet. Then Soleil produced a cyclone to kick up the potent benzodiazepine powder so it shrouded the man in a cloud of dust. As he waved his arms trying to fan the powder away, Soleil unraveled his ski mask. The man took in a breath of the powder and fell to the floor.

Soleil pocketed the empty capsaicin vial, reconstructed the wall, and prepared to take out the guard in the last upstairs room. He took out a vial packed with a material that looked like cotton. Some of the leaves on Soleil's tree were rich in cellulose, which he'd used to produce highly combustible nitrocellulose. Soleil placed the vial on the floor and pushed the door open slightly as he made his body invisible. The door opened wider, and the man looked out. He held his gun in front of him as he scanned the hallway and noticed the vial. As soon as he looked at it, Soleil increased its temperature, igniting a small flare that flash-blinded the man with its intensity Soleil ceased to be invisible, rushed into the room, and delivered a flurry of punches until blood seeped through the man's mask and he fell to the floor.

Soleil knew there were three on the first floor and two in the basement. He heard someone running up the stairs and took the gun of the man he had just beaten. The two met at the top step, but before the man could fire, Soleil swung the gun and hit him in the temple, sending him tumbling down. Another guard rushed to the body at the foot of the stairs. Soleil whistled to get his attention, and when their eyes met, Soleil raised the gun and squeezed the trigger. The man instinctively threw his arms above his head, but the bullets never hit him because Soleil deconstructed them first. Realizing he hadn't been shot, the man lowered his hands, and Soleil threw the gun, hitting him in the nose. The man staggered back, blood dripping from his face, as Soleil ran down the stairs and punched him in the throat. Then he grabbed the man's arm, dislocated his shoulder, and snapped his wrist before letting him fall.

There were three people left. Soleil turned to see them all behind him. They opened fire but Soleil deconstructed the bullets. The three stared in confusion as the metal shavings fell to the floor.

"Here comes the sun, assholes," he taunted as he drew a vial and unraveled their masks.

The three men holstered their weapons and advanced on Soleil with their fists raised. He took out a vial with a compound that stimulated histamine production and led to bronchoconstriction when inhaled. As the three gunmen surrounded him, he flicked off the cork and controlled the flow of air to create a cyclone that pulled out the powder and expanded it outward, creating a ring of poison. Inhaling it sent the three men into instant anaphylactic shock.

"You deserve a lot worse than this," said Soleil as they fell. "I have worse toxins than the ones I used tonight. I could have killed all of you."

FLARENCE

While Soleil was throwing his herbal artillery around, Flarence and Claire were busy with their own opponents. They had also decided to start at the top floor and work their way down. With Claire's hand in his, Flarence summoned them to a wall in the middle room, where one guard was stationed. Claire snuck up behind and trapped him in a headlock, holding him still while Flarence knocked him unconscious with his Wrist Cannon. Without a word, Claire and Flarence went to opposite sides of the room. Flarence tapped his thigh once, then twice, and on the third tap, he turned both walls to dust. He heard the puff of the Stakehail Colt going off behind him as he rushed into the room, and almost caught the man inside by surprise. Instinctively, the man raised his gun. Flarence used a disarming technique, kicked the gun across the floor, and tried to kick the man in the head. The man moved backward to avoid the attack, drew a knife, and lunged. Flarence smirked as he happily extended his hand and let the blade penetrate his palm, then curled his fingers around the man's hand and squeezed until he heard the knuckles pop. The man's head went back and he let out a scream, which was cut short as Flarence brought the Wrist Cannon down on his throat. His hand went limp. Flarence drew the blade out of his palm and let the wound heal. Then he turned to Claire as she brought the butt of the Stakehail Colt down on the head of her opponent, who also had an icicle protruding just below his right knee.

Flarence and Claire returned to the center room and stood back to back. They could hear someone coming up the creaking stairs to investigate the commotion. Flarence deconstructed the boards below their feet. When they hit solid ground, they took a second to assess the room and then lunged simultaneously for the first person they saw. The man was armed with a twelve-gauge shotgun. Flarence became invisible and dashed to his right, which made the man pause. When Flarence became visible again five feet from where the man had seen him a moment ago, the gunman re-aimed, but Flarence turned invisible again. This time, he dashed to his left before reappearing. The man turned, but before he could aim again, Flarence disappeared a third time and rushed behind him. The man kept the shotgun steady, expecting Flarence to appear in front of him again, but instead, Flarence struck him in the back of the neck with the Wrist Cannon.

"Reload!" shouted Claire from the other side of the room. He turned and saw her holding a man hostage as two others aimed their guns at her, looking for a clear shot without harming their partner. Claire held the Stakehail Colt behind her back where Flarence could see it clearly. She had pressed the release button to expose the gas canister and cylinders. Flarence refilled the canister with gas and the cylinders with ice stakes and shouted, "Y'er good!" Claire whipped the gun into the chest of the man she was holding, which snapped the gas canister and cylinders into place.

Flarence was about to help her when he felt an intense pain. He looked down and saw a hole in his suit jacket, then turned to see a man with a .44-mm in his hands who had shot Flarence below the ribs, sending the bullet straight through him. Flarence sighed as the wound healed and casually held out his hand over the man he had just hit. The shotgun rose off the ground and he caught it by the handle, his finger on the trigger. His shot caught the man in the thigh and tearing off a chunk of meat and flesh. Dropping his gun, the man fell down the stairs. Flarence positioned him so his forehead was resting on the edge of a step and drove his heel into the man's neck. He felt the bone break.

Flarence turned to see Claire standing in front of a man with a razor blade against his throat. His gun was lying near his feet, and his eyes showed his fear through the mask. Claire placed the Stakehail Colt directly against his shoulder and pulled the razor away a moment before she fired. The man screamed and squirmed for a moment before she kicked him into unconsciousness. Claire slipped the razor back into her scarf. "Reload," she said as she clicked the Stakehail Colt open.

Flarence reloaded it. "You're good."

He placed the gun on the floor as she flipped the canister into position. "We got all the people in this place. We should go to Soleil's house and make sure he's all right. If all the gunmen in his house are either dead or immobilized, we'll go to Darren and Tymbir." Flarence crossed the room, took Claire by the hand, and summoned them both out of the house.

-10-

DARREN

Darren went to the house where Lucy was being held captive. He didn't see any point in being subtle, and stomped to the top floor, where he kicked a door open. He expected to be shot the moment he walked in, but nobody was in front of him. He was about to turn around when he felt a stabbing pain in his back. He flailed his arms and struck his assailant, who staggered away. Darren yanked out the knife that was lodged near his spine and stabbed the man five times, then deconstructed a wall and went to the next room. He was shot as he did but didn't care anymore. He let the bullets smash into his body as he walked toward the shooter. The man backed up as he continued firing. Darren deconstructed a part of that wall as well and the man tripped. He tried to keep firing but was out of bullets. Another gunman unloaded at Darren as well. He just closed his eyes and waited for the shooter to run out of ammo. He didn't know how many times he was hit, but it didn't take long before the loud banging was replaced by soft clicks. Darren opened his eyes to see both men cowering in a corner. He slit their throats with the knife and placed a hand on each of their necks so he could feel their pulses slow down as their blood drained. When they were dead, Darren summoned the bullets in his body to theirs. Soleil had told him there were only three armed men on this floor, which meant all he had left to worry about was Tymbir.

The wooden stairs to the basement creaked as he descended. He found Lucy with a ball gag in her mouth bound to a metal rectangle that looked like a bed frame with a mesh of wires filling the middle space. She was spread-eagled with zip-ties on her wrists and ankles. There were faint marks on her arms, neck, and face. One end of a chain was attached to the board that kept Lucy suspended above a series of sharpened pipes bolted to the floor, and the other end was wrapped around a thick leather glove Tymbir was wearing that went halfway up his forearm.

He gave a light tug to the chain, which clanged as it went taut. Lucy let out a muffled scream, but the frame didn't fall. "Come at me if you want," he said, "but if I move too far, the board will be dragged away and she'll fall onto the spikes. And if you take one step toward me, I'll yank on the chain anyway. I'm armed too, so don't get any ideas about turning the spikes to dust. If anything happens that's not according to plan, I'll shoot her."

"Go ahead and try," said Darren. "I'll deconstruct your gun the second you pull it out."

"Interesting. What do you think is faster, your powers or my trigger finger?"

Darren considered his options and realized that the only way to save Lucy was to cast multiple spells at the same time. He would have to take the gun, spikes, and constraints out of the equation. With enough practice, it might be possible, but he wasn't confident enough in his abilities yet to try.

"That's what I thought," said Tymbir. "Now drop the knife."

Darren knelt down slowly and placed the knife on the floor, then stood up and kicked it away. He examined Lucy. She was sweating heavily and struggling to breathe through the ball gag as she sobbed. "Listen, Officer Tymbir . . ."

He gave the chain another threatening tug. "Don't call me 'officer.' Not here."

"The others weren't cops, were they? What is this place?"

Tymbir puffed his chest. "To most people, we're just ordinary people who've watched one too many movies. Everyone here believes in things like aliens and government cover-ups, and they're ridiculed for it. But nobody here's stupid, and nobody here's crazy. The truth is, we have the guts to imagine the extreme. We're prepared to face threats most people refuse to believe are real."

"I'm no threat to anyone."

Tymbir rattled the chain again. "Tell that to the one you used that knife on."

"I'm only here tonight because of you. Besides, this can't be about me being inhuman. You kidnapped Tyrell before you knew about my abilities."

"You got me," Tymbir said with a shrug. "This started off as something else. I had you in my crosshairs before I discovered your secret."

"But why? What did I ever do to you?"

"A lot of people treat your neighborhood like it's a lost cause. Stores could get robbed, people get shot, and most don't give it a second thought because that's become normal. I haven't given up. I know what that 'hood has the potential to be, but it won't get better as long as your gang act like they own the streets. When you gave me the slip, that was the last straw. I decided to fight fire with fire."

"So that's it? You kidnapped my son, stalked my wife, and abducted an innocent high school girl just because I escaped from jail?"

"It's not that simple. The way the evidence was destroyed was unreal. One man who can do all that is more of a menace than any gang. I wasn't going to let you get away with it."

"So you got your friends involved."

"I took you for a mastermind, figured I'd have to go outside the law to take you down. I didn't realize how right I was until that day in your apartment. I couldn't make sense of the things you were doing, and yet it explained everything. You used magic to escape. I didn't see that coming. But now that I know, there's no way I'm going to rest while a wizard is loose on the street and is part of a gang."

"And what was your plan to stop me? Did you think there were enough people here to take me down? There weren't."

"I figured that the moment you walked into this room."

"I also figured you would come here unarmed. When I watched you practicing in your apartment, I never saw any physical power sources like a wand or a religious artifact. I'm guessing your powers are a matter of focus. If my hunch is right, your greatest enemy is . . ." he drew his gun mid-sentence, ". . . surprise!" he said as he pulled the trigger.

The bullet traveled to the top of the doorframe. Darren looked up as it struck a glass bottle. The liquid inside ignited as it shattered. It happened so fast that instead of thinking of a way to snuff the flames, he threw his hands up over his head.

There was no burning sensation when the liquid hit Darren; in fact, it was cold to the touch. He felt a hand on his right shoulder and turned to see Soleil next to him. He looked to the left and saw Flarence and Claire.

Tymbir fired again, each shot aimed at a different person until the gun was empty. Every one of the bullets turned to dust before finding its mark. Tymbir dropped the gun and pulled out a walkie-talkie clipped to his belt: "Everyone remaining, report to the holding room."

"There is no one remaining," said Flarence. "Between the three of us, we took them all down while you were talking to Darren." He turned to Soleil. "By the way, did you kill anyone in the house?"

"No," said Soleil, "but it was tempting."

"Well, Tymbir" said Darren, "it looks like you're completely out of firepower."

"Not yet," said Tymbir as he jerked the chain.

"I got her," shouted Soleil. The spikes disintegrated as he dove to the mattress, which he caught just before it struck the hard floor. Claire fished a pocket knife out of her jeans as she ran to Lucy and cut the zip-ties.

Tymbir swung the chain around his head like a whip and tried to hit Lucy with the board. It was heading for Lucy's head until it changed direction and flew toward Flarence, who caught it. Tymbir pulled his hand out of the glove and charged in Lucy's direction.

Darren didn't want to find out what he planned and intercepted him with a flying tackle.

Claire finished cutting through the zip-ties, helped Lucy off of the wire mat, and took the gag out of her mouth. "I'm sorry for what you've been through. Can you walk?"

It took Lucy a moment to recognize the voice. "Claire? Is that you?"

"Call me Razor Punk," said Claire, as she and Soleil went over to Tymbir. Flarence approached him as well. The four of them had him surrounded.

"Good for you," said Tymbir. "You saved the kid. Unfortunately, there's something you overlooked: By coming here, you left your loved ones wide open." He brought the walkie-talkie to his face again. "Clark, put his wife on the horn." There was no response. Tymbir pressed the button again. "Clark, respond. Tell me you got Darren's wife and son."

The voice at the other end could be heard through the static. "There's more than one, sir."

"Clark, where are you?" Tymbir shouted.

"I'm sorry, sir. Atalissa and Tyrell weren't at the apartment, but two other monsters were. The government must have made more to hunt down the one that got away."

Tymbir shouted into the device. "It's not the government this time, Clark. We've been over this. Focus on your targets!"

"We're looking, sir. We don't know where they went."

"You won't find them," said Darren. "You lured me out of the apartment, but Razor Punk stayed behind and made sure they were safe. You couldn't kidnap my family, your army has been quashed, Lucy is safe, and your gun is empty. You lose."

Tymbir spun in circles. His legs tensed, and it looked as if he was going to make a move, but Claire stepped in and cut him deep in the lower lip. He placed his hands over his face and staggered back toward Flarence, who hit him in the back, activating his Wrist Cannon so the doorknob struck him in the spine. The impact made Tymbir's hands drop from his face as he stumbled forward toward

Soleil, who pulled a vial out of his poncho, flicked the cork off with his thumb, and splashed the liquid inside on Tymbir's forehead. Tymbir screamed and clawed at his face as a series of welts appeared on his skin. No matter how he rubbed them, it did no good. Darren placed his left hand on Tymbir's shoulder to hold him still and delivered a right uppercut to the jaw that knocked him down. As he tried to get up, Lucy ran over and brought her right foot up between his legs. Tymbir coughed, rolled over, and curled into a ball as he wrapped his arms around the middle section of his body. The five of them moved closer until they were almost standing on top of Tymbir. Soleil had a new vial in his hands filled with a light blue powder which he was twirling between his fingers, Flarence was standing with his Wrist Cannon raised, and Claire had both her weapons pointed at Tymbir, the Stakehail Colt in one hand and a razor in the other.

"We could kill him," said Flarence. "He deserves it."

"No," said Soleil. "This has gone far enough." He lowered his vials and backed away.

"You're a long was from the peace and quiet of your indoor garden" said Flarence. "This is how I do things."

"It wasn't always how you did things," said Claire. She lowered her weapons and backed away as well. Darren did the same. "I don't care what you do. I've already won."

Flarence looked at them, keeping his eyes on Claire a little longer than the rest. Soon he stepped away from Tymbir as well.

"What if he comes after me again?" said Lucy.

"He won't," said Flarence. "Are you still conscious enough to hear me, Tymbir?" Tymbir let out a deep groan. "Good. Now let me make this perfectly clear. There isn't enough firepower in the world to bring us down. There isn't a trap too elaborate for us to neutralize. We're Genies. We have powers beyond your understanding. To top it all off, we just found out we're free to use our powers any way we see fit. If we have to come after you again, we won't hold back. Keep that in mind the next time you try setting one of us up."

"Did he just say he was a Genie?" said Lucy.

Darren held his hand out to her. "Listen, Lucy, I know you've been through a lot, but the night isn't over yet. You heard Tymbir—there are still a few of his crew out on the street. I don't want you going home alone right now. Take my hand, and I'll get you out of here."

She hesitated.

"Lucy, we can explain everything," said Soleil.

"I don't want to talk to any of you right now," she replied.

"We'll take you to Tyrell," said Claire. "Would you like to hear it from him?"

Lucy slowly walked toward Darren and took his hand.

"We'll meet back at the cafe," said Darren. "That's probably where Tyrell and Atalissa went."

"Sounds good to me," said Flarence, as he and Claire held hands. Lucy jumped when the two of them disappeared, and jumped again when Soleil did as well.

"Hold on tight," said Darren. "This is going to happen really fast." He summoned his body to Soleil's Cafe, bringing Lucy along with him.

SOLEIL

The five of them appeared by the counter. Claire gave the Stake-hail Colt back to Flarence, who pocketed it along with the Wrist Cannon. Physically, she was unharmed, but when she untied the shirt from around her waist, she noticed holes in it. She tried putting it on anyway, but the tears were large enough to reveal the chains. "Could I borrow one of your shirts, Soleil?" she asked. Any of his shirts would be too big, and would hide the chains well.

Soleil pulled the poncho off over his head. "Sure, I have to find space in my closet for this anyway. There's no point in keeping it hidden anymore."

"What is that thing anyway?" said Darren.

Soleil gave him the shortest explanation possible. "I Enchanted a tree, and it became the most toxic plant on Earth. I extracted its poisons and used them to hurt Tymbir's people." He went up the stairs to his room with Claire behind him. "Help yourselves to anything in the refrigerator," he called over his shoulder. "I think everyone deserves a free drink." He found a long-sleeved Jefferson Airplane shirt and gave it to Claire.

"You really surprised us tonight," she said. "Flarence is proud of you. So am I."

"Did you really think I was as innocent as I made myself out to be? We all have dark sides. I always knew it was only a matter of time before you and Flarence saw mine."

"Don't let tonight get you down. I won't say we couldn't have saved Lucy without you, but you were a huge help. I wouldn't mind seeing you let your dark side out more often."

Soleil smiled as he hung his poncho in the closet and ran his fingers over the vials. "I'm going to need to replace some of the poisons."

Claire walked over to take a closer look at the poncho. "Where's your tree anyway?"

"It's not too far from here. If you walk down the jogging path you'll find a wooden bench with a ring carved into it. From there, the tree is about fifty paces off the trail."

"You've hidden a tree in a forest?"

"What can I say? I like hiding in plain sight. As far as I know, nobody's found it yet, at least nobody human. I walk by the tree periodically to clean up the dead wildlife. Sometimes I examine the birds and rodents to find out how they died. It's how I learned what the poisons do." He pulled out a vial that was filled with light brown syrup. "This is some of the tree sap. I found out it acts as a neurotoxin. The bark contains a chemical that makes blood coagulate."

"You'll have to show me how you extract the poisons someday," said Claire, "and you'll have to work with us again sometime." She found a piece of paper and a pen. "Here's my cell number." Soleil put the paper near a plant, and they went back downstairs. Lucy was sitting alone at a table, while Darren and Flarence were at the counter. Flarence had helped himself to a bottle of water, while Darren was drinking a can of soda. Flarence seemed relaxed, but Darren looked worried.

Soleil sat next to Darren. "I'm sorry I don't have any more pot. I bet you could use some right now."

Darren flipped the phone shut loudly and slid it across the counter toward Flarence. "She isn't picking up. I just called Atalissa twice, and she didn't pick up."

"She's probably driving," said Soleil.

"Then Tyrell would have picked up," said Darren.

"I'm sure she's fine," said Flarence. "She left the house in a hurry, and she might have forgotten her phone."

"No, she didn't," said Claire. "I made sure she had her phone before she left so we could contact her when everything was over. I even asked her to check her battery."

"Then she has it on silent mode," said Soleil. "It's in her purse, and she can't hear it."

"Maybe," said Darren, "but I'd like to be sure. I've got to get the hang of this sometime." He laid his head on the counter.

"What's he doing?" said Lucy.

Claire flicked Darren hard in the temple, but he didn't respond. "He's performing an astral projection. It's about time he figured it out."

The room was silent except for Darren's deep breathing. "This is a little creepy," said Lucy.

"I agree," said Claire. "I don't like watching Flarence do it either, but it's a useful skill. He should find Atalissa and Tyrell soon."

As soon as she said it, Darren jerked his head up, his eyes wide. Soleil reached out and grabbed his shoulder to comfort him, but before he could ask what was wrong, he felt himself being pulled away. Instinctively, he tightened his grip and held onto Darren as they flew through the city. A moment later, they stopped, and Darren tried to break Soleil's grip, but he was holding on too tightly.

"Darren, calm down. Where are we?"

"We're at the hospital," Darren shouted. "She's in there. They're both in there."

Soleil let go and Darren ran off. He looked around and saw that he was standing next to the large, white brick wall of the hospital Darren had been taken to when he was shot.

FLARENCE

"I'm not doing anything until Tyrell gets here," said Lucy.

Flarence was holding Claire's hand and extending his other to her. After Darren and Soleil disappeared, he had used his own astral projection to find Atalissa.

"That's the problem," said Flarence. "Tyrell isn't coming. He's alive, but he's hurt."

"What about Atalissa?" asked Claire.

"I think the term is flat-lining. When I saw her, the doctors were charging a defibrillator. Lucy, it doesn't look like Tyrell is going to be able to hang out with you for a while. You can walk to the hospital, but it would be faster if we did it my way." Reluctantly, Lucy took his hand.

It didn't take long to find Darren. He was in the lobby struggling to get out of Soleil's headlock as three security guards approached. He waved them away with his free hand. "Just give him a minute," Soleil shouted to the guards. "He'll calm down."

"Soleil, if you don't let me go right now, I swear I'm going to beat up everyone in this room," said Darren.

"Please don't do anything stupid," Soleil begged.

"It was stupid to leave them alone," said Darren. "I'm not doing that again."

Flarence walked between Soleil and one of the guards who was reaching for a weapon. "Soleil, let go of Darren. Darren, calm down. We've been able to keep our heads straight all night, and we're not going to fall to pieces now." Soleil let go of Darren, who straightened up, his face flushed and his breathing deep. He was in control for the moment, but if he didn't get what he wanted fast, he was going to go crazy. Florence approached the front desk and put on his most charming smile. "I'm sorry about my friend. He's found out his wife and son have been involved in an accident and were brought here. Their names are Atalissa and Tyrell Raleigh. Can you give us any information on them?"

The woman at the desk glanced briefly at her computer. "Sorry, I don't have any information at this time. If you'll have a seat ..."

Darren wasn't in the mood to wait. He ran past the guards toward the operating rooms. The guards couldn't react in time, but Soleil and Florence were right behind him. Darren rammed his shoulder into the doors leading there from the lobby, knocking them off their hinges, and ran down the hall. Soleil followed him, but Florence stayed behind and examined the door. Even though the Council of Elders had been debunked, he felt secrecy was still important. The more the public knew of the existence of Genies, the more motivated people like Tymbir would be to track them down.

"Sorry about that," he said as he repositioned the doors and reconstructed the hinges. But he didn't reposition them right so it would look as if Darren had actually broken the door down. "He's a big guy and he's really stressed out. It looks like you have some maintenance to do," Florence said. He was about to offer to pay for the damage, but the guards pushed him out of the way as they chased after Darren. Florence followed. them and arrived at the operating room where Atalissa was being held. Darren was pounding on the operating room door while Soleil was trying to calm him down. Florence and the guards approached the room as a doctor emerged with his gloves and coat stained with blood.

"I'm not supposed to be in the hallway until I'm cleaned up," said the doctor, "but what's going on?"

"I'm her husband, and I want to see her," said Darren. "Step aside or I'm busting in there myself."

"Her husband?" said the doctor. "Listen, we brought her in as soon as possible."

"I don't care what happened," said Darren. "Open the door."

"I'm afraid there was nothing we could do," said the doctor. He still seemed surprised by the situation but opened the door to let Darren go in, along with Florence, Soleil, and the guards. The first thing Florence noticed was the steady pitch of the machine Atalissa was attached to, She no longer had a pulse. Darren noticed it as well, and froze halfway to the bed.

"As I was saying," said the doctor, "we did all we could, but her injuries were too severe. We lost her just a moment ago."

Darren didn't move. Florence and Soleil each put a hand on his shoulder, and the three of them approached the bed together. When they stood above her body, Darren took her hand in his. It was subtle, but Florence noticed that Darren's hand had stopped inches away from hers. He had summoned her hand to his body in an attempt to expose her to magic and enable her to heal. The three of them were still for a moment, but Atalissa didn't move. Darren lifted one of her eyelids. Florence watched the color turn from brown to blue to green and back to brown. Still, Atalissa didn't stir.

"I'm sorry Darren," said Florence, "but at this point, there's nothing anyone can do." He turned around to the guards and doctors. "Could we have a minute alone, please?" The guards didn't move. "The man just lost his wife. Give him some time. You can wait right outside in case he does anything rash."

The room emptied, and the three of them were alone with Atalissa. The high-pitched tone still filled the room, and Soleil unplugged the machine. Eventually Darren backed away from the body, and they went back to the lobby together. Claire and Lucy looked at Darren hopefully. Florence shook his head.

"What about Tyrell?" said Lucy, which made Darren snap out of his spell. He bolted out of the chair and was about to make another run for the operating rooms, but Florence held him back.

"He's fine," said Florence. "It doesn't look like he took as much damage as Atalissa. The doctors can patch him up."

"How do you know?" said Lucy.

202 Made to Be Broken

"We just do," said Soleil. "Darren, take a look for yourself before you cause another scene."

Darren sat back in a chair, and his body went limp as he performed another projection to confirm his son's condition. "You're right," he said when he came back to his senses. "He doesn't look as bad as Atalissa. I'm going to keep checking on him, though. If it looks like the doctors are losing him, I'm charging in there."

Nobody said anything. They just sat quietly and waited for news to come. Every few minutes, Darren would lean back in his chair and go limp as if he were sleeping. They waited hours before a doctor came and told them Tyrell was stable and that they could visit him.

It seemed as though the doctor had more to say but Darren didn't wait to hear him out. Flarence, Soleil, Claire, and Lucy rushed to keep up with him. Tyrell had a bandage on his head and bruises on his face, as well as cuts on his cheeks and nose that had been cleaned and covered. His left arm was in a cast suspended over his bed. His lower lip was puffy, but he managed a half-smile as the group walked in. "Is that everyone?" he slurred. "My eyesight's a little blurry. I can't feel my legs. I can't feel anything."

Darren walked over to the bed and bent close to Tyrell. "Growing up under my roof you were bound to go on a drug trip eventually. I'm glad it was morphine instead of crack." It looked like Tyrell tried to laugh. All Darren could do was let out one small sob. "Do you remember what happened?"

"Mom got scared," said Tyrell. "We were driving away from the apartment, and she saw a van behind us. She thought those guys were following her again. She wanted to lose them. She drove fast and was weaving in and out of lanes. We were on Lake Shore Drive. You know that part where it makes a sharp turn and the signs tell you to slow down? She didn't slow down. She lost control, and we hit something. It happened so fast. Is she all right?"

Darren backed away. He couldn't speak the words that would tell Tyrell what had happened. Lucy approached the bed. "Tyrell, I'm sorry, but your mom didn't make it." Tyrell scrunched his face. Darren rushed out of the room before anyone could see his eyes fill with tears. Tyrell focused back on Lucy's face, then his gaze drifted down her neck and arms.

"I know I'm a mess," she said as she covered her marks. "A bunch of guys grabbed me earlier. I think you know what it was about."

"There's no point in staying quiet anymore," said Soleil. "You might as well come clean about everything. She knows about Tymbir, and she's seen what Darren can do."

"Lucy, ask Soleil. He knows more than I do anyway."

"I don't want to hear it from Soleil. I want to hear it from you."

"He isn't in the best condition to talk right now," said Flarence.

"I'll stick around and help him fill in the details," said Soleil. "If a nurse comes in and kicks us out for the night, I'll give Lucy a lift home."

"Fine," said Claire. "Is there anything else we can do?"

Soleil sighed. "Not unless you think you can comfort Darren."

Flarence and Claire went outside but didn't see Darren. The doctor from the lobby passed by them and entered the room, a solemn look on his face like he was preparing to deliver bad news. Instead of waiting to hear what the doctor had to say, he and Claire went to the lobby. Darren wasn't there either. "He just needs some space," said Claire. "Let's go back to the hotel for the night, and we'll see how he's feeling later."

When they were there, Claire started to go straight to bed but stopped and turned. "Do you think Darren will be all right?"

"No," said Flarence. "I was impressed with how he handled himself against Tymbir and his goons, and it was great working as a team for one night, but there's no doubt in my mind that he's going to go after Tymbir and do what we decided against doing tonight. Maybe not right away but eventually."

"What do you think we should do about it?"

"There isn't anything we can say or do that will bring Darren's wife back. We can try to comfort him, but I doubt anything we tell him will do any good. Also, we found out that Tymbir is more than just a bully. He's crazy, and so is everyone we met in those houses tonight."

"Agreed. So what do you think we should do about it?" she repeated.

"I say we let Darren finish the job and hope that's where it ends." He went to his room and closed the door before Claire could say another word.

—11—

DARREN

Sulking in his apartment after coming back from the hospital, Darren lost track of the days. Soleil visited and told him the main points of Mohinaux's story, but that was his only contact with anyone else. Time passed slowly in the deathly quiet apartment, but he couldn't find the energy to leave. It had been a long time since Darren had spent a night by himself. When Tyrell cried constantly as an infant, Darren and Atalissa had wished he'd stay asleep for just one night, but now, Darren would give anything to be dragged out of bed again by Tyrell's crying.

Suddenly his loneliness was replaced by guilt. Four days had passed and he hadn't visited Tyrell. He also had no plans for Atalissa's funeral. He put his shoes on and walked to the nearest bus stop. Magic had been nothing but trouble lately, and he wasn't in any mood to summon-travel to the hospital.

Crossing the hospital parking lot from the bus, Darren didn't notice who was walking near him. "Well," said a voice, "look who decided to show up." Darren turned to see his in-laws, which made his spirit sink even lower. He had never gotten along with Atalissa's parents. When he was young, they thought he was a bad influence on their daughter, but Atalissa would always defend him and say Darren was really a good and caring person, and that nobody knew him like she did. He would do anything to have her with him now.

"Hello, Mr. and Mrs. Walker," said Darren. "I'm sorry about what happened to your daughter."

"You should be," said Atalissa's mother. "You were the reason she kept living in that awful neighborhood. I told her for years to move to a better place. I knew it would be the death of her someday."

"It wasn't the mean streets that killed her," said Darren.

"You want to tell us how she died?" said Mr. Walker. "The police aren't telling us anything except it was a car crash. Tyrell told us someone was following her. Who could be frightening enough to make her crash her car, if not someone in that gang of yours?"

"It's not what you think. There's more than one violent group in Chicago, and not all of them are street gangs. Anyway, I came by today to talk to someone about what's going to happen to her body."

"She died four days ago," said Mrs. Walker. "Don't you think we took care of it by now?"

"You've been making plans for her burial?" said Darren. "Why didn't you tell me?"

"You pretty much went off the grid," said Mr. Walker. "We didn't see you around here, and you didn't pick up the phone."

"I was at my apartment," said Darren. "You could have stopped by and asked for my input on how and where my wife would be buried."

"This is our daughter we're talking about," said Mr. Walker. "Excuse us for not being in a hurry to go to the apartment that she lived in and look at what remains of her life. We'll be by when we can go into her room without breaking down, but right now, we still look at pictures of her before we go to sleep."

The two turned and started walking across the parking lot. "Wait," Darren called out, "what did you decide to do with Atalissa's body?"

"Cremation," said Mr. Walker. "Did Atalissa ever tell you it's been a tradition in our family for generations?"

"No, she didn't, but where is she now? When is it happening?"

"It's already done," said Mrs. Walker.

"What?" Darren shouted. "You didn't consider letting me have a chance to see her one last time before you burned her body?"

"You shouldn't have wallowed around for so long," said Mr. Walker. "Atalissa always said you cared about your family. If that's true, you need to get your act together. Go visit your son. He needs your support right now." They left Darren standing alone.

SOLEIL

Soleil and Lucy sat on opposite sides of the hospital bed. They were talking and laughing, but the moment Darren walked in, Lucy stopped. She'd had a similar reaction to Soleil when they met earlier that day. It seemed she still hadn't gotten accustomed to the idea of her friends being Enchanted.

Tyrell held up a piece of paper. "It's an application. Lucy's helping me to complete them."

"I've been printing them out and bringing them here," she said. "And I've been asking teachers to write him recommendation letters."

Tyrell held the paper close to his face and scanned through it. "And you don't have to worry about me falling behind with my homework. Lucy's been bringing it here after school every day, and we've been doing it together. It hasn't been easy writing with a bad arm, but I'm not going to have to rush to catch up with the other kids when I get out of here."

"Thanks, Lucy," said Darren. He looked up and down Tyrell's body. The cast was still on, but the cuts and swelling on his face looked better. "How long will it be until you get out of here?"

"It's going to be four to six weeks until the casts come off, not that it will help my legs feel better. I really appreciate you giving me a few days to breathe, dad. I was upset at first, but it's a good thing we took time to relax before doing something we'd regret."

Darren looked confused, and his eyes went back and forth from Tyrell to Lucy.

"Nobody had a chance to talk to you after the accident," said Soleil. "You left in a hurry the night of the accident, and afterward, well, I guess I didn't know if you were ready to hear it."

"Nobody told you?" said Tyrell, biting his lip and trying to fidget nervously although the casts made it difficult. "Dad, there's something you need to know, but I need you to promise you won't panic when you hear it. By panic, I mean don't use magic on me. I don't want to be Enchanted, no matter how bad my injuries are."

"I figured you wouldn't, considering all the trouble magic has been so far," said Darren. "I was never worried about you, though. Like you said, four to six weeks. You'll be back on your feet then, right?"

Soleil led Darren out of the room. They stared at each other a moment. A thought suddenly struck Darren. "Why's Tyrell still in bed? It didn't look like he was banged up that badly."

"Tyrell got more than a broken arm in that crash. He also suffered a spinal injury. He's not going to walk out of this room. He's going to be in a wheelchair. Permanently." Fear and frustration filled Darren's face, and he started back into the room. Soleil grabbed his arm. "Darren, don't."

Darren shook his arm free. "Don't tell me how to raise my son."

"You've been a great father, and everyone knows how much you care about Tyrell, but this isn't a decision you can make for him. He said he doesn't want to be Enchanted."

"He might think differently after he spends a few weeks not being able to walk," said Darren as he went back into the room with Soleil close behind.

The moment he approached the bed Tyrell's expression paled. "Dad, wait," he pleaded. "I said I didn't want this!"

"It's for your own good," said Darren.

Soleil lunged at Darren and tackled him before he had a chance to Enchant Tyrell. With his arms wrapped around Darren, Soleil summoned them to the cafe.

Darren swung his arms wildly and broke Soleil's grip. With his hands in a pleading gesture, Soleil said, "You're not thinking clearly. I'm not saying you shouldn't Enchant Tyrell, I'm just saying you should sleep on it. Magic has benefits, but it also has consequences.

Talk it over with me, along with Flarence and Claire. Most important, talk it over with Tyrell."

"I'm not going to regret this," said Darren. "I regret not being able to protect my wife when she needed me most. Now my son is on the verge of being paralyzed for the rest of his life, and I can help him."

"I can't let you do that," said Soleil.

"You can't stop me," said Darren. "I'm getting the hang of my powers. I don't think I need to be next to Tyrell to Enchant him."

Darren's brow wrinkled, and Soleil lunged at him again, twisting Darren's wrist and pinning him against a wall. "Maybe not, but you do need to be able to focus, which is hard to do when one of your joints is being dislocated." Soleil twisted harder.

"He's my son," said Darren through gritted teeth. "I'm going to help him any way I can." A salt shaker flew across the room into Darren's free hand. He broke it against the wall and jammed the shattered glass into Soleil's thigh. It made Soleil loosen his grip but not enough break it.

"You're going to need to do more damage than that," said Soleil.

"How about this," said Darren, driving them up and smashing Soleil's back into the ceiling. They fell to the floor and Soleil's grip on Darren's arm slipped. He grabbed Darren's ankle, fearing he would use a summoning spell to get away. Darren kicked Soleil in the jaw but Soleil wouldn't let go, and Darren kicked him again. Soleil slapped his foot away and jammed his knee into Darren's solar plexus.

Darren's face scrunched again, and Soleil could tell he was making another attempt to Enchant Tyrell. He punched Darren in the nose.

"My son needs me," shouted Darren as his nose snapped back into place.

"You're not helping him," said Soleil. "You'll heal him, but the price of immortality is being alone. I was reluctant to Enchant you, and a part of me regretted it as soon as it was over. You want to know why I've been laying low in my run-down cafe for so long?" He punched Darren again to keep him unfocused. "It wasn't just because of the rules. It's just the way it is for people like us. Nothing lasts forever, not even relationships. I've loved people before, but love fades and friendships crumble." He punched him in the throat before continuing. "If you Enchant Tyrell, that's the kind of life you'll expose him to. He'll outlive Lucy and any other friends he has. Sure, the two of you will have each other, but that won't last forever. Flarence and I are brothers, and we haven't always been on the best of terms. In fact, we've gone decades without seeing one another. Do you really want to live long enough to see you and Tyrell grow that far apart?"

There was a moment of silence, and Soleil thought Darren was calming down. He lifted his knee and started standing up. Suddenly Darren's calm disappeared. "It won't be that way with us," he spat at Soleil, who immediately drove his knee back into Darren's gut.

"I can do this all day," said Soleil as he grabbed Darren by the neck and slammed his head into the floor.

Darren's grabbed Soleil's wrists. "No you can't."

Darren performed a summoning spell, and they stopped in a poorly lit room. Before Soleil could figure out where they were, a bolt of pain surged through every cell of his body, and he was thrown backward. He felt numb and lay still on a cold, uneven floor. The feeling subsided quickly, but the dizziness lingered.

"I'll think about it," said Darren. His voice echoed and sounded distant. Then he was gone.

Soleil became aware of a rumbling behind him. He turned and saw two rings of light approaching. He realized where he was. Darren had brought them to a wall of the subway and they had been sitting on the tracks. The pain Soleil had felt was from Darren grabbing one of the rails and electrocuting them both to make Soleil let go. He summoned his body out of the tunnel and arrived safely in Tyrell's room, faintly aware of Lucy's gasp as he appeared in front of her.

"Where's Dad?" said Tyrell. Soleil looked around. Darren wasn't there, and Tyrell was still in his casts with the shadows of cuts and bruises still on his face. He had not been Enchanted.

"Lucy, give me your phone." Soleil punched a number hard. "Come on, come on . . . Flarence? It's Soleil. Get to Tyrell's room. It's safe to summon. There's no one here but us."

He ended the call as Flarence appeared with Claire next to him. "Darren just got some bad news and didn't take it very well," Soleil explained. "I'm going to look for him, and I need you to stay here and watch Tyrell. Call me if anything weird happens. This is Lucy's phone. She'll give you the number."

"Define weird," said Flarence.

"Let me know if Tyrell becomes Enchanted," said Soleil. "And if Darren shows up angry, make sure he doesn't do anything crazy." Soleil was gone.

FLARENCE

"I never said he could take my phone," said Lucy.

"Yeah, well, I never said I was available tonight," said Flarence. "There was a mugging downtown last weekend that I wanted to look into."

"I did tell Soleil he could call us if he ever needed backup," said Claire. "I didn't think he'd take me up on the offer so quick. What's all this about Tyrell being at risk of Enchantment?"

"Darren found out the car crash paralyzed Tyrell from the waist down," said Lucy. "He thinks his magic can make Tyrell better."

"He's right," said Flarence. "Enchanting Tyrell would fix him right up, but Darren hasn't had his powers very long, and he doesn't really understand what this kind of life is like."

"Claire, what do you think?" asked Tyrell. "You've been working with Flarence, helping him chase criminals. Having powers would make your life easier, but you said you don't want to be Enchanted."

Claire sat at the foot of Tyrell's bed. "Being Enchanted would make my life easier in some ways. I'd be able to run longer and wouldn't have to worry about getting hurt. You want to know how

I got involved with Flarence, why I stick with him, and why I don't want powers? It all started after my dad was killed."

"I'm sorry," said Tyrell. "I shouldn't be pushing. You don't have to tell me anything."

"I don't mind talking about it," Claire replied. "I don't know why, but my mom left before I was old enough to walk. All my dad ever said was that she had personal issues. He never remarried, but we did all right on our own. I was about your age, Tyrell, when I lost him. He saw a man assaulting a woman one night and tried to break it up. Things escalated, and the man hit him several times in the head with a hammer.

"It turns out the man was the Tool Shed Killer, a serial killer who targeted women and killed them with common hardware tools, which he would leave with the bodies. He'd killed four women before murdering my dad: One was decapitated with a saw, one stabbed repeatedly with a screwdriver, one suffocated with a clamp that was tightened around her neck, and one had holes drilled through her wrists and was tied to a sawhorse where she bled out.

"I still remember the night two cops came to the apartment and told me what happened. I waited for months, but the psychopath wasn't caught. I became obsessed and tried to find him myself. I was frustrated when there was no sign of him for so long, and I started to believe he'd never be captured. Then one day, there was a story about a woman who was found naked and most of her skin had been removed abrasively. The killer left the power sander he used to do it at the scene of the crime."

"That's when I showed up," said Flarence. "The sandpaper victim was the first time I'd heard about the Tool Shed Killer, and I decided to look into it. I soon found out that the guy was careful, and the cops didn't have enough information to catch him. They tried tracking down the power tools, but each one led to a different person, each with an alibi. It turns out the killer had been stealing his murder weapons rather than buying his own. The guy was slick, but I knew that if I snuck into the police evidence locker and grabbed one of the tools he'd used as a murder weapon, I'd be able to find him. That's when I met Claire."

"I was stealing the murder weapons too," said Claire. "My plan was to track each one to its owner so I could find out if there was a certain area where the killer was getting his supplies. I was able to grab the hammer and the drill before Florence showed up. Once I saw him, I ran off."

"She really caught my attention," said Florence. "I let her get away at the evidence locker and grabbed the screwdriver. I followed Claire's progress as she tracked down the owners of the tools and didn't find any pattern. But I knew who the killer was thanks to my psychometry, and I could monitor him with my astral projections. Using those powers, I also found out the motive behind the killings. It seems that John Klarbel—that was his name—had a rebellious daughter, and every time he felt he was losing control over her, he hunted down a girl and killed her in order to get a sense of power back.

"Every time he kidnapped a victim and took her to a quiet place, he talked to them as if their name was Ariel, which was his daughter's name. He also told his victims why he was punishing them, and it was always related to something Ariel had done. At the time I was following Claire, Ariel was spending her summer vacation out of town, so I knew we had some time before John would be motivated to strike again."

"And you spent your time recruiting Claire to be your partner?" said Tyrell.

"No," said Claire, "he didn't try to recruit me. At first, he just wanted to get to know me. He walked up to me one day, completely casual, and asked me how my investigation was going and if I needed help."

"You tried to kick my ass right there on the street."

"I almost succeeded too," said Claire.

"I was holding back," said Florence.

Claire rolled her eyes. "What a prince you are," said Claire. "Florence kept approaching me and offering help, but I had developed trust issues. I even broke off all my connections with my old friends. My life revolved around studying the tools I'd stolen and rereading old news reports about the murders. The problem was that thinking about the tools and rereading news stories about the murders wasn't providing any new information."

"So I caved and accepted Flarence's offer. He told me he knew the houses where the Tool Shed Killer got his murder weapons, but he didn't tell me their addresses right away. Instead, he made me watch the victims' families. Some of the women Klarbel killed had boyfriends who Flarence and I spent some time shadowing. We also shadowed the victims' siblings as well as their parents. Later, he took me to follow Klarbel himself. His daughter was still away. When Flarence first told me Klarbel was the Tool Shed Killer I almost went after the son of a bitch right on the spot, but Flarence held me back. Literally. He forced me to watch Klarbel and his wife from afar, for a full day. Then he asked me what I noticed."

"I think your exact words were, 'I noticed a sociopathic bastard who deserves to bleed,'" said Flarence.

"Which wasn't what he wanted to hear," said Claire. "Flarence dragged me back to his apartment and kept an eye on me the whole night before taking me back to Klarbel's the following day. We kept it up for about two weeks until my opinion finally changed."

"What was the point of all the watching?" said Lucy.

"When I was hunting down the Tool Shed Killer, I was in it for the gore and the eventual joy of knowing I would have payback for what happened to my dad. After following Klarbel around for two weeks, I noticed how happy he and his wife were together. I realized that if I had killed Klarbel the way I'd dreamed, his wife would be subject to the same pain I was going through."

"So Flarence's lesson was to make you feel sorry for the man who killed your father?" said Tyrell.

"No," said Claire, "I didn't feel sorry for him at all. But I realized what was happening was bigger than me. When I started hunting the Tool Shed Killer, I was driven by anger. Flarence taught me how to be driven by empathy. I still wanted to give Klarbel what he deserved, but I wasn't just doing it for my dad anymore. I was thinking about the other people he'd hurt, and also the people he loved."

"Klarbel did get what he deserved," said Flarence proudly, "but we didn't kill him or even send him to jail. We exposed him to the people he cared about. When he kidnapped another victim, we made sure his wife and daughter caught him in the act. Klarbel went into hiding and eventually committed suicide. The cops never found his body. I did, though. The sicko jacked up his car, positioned his head right under the tire, and then knocked the jack out of place."

"When it was over, Flarence told me to move on with my life, but I didn't have anything to move on to. I'd lost both my parents, I never really took the time to get to know the rest of my family, and I had been so obsessed with catching Klarbel that I hadn't kept up contact with any of my friends. Flarence was reluctant about letting me stay with him, but I insisted. I also threatened to go to the cops and tell them all about how Flarence stole evidence."

"She also started asking about my methods," said Flarence. "She was curious as to how I knew so much about the Tool Shed Killer and the victims' families. That's when I revealed to her that I could use magic. I was hoping it would scare her away, but instead it just made her want to stay even more."

"And, obviously, he let me," said Claire. "We've been chasing criminals together ever since."

"But why don't you want powers for yourself?" said Tyrell.

Claire held up her arm and squeezed her bicep. "For one thing, I don't need powers. I'm tough enough to take bad guys out all on my own."

"For the record, I could hold my ground without powers too," said Flarence. "I just wasn't given a choice in whether or not to be Enchanted."

"Fine," said Tyrell, "you're both awesome. What's the other reason?"

Claire's face sobered. "The other reason is that power changes people. I chase criminals because I know what it's like to be a victim. Sure, if I had Flarence's abilities I'd be safer, but understanding danger, pain, and loss made me who I am."

"You could still hold on to your feeling even if you were Enchanted," said Lucy.

"I'm not so sure," said Claire. "I think that if I gained that kind of strength, I'd lose my respect for the weak. While we're on the subject, Flarence, I'm worried about you. When we had Tymbir cornered in the basement, you were on board with killing him. You also killed a homeless man recently, as well as a gang member when you were investigating Tyrell's apartment." She faced him. "And you didn't see the carnage your father left behind when he was trying to save Lucy. I know he had good intentions, but it was a massacre. Everything Darren's done lately has been to protect his family and friends, but what about the people he killed that night? What about their families and their friends? Even killers have people who are important to them, and their feelings matter just as much as yours."

"You still haven't explained why you carry that scarf with you," said Lucy.

"Flarence doesn't have to worry too much about being caught," said Claire. "His summoning ability lets him travel great distances in short periods of time without leaving a trail, so if things ever start getting too hot, he can get out in a second. I lack that ability, so I have to take measures to conceal my identity. As for the weapons, the razors on the scarf aren't long enough to be lethal. They're sharp enough to cause pain, but they won't kill anyone unless I go right for the neck. Small blades are one of the few weapons I feel comfortable using. They keep me from being tempted to kill. Anyway, that's my story, Tyrell. That's why I work with Flarence and why I have no interest in being Enchanted. What do you think? Do you want powers yourself?"

"Did dad really slaughter dozens of people in the houses while rescuing Lucy?" said Tyrell. "You don't really think he's losing control, do you?"

"I don't know," said Claire. "But he is becoming more dangerous as he gets comfortable with his powers. Let's hope Soleil finds him soon, before things get worse."

−12−

DARREN

Darren leaned a chair on its two back legs with his hand folded on his lap in Mike's apartment. Juan and Josh were both there and sat in silence. Darren chose to meet at Mike's place because Soleil would look in his apartment, as well as at the cafe and the hospital. He'd promised to explain everything that had been going on with him and his family, including the details of his prison break and Atalissa's death, but he didn't want to say anything until the five of them were together. Everyone was nervous, and when there was a knock at the door Mike all but leaped from the table to answer it.

Darren let his chair fall to all four legs and slid his right hand forward, palm up, to the center of the table. "Someone give me a coin." The four of them looked frustrated, not happy with what seemed like his stalling. "Humor me," Darren continued. "You're not going to believe a word I say unless I show you this first."

Danny placed a quarter in Darren's palm.

"Call it," said Darren.

"I don't know, heads," said Danny.

The coin made a loud ping as Darren flicked it up. The group stared and waited for it to fall back down, but it stayed in the air, flipping over and over for several seconds before landing gently on Darren's palm, heads side up.

"Gravity manipulation," said Darren. "It's one of the things I can do now. He turned his hand palm down so the coin was resting on the table. He moved his hand away and the coin turned to liquid metal which oozed into the shape of a throwing star and then became solid again. "I can also control the temperature of objects, so I can make metals melt on demand. Once they're melted, I can control their flow and remold them any way I want." The star liquefied again, rearranged back into a quarter, and he slid it across the table back to Danny. "I can do other things. A lot of other things. My powers are what brought me back after being shot."

Juan stood up and backed away.

"Sit back down," Darren demanded. "I'm not going to continue unless we're all here."

Mike took Juan by the wrist and pulled him back to his chair. "What are you?"

"I'm a Genie. At least I thought I was. When I acquired these powers, I was under the impression that it was my responsibility to use them to help those who lacked the means to help themselves. I thought there was a system, an order. I thought there was a reason all this was happening."

"Is that why you're talking to us now?" said Josh. "Are you here to help us with something?"

"Actually, I'm the one who needs your help," said Darren. "A lot has happened, and I need to talk to someone about what to do next."

"We've been friends for a long time," said Juan, "and we've had a lot of experiences together, but none of us can control gravity or turn quarters into weapons. I don't think we're the right people to go to for advice right now."

"I'm not coming to you for advice," said Darren. "I've decided what I'm going to do. I'm coming to you for approval. I feel like it's me against the world, and I just want someone on my side."

"Whatever you need, we're with you," said Mike.

Darren leaned over the table and looked Mike in the eyes. "I'm going to kill a cop." The quarter he had slid to Danny was still on the table. He melted it again and this time molded it into a small hook before he summoned it to his body. He caught it and held it at face height with his elbow on the table. "I'm going to do it in the most painful way I can think of. I'm going to scoop both his eyes out and shove them down his throat. Or maybe I'll drag him outside, nail him to the hood of his own car, and publicly disembowel him. Are you still with me?"

"That doesn't sound like you're using your powers to help people," said Josh.

"It's going to help me," said Darren as he slammed the newly formed hook onto the table. "This is going to help me feel a lot better. The cop I'm going to kill is Officer Tymbir. He's the reason my wife is dead and my son is a cripple. He found out about my powers and assumed I was evil. I can understand being afraid of things that are unfamiliar, but he took it too far."

"And now it sounds like you're taking it too far," said Mike. "There's got to be another way."

"You're right," said Darren, "there probably is another way, but I want to do this my way. It used to be our way, before we all went soft. Look at us; we're sitting around discussing the proper course of action against a man who tried to kill me. When we were kids and someone messed with us, we brought a world of hurt on them. This isn't just about giving that son of a bitch Tymbir what's coming to him, it's about bringing us back to the way we used to be when we were young.

"I have powers now, and I can use them to take this gang to a whole new level. Are you happy here, living in small, dilapidated apartments on a crumbling street? If you stick with me, I can expand our territory. We'll take over more than this neighborhood. I can help us take over this whole city. With me on your side, you'll be bulletproof. Nobody, police or rival gang, will be able to stop us. Now I'm going to ask you this one more time: Are you still with me?"

Juan nodded. "If you think you can improve our status, you should go for it."

"If this Tymbir guy attacked you, he should pay," said Mike.

"We've all got your back," said Danny. "You wanted approval, you got it."

"Good," said Darren. "This is the start of something big. For now, just sit tight. I'll be right back."

Darren summoned his body to a car in a hardware store parking lot. He didn't care if anyone saw him appear; in fact, he was hoping people did. He was on a mission to get attention. He casually strode into the power tools section, found an electric saw, and deconstructed it. The frame turned into hundreds of small plastic beads which fell to the floor. The wires, now exposed, fell next, and Darren was left with just the circular steel blade. An employee approached and asked what was going on. Darren swung the saw blade into the man's cheek. He fell to the floor as blood pooled beneath him. "This'll work," Darren said as he walked away.

In the aisle, a man grabbed his arm. Darren spun and drove the saw blade into his neck. He walked away again but then noticed his hand. The impact of slicing the man's throat had cut Darren below his knuckles. "Hmm," he said as the wound healed, "that's going to get annoying." He focused on the blade, melting and bending some of the teeth to make a smooth part he could hold when he struck people. Then he made a handle above the new smooth section. "That's better," he said to himself, as panicked shoppers gathered around the two bleeding men in the store. Darren threw the blade into the crowd. The man it hit in the back screamed and frantically tried to remove it but couldn't. A woman next to him pulled it out. But as soon as it left the man's skin, Darren summoned the blade, slicing the woman's fingers as it flew to him. He caught it safely by the handle.

As Darren approached the doors, he looked up at a television monitor showing what the security cameras were recording. He turned to give the screen a clear view of his face and waved with his right hand which was holding the bloody saw blade.

"Don't move," said a voice. The security guard was holding a Taser.

Darren pointed at the monitor. "I wasn't moving. I wanted to make sure the camera got my picture."

"Put the blade down. Get on your knees. Put your hands behind your head."

"That's not happening," said Darren. "I cooperated with an officer before. It was the biggest mistake of my life."

"This isn't a joke. Drop the blade. Now."

He tossed the blade in front of his feet. As the guard approached, he summoned it to a grill in the distance. The blade traveled fast, but the guard avoided it.

"Impressive reflexes," said Darren. The guard turned back to him. Darren summoned the blade back to his body, sending it through the guard's liver. Darren caught the blade and summon-traveled to a wall of Mike's apartment.

Mike, Josh, Danny, and Juan were exactly where he had left them. "How long was I gone?" he asked, but the four of them were speechless as they stared at the bloodstained saw in his hand. "Never mind, it doesn't matter," he said as he took his seat. "Anyway, as long as we're all sitting in a circle, everybody link hands." Danny hesitated. Not wanting to put his hand near the saw, he gripped Darren's arm near the elbow. "Hold on tight," said Darren. "I should see the skin around your fingers lose color." He waited until the whole group had obeyed, and then brought everybody out of the apartment.

They arrived in a vacant room with only a bed and a wardrobe. "What happened?" asked Josh.

"Where are we?" Danny said.

"Oh, damn, there's a dead body!" shouted Mike.

"Good," said Darren, "that means he hasn't found time to clean up yet." He approached the wardrobe and opened the door, revealing three rifles on hanging racks, along with boxes of bullets on the shelves. "We're at the spot where it could have all been over. I met Tymbir in the basement of this very house, and I could have killed him then. I chose to let him live, not knowing at the time that his actions had led to Atalissa's death. Now Tymbir's going to make up for it by supplying us with ammunition."

"There are only three guns," said Mike.

"I'm sure there's a firearm on the body you saw a moment ago," said Darren. Mike was hesitant about taking a gun from a corpse, and when he took too long, Darren summoned the dead man's gun, caught it, and handed it forcefully to Mike. "Here. Take it and man up. Now everybody grab my arms again. We're leaving."

"Wait," said Mike, "I don't have any spare bullets."

"We'll be back," said Darren. "You just need to be able to hold a small crowd still for a little bit." Mike walked behind Juan and grabbed his shoulder, Juan grabbed Danny's shoulder, Danny grabbed Josh's, and Josh grabbed Darren's. "Everybody holding on tight?" said Darren. Once again, the group was summoned away.

Darren arrived in Jordan's apartment, his friends behind him, in the room where he had gone for questioning. At the other end, he could hear a television with two people arguing about nonsense, probably some kind of reality show. Jordan and Rookie were on a couch watching it while two others stood nearby with their arms crossed. A floorboard creaked under Darren's feet, and the guards turned to him. One pulled out a pistol and the other a knife. "How did you get in here?" the one with the gun asked. Darren summoned the knife to his body, caught it with his free hand, and threw it into the gunman's eye. The guard who'd lost his knife was confused but instinctively raised his fists in front of his face. Darren threw the saw blade into his thigh, and the man fell. Darren snapped the downed man's neck and pulled the saw blade out of his leg before going to the gunman and driving the knife deeper into his head.

Darren tossed the dead man aside and looked toward the couch. Jordan was standing near the television with a shattered beer bottle in his hand while Rookie was on his butt leaning back on his hands. Looking at Rookie, Darren moved away from the door and gestured toward it with his chin. Rookie bolted for the door. Darren locked it and turned around to see Jordan cautiously moving toward him, the bottle held high and ready to strike. Darren became invisible, and Jordan stopped in his tracks. Darren held his breath and moved quietly until he was a few inches from Jordan, then suddenly became visible again. Before Jordan could swing the bottle, Darren grabbed his arm and moved the saw blade against his throat.

"Drop it."

The bottle clattered to the floor. Darren took the blade away from Jordan's neck and shoved him. "Get into the interrogation room."

Jordan rubbed his neck. "If you have something you want to ask me, ask me here."

Darren grabbed Jordan by the arm and pulled him into the room with the chair. "You're not in a position to give me orders anymore, so stop trying to act like you're the boss."

Jordan looked around and saw the other men. "Danny, Juan, Josh, Mike! You're all in on this too?"

Darren shoved Jordan into the chair. "They didn't have anything to do with this. Right now, you should be focused on me."

Jordan started to stand up. "This is out of line, Darren. If you don't stop right now, I'll …"

Darren swung the saw blade in a downward arch into Jordan's left shoulder. He collapsed into the chair. "Sit down or the next blow's going to be to your skull," said Darren. He removed the blade. Screaming in pain, Jordan gripped his shoulder tightly.

"I devoted years to this gang," Darren said. "I risked jail time to bring you profits from drug sales, and fought off our rivals whenever our territory was threatened. Where do you get off questioning my loyalty?"

"Oh, was I too rough with you?" said Jordan sarcastically. "I needed to know you were the same person you were when you were young. I needed the facts."

Darren slapped him with the flat of the blade. "The fact was I had a wife and son I needed to take care of. The fact was that when I joined this gang, you told me it was a family. A brotherhood. So why didn't you protect me when I had a target on my back? How did nobody notice or do anything when a cop was spying on my apartment? Why didn't you call me after Atalissa died?"

"We tried calling you," said Josh. "We were always there for you."

"I know," said Darren, "which is why you're here." He walked around the chair with his arms spread wide. "Look around the room,

Jordan." The man in the chair started to stand again but stopped when Darren placed the blade against his other shoulder. "I didn't say get up. I said look around." Jordan sat back down and turned his head. "These four people represent what it truly means to be part of the gang," Darren said. "Most of you turned your backs on me, but when I was down, these guys helped me back up. It's true that Josh kind of screwed me over by not telling me about how drugs were being transported through his dad's shop, but he apologized for it, and we're still friends. You abandoned me, and I didn't get so much as an 'I'm sorry' out of you."

"It was about more than the money," said Jordan. "There was evidence that you were linked to a man who was attacking us."

"What is he?" said Darren. Jordan looked at him confused. "The man whose picture's been circulating the neighborhood. What is he?"

"We know his name is Flarence," said Jordan.

"Not who, what?" said Darren. Jordan didn't answer. "You don't know what you were dealing with, do you?"

"We know Flarence is trouble," said Jordan.

Darren moved in front of Jordan and grabbed him by the chin. He forced his head up and looked him in the eye. "Trouble has plagued this neighborhood before, but we persevered. There was no reason for you to think the situation with Flarence would be any different. It could have been handled without making me a pariah. You punished me because I wasn't bringing you enough money. You don't see me, or any of us for that matter, as a brotherhood. You see us as a delivery service."

"I see you as followers. You all follow me because I know what I'm doing. I know how to survive."

Darren tipped the chair, and when Jordan fell out, he threw it across the room through the window to the cement below. He dragged Jordan to the broken glass. "You think the ability to survive qualifies you to be a leader? Tell you what, whoever survives this is in charge." Darren lunged forward and dragged Jordan with him over the edge. Darren released his hold and let Jordan plummet to the concrete, but he made himself lighter. He floated down and landed gracefully on his feet next to Jordan's broken body. Mike, Josh, Danny, and Juan all rushed out, still holding their guns.

A crowd started to gather. There were about twenty people when Darren broke the silence. He pointed to the apartment building. "Everyone get inside. I'm taking charge of this gang, and there's going to be some new ground rules." Nobody moved at first, and Darren raised the saw blade. "Get in there now, or you're going to be next." The crowd went into the lobby.

"Rookie already got away," said Josh. "He looked scared enough to go to the cops."

"I'm counting on it," said Darren as he followed his friends to the apartment. Inside, he turned to them. "This is why I gave you those guns. If anyone tries to get away, shoot them. I'll be right back."

"I thought we were going back to the house to get more guns," said Juan.

"We will," said Darren. "We need to have enough guns and bullets for everybody. But there's something I think I should do first."

Darren summoned his body out of the apartment and into a room filled with metal cabinets and tables and little else. Dead bodies were entombed in the drawers, and he was about to select one when an attendant came in wheeling a new corpse. "What are you doing here?" he asked.

"Gaining the element of surprise," said Darren as he threw the blade deep into the man's skull. He examined the dead attendant, who was short and didn't look like Darren, the eyes too close together, his nose too small. "Too much work," said Darren. "Let's see what you brought."

Darren unzipped the bag. The man inside was closer to his own appearance. "You look much better," he told the dead man, then zipped the bag back up, placed the saw blade on top of it, and walked out. He ignored the employees who eyed him suspiciously when they saw the blood on his hands. In another room, Darren found what he was looking for. He deconstructed part of the red container medical personnel used to dispose of used needles, pulled one out, and went back to the morgue. Gripping the bag with one hand and his saw blade with the other, he summoned his body back to Jordan's apartment building.

The twenty or so people he had pulled off the street were cowering on the floor of the lobby with his friends' guns pointed at them. "Feeling young again?" Darren said loudly.

"Who's in the bag?" asked Juan.

"It's just a little ace in the hole for later," said Darren. "Now let's get some more guns."

SOLEIL

Soleil wished he knew Darren better. He wasn't in either of the places Soleil could think of to look: his apartment and the cafe. Astral projections were also useless since he didn't know any of Darren's friends. He walked the streets looking for anything suspicious. His thoughts raced as he tried to find a hint of where Darren would go, struggling in the back of his mind to remember the name of the gang's leader which Tyrell had mentioned. Soleil thought it was Jimmy or Johnny, but that didn't help. Just as he gave up, Lucy's phone rang. Several people stopped and stared when they heard the pop song ring tone. He slid his finger across the screen to accept the call and had barely finished saying "hello" when Flarence interrupted him.

"I thought you were looking for Darren."

"I am."

"Get back to Tyrell's room," said Flarence, and he hung up. Soleil ducked behind a trashcan, and summoned his body to the hospital. Flarence, Lucy, Claire, and Tyrell all had their eyes glued to a television on the wall. A reporter was talking with a man who was trembling and speaking in a shaky voice.

"He just walked into the store, picked up an electric saw, and started cutting people," the man said. "But he only used what he needed."

"What do you mean 'only used what he needed?' " asked the reporter.

"He didn't use the whole saw. He just took out the blade."

"You mean he disassembled the saw in the store and then used the blade as a weapon?"

"He didn't disassemble anything. He just, I don't know, got rid of it. One minute there was a tool; the next, there was nothing but the blade."

"There was a description of the killer earlier," said Flarence. "There hasn't been a picture released yet, but it sounds a lot like Darren. That business about the killer deconstructing the saw is a red flag too."

Soleil turned to Tyrell. "Do you feel any different?"

"I haven't been Enchanted," said Tyrell. "If I were, I'd probably be able to feel my legs right now."

Soleil paced around the bed. "So Darren finds out you're paralyzed, he tries to heal you, but I stop him, and so he goes on a killing spree?"

"That isn't like him," said Tyrell. "Dad's not the kind of guy who loses control."

"It looks like he's trying to send a message," said Claire, "or prove a point."

"He's drawing attention," said Flarence. "He's daring the police to come after him and hoping a specific officer will show up. He is calling out Tymbir."

"If that was true, then he would have stayed in the store," said Claire. "He would have kept attacking people until the cops showed up. This is about something other than Tymbir. There's something else he wants to do that takes precedence over revenge. But I can't imagine what that can possibly be."

"I think I can," said Tyrell. "The only person in the world dad could possibly hate more than Tymbir is Jordan."

Soleil stopped pacing and snapped his fingers. "That's his name!" he shouted as he performed an astral projection without bothering to sit down. He caught a glimpse of his body falling in a heap on the floor before he drifted through the wall of the hospital.

His projection was drawn to an apartment. When it drifted inside, it hovered over a bed sheet on the lobby floor with a large lump in the middle. He knew it was the man he was looking for. The trail of blood from the building's front door to the body told Soleil that Jordan had been killed outside and dragged inside. His projection followed the blood to a pool of it outside, surrounded by shards of broken glass. It rose to a broken window and floated inside, where he saw Darren standing in front of a crowd of about twenty people, each with a gun in their hands. Darren was holding a serrated blade that appeared to have come from an electric saw.

"The police will be here soon," Darren said, "but I'm only interested in one of them: a man named Officer Tymbir. You don't need to know what he looks like. I'll let you know when he comes. If he's not among the cops who arrive, kill all the ones who do show up, and then wait for reinforcements. We'll stay here until Tymbir comes. When he does, I'll kill him and get you all out of the building safely. Don't worry about the cops returning fire. I can disable their weapons from here. All the cards are in our hands. We can attack them all we want, and all they can do is run."

Soleil's projection returned to his body. "I used my astral projection to find Jordan," he explained. "He's dead, but Darren was nearby, and I was able to listen in on what he's planning to do."

"Yeah, so was I," said Flarence. "I projected right after you left. I feel a little embarrassed for not thinking of finding Jordan earlier." He pulled the Stakehail Colt out of his coat pocket and loaded it. "Let's get him."

"No," said Soleil before Flarence summoned his body out of the room. "I'll take care of this alone."

"Why?" asked Flarence.

"Because you're holding a gun," said Soleil. "I'm worried that if you do this, you'll end up killing Darren."

"I'm sure as hell going to try," said Flarence. "He's a psychopath."

"No," said Soleil. "He's convinced the world is out to get him, and now that he has powers, he's trying to take what he feels he deserves."

"Oh," said Flarence, "and what did I say?"

"Hey," said Tyrell, "this is my dad you're talking about."

"That's right," said Soleil. "He doesn't deserve to die. He just needs to know that this isn't the way to get what he wants."

"Darren is in no state to be reasoned with," said Flarence. "The man wants blood. You can't just go into that apartment and talk some sense into him."

"No, but I can remind him that he's not the only one with powers. I can show him I won't stand for what he's doing."

"You're going to fight him?" said Claire.

"I'm going to neutralize that army he's building," said Soleil. "It won't be pretty, but not all my toxins are deadly. I'll do enough damage to prove my point and then I'll leave. Flarence, I need your word you'll let me try this my way. Stay out of it for now."

Flarence clicked the release button on the Stakehail Colt. The ice turned to liquid, and he clicked the empty cylinder and gas canister back into position, then placed the gun back in his pocket and held up his hands. "Fine. You have my word."

Soleil summoned his body to his cafe to retrieve his poncho.

FLARENCE

When Soleil had left, Flarence went into the hallway. Claire followed close behind. Lucy stayed with Tyrell.

Claire grabbed his arm. "We're not going after Darren."

"I am. Do you really think Soleil can pull this off on his own?"

"I think we need to give your brother a chance," said Claire. She lowered her voice as two doctors walked by. "You're doing it again, Flarence. You're not showing compassion to anyone anymore."

"Listen, I'm sorry about what happened with Tymbir."

"And the homeless man?"

"Fine, I'll admit killing the bum was a mistake too. But this is a special situation, and I'm not out of line. You need to understand that I've been holding back all this time because, in spite of everything I said, a part of me was worried that the Council of Elders was watching me. Darren is powerful, pissed, and knows the council doesn't exist, which means he has no reason to go easy on anybody. Soleil and I are the only two who can scare him straight."

"That's exactly what Soleil wants to do," said Claire. "Like I said, give him a chance to do things his way."

"I intend to," said Flarence, "but I'm also going to be ready in case Darren doesn't listen. If Soleil can't calm him down, a lot of shit is going to hit the fan, and when that happens, no matter how it looks when the smoke clears, I have a pretty good idea of where he'll go to unwind." Flarence turned and started walking down the hall. Claire followed him until he stopped and turned. "You're not coming with me."

"I've held my ground against plenty of different enemies," said Claire, "and you taught me how to stand up to magic."

"I didn't teach you well enough," said Flarence. "The Student … I mean dad, roughed you up, and you weren't even fighting the real him. I'm sorry, but I don't feel comfortable taking you with me to fight Darren."

Claire hurried after him, but he walked into a men's room, and by the time she opened the door, he was already gone.

-13-

DARREN

"**K**nock it off, Darren, that's gross," said Josh, as Darren stabbed the syringe into his arm and pulled out more blood.

He inserted the needle into the body he'd taken from the hospital. "I'm doing this for a reason. There are other people in the world who have powers like mine."

"Are you kidding me?" said Josh. "There's another one of you?"

"Three that I know of," said Darren, "and I have reason to believe every one of them is against what I'm doing here. Controlling dead bodies is one of our powers, and I know from experience that it's an effective trick. If I can make this body look like me, it might give me an edge if another Genie tries to interrupt our assault on the cops." Darren slid the needle out of the body and stood over it. He was wearing a simple black T-shirt and jeans, and the corpse was too. The dead man's skin was clammy, but Darren focused on it and changed the color to match his own. Then he deconstructed sections of the dead man's hair to make their cuts match.

"That's cool," said Josh, "but why did you inject him with your blood?"

Darren shrugged. "Call it paranoia, I guess. I haven't had my powers for long, but the other Genies have had hundreds of years to practice. The worst thing I can do right now is underestimate them. If I'm going to do the Corpse Puppet spell, I need it to be as realistic as possible, outside and in. I also need to remember to inflate its lungs and regulate its temperature. Those two things shattered the illusion the last time the spell was used."

"I still think its gross," said Josh.

"Well then don't stand around watching me. Is everyone in their positions?"

"Danny is in the lobby, Mike's on the first floor, Juan on the second, and I'll be on the third along with you. We each have five guys on the floor with us, all armed."

"Good," said Darren. "Remind them to hold their fire when the cops show up. If I turn their cars to dust, it means Tymbir wasn't with them and you can open fire. If Tymbir does show up, I'll heat the gas in the tanks to set fire to the cars. Once we get Tymbir, we'll meet in the lobby, link arms, and I'll summon us out of here."

"We only assumed Rookie went to the cops after you showed up in Jordan's room. He might have gone somewhere else, or he might've been scared enough to skip town. Even if he went to the cops, there's no guarantee Tymbir'll show up."

"I'm hoping Tymbir will be too scared to show up," said Darren. "I could just summon-travel to his house and hack him to pieces. The longer Tymbir waits to come, the more police officers die. Their blood will be on his hands. Now get to a window, and be ready for whatever happens." Josh left the room, and Darren was alone. He pushed the body behind a sofa. If there was a fight, he would have to find a way to distract his opponents, then hide and make the corpse crawl out. He looked out the window at the street below. For now, everything was still calm, and there were no sirens in the distance. He began to wonder if Rookie had in fact gone to the police.

There was a creak behind him. He spun around to find Soleil in the room, wearing the poncho with vials of poisons that he had used the night they saved Lucy. "It's amazing how you can travel across the city without being seen," said Darren, "but you're careless enough to step on a loose floorboard."

"I wasn't making a sneak attack. I didn't come here to fight you. I came here to ask you, nicely, to please stop what you're doing."

"You're wasting your breath."

Soleil held his hands in a pleading gesture. "I'm sorry about what happened. I can tell it was painful to lose Atalissa, but it doesn't make this right. I heard you when you were talking to your army. I know you're going to massacre any police officers that show up."

"It doesn't have to be a massacre. I'm only after one person, but I'm going to kill however many are necessary to accomplish my goal. Who knows, maybe Tymbir will show up on his own, and he'll be the only person who has to die."

"Even if that's the case, and I doubt it will be, I can't let it happen. I can't let you use your powers to kill even one person in cold blood."

"These are my powers, and I'll use them any way I want. You're the one who told me the Council of Elders doesn't exist. There's nobody around to keep me in line."

"I'm around."

Darren scoffed. "What're you going to do? Throw your vials at me? I've taken barrages of bullets and I'm still walking around. You can't kill me."

Soleil pulled two vials out of his poncho. The floor beneath his feet turned to dust, and Darren watched him fall to the level below.

SOLEIL

When his feet touched the ground, two people were facing him. They'd heard him land and turned, but before they could shoot, Soleil threw a vial against a wall. When it shattered, the powder scattered, a protease that was highly reactive to ocular tissue, and the victims fell to the floor screaming as their eyes turned to mush and oozed down their faces. Darren fell through the floor and landed in front of Soleil.

"Too slow," said Soleil as he ran into the hallway. Four more members of Darren's army greeted him. He ran toward them, and when one raised his gun, he became invisible and dove onto his stomach as the trigger was pulled. The bullets flew over Soleil's back and struck Darren in the stomach. The man rushed to Darren to make sure he was all right.

"Juan, no," shouted Darren as Soleil restored his visibility. In a smooth motion, he leaped up and flicked a vial of liquid in Juan's face, which was quickly covered in chemical burns. The other gang members raised their guns, but Soleil grabbed Juan as a shield. Everyone held their fire, and Soleil grabbed another vial with his free hand and threw it at the ceiling. When it broke, he increased the weight of the liquid and made it rain down on their faces and hands, causing whatever body parts it touched to go numb. The shooters dropped their guns and stood dumbly in the hall, their hands unable to grip their weapons or throw a punch. Soleil slammed Juan's head against the wall and let him fall to the floor.

"Not so much of a hot-shot now, are you?" said Soleil as Darren looked at his fallen comrades. "Have I proven my point, or should I keep this up?"

Darren was about to strike Soleil with the saw blade, but suddenly, there was gunfire from the floor below.

"Cops!" said Darren as he ran into the closest room and looked out the window.

Soleil followed him. "Darren, I swear, if Tymbir is outside and you kill him, everyone in this building is going to die vomiting their own blood."

"Tymbir's not here," said Darren. "Nobody's here."

Soleil stood next to Darren. Sure enough, there were no police cars on the street, though they still heard shooting from the floors below. With a quick glance at each other, Soleil and Darren deconstructed the floorboards they were standing on.

They landed in an empty room and instantly rushed into the hallway. Darren was out first and narrowly avoided colliding with Mike. "What's going on?" said Darren.

"Don't know," said Mike. "No cops outside to shoot, but there's something goin' on in the lobby."

Darren, Soleil, and Mike leaped down the steps three at a time. Mike ran into the door shoulder-first and knocked it open, only to fall back a moment later, screaming and clutching his face. Darren forced his hands away to see what had happened. There were third-degree burns on Mike's forehead, left eye, and most of his left cheek.

Soleil looked away from Mike and saw a man in the doorway wearing brown boots and black denim jeans. His navy blue shirt clung tightly to his skin. His black gloves each had a white W on it, the left with a plus sign superimposed, the right with a horizontal line running through it. The man's shirt also had white symbols. A large χ was on his chest while his right shoulder had a λ symbol and his left shoulder the letter Z with a ring around it. The black bandanna hiding his face had a white symbol of a ring surrounding two lines, one pointed to 12 if the ring had been a clock and the other trailing close behind. He was armed with two revolvers, each with a spinning cylinder that held six chambers. Like Flarence's Stakehail Colt, the guns had been modified. The hammer was gone, and wires flowed out of the empty space, each running to a hole in the grip.

Soleil stared at the man and didn't react when he pulled the trigger. Soleil braced himself for the bullet's impact, but it never came. Instead, a transparent wave emanated from the barrel like heat from a fire. The wave hit him, but all he felt was a tingle, like a thin layer of cold mist washing over his body. Soleil stood still for a moment, confused. The man pointed the gun above Soleil's head and fired again. Soleil was thrown backward and up the stairs, as if pulled by an invisible tether. He smashed into the wall, knocking the wind out of him, but it quickly came back. He stood up, ready to charge the man with the guns, but then stopped, as the reality of what just happened sank in. *That guy just summoned me*, Soleil thought, *with his gun.*

He was brought back to his senses by the sound of Darren's screams, and saw that the man had shot him in the face with his other gun. Darren's skin was severely burned, just like Mike's. The man walked over Darren's body and started moving up the stairs toward Soleil, but Darren grabbed the man's ankle and pulled. The man fell to the steps and rolled over, pausing as he watched the burn on Darren's face rapidly disappear. Darren tried to take advantage of the attacker's confusion and lunged, but the man shot Darren with his first gun, then fired above his head. Darren flew into the same wall Soleil had been summoned to. He got up with the saw blade in his right hand, ready to fight.

"What are you?" said the stranger. He pressed a switch on the grip of the gun in his right hand four times. The cylinder rotated clockwise with each click. Darren moved his arm back to throw the blade, but the stranger pulled the trigger. Darren grabbed his wrist as he fell to the floor. The man released the trigger, and when Darren took his hand from his wrist, Soleil saw dark marks running up his arm. They were quickly healing, but it was obvious they were electrical burns.

"Stay close," said Soleil as he took a vial from his poncho.

"What, we're a team all of a sudden?" said Darren. "Five minutes ago, you were killing my crew. I don't know what's going on here, but if you want this guy, you're on your own." Darren vanished.

Soleil was about to perform a summoning spell of his own but was stopped by a searing pain in his neck. The stranger had once again set the gun to burn, and this time, he wasn't so quick to let go of the trigger. Soleil ran into the hallway to put the wall between himself and the attacker. As he waited a moment for the burns to heal, he heard a dull, rhythmic clunking and looked up to see the stranger walking toward him. The man raised a gun and fired, but Soleil pushed away with his heels and crawled back to avoid the blast. The shot singed the carpet. The stranger's bandanna shifted, as if he was grinning underneath it, and he pulled the trigger again, holding it down while aiming in front of Soleil, and the floor burst into flames. Soleil backed away and regained his footing as the stranger swept the barrel along the floor and walls to spread the blaze. Soleil tried to focus on the air in the room and concentrate carbon dioxide around the fire to extinguish it, but the stranger made new flames grow as quickly as Soleil could put them out.

The fire became too much to handle, so Soleil decreased his weight and leaped off the ground. He passed through the ceiling and restored his weight as he reconstructed the hole he'd made. His plan was to run down the hallway before deconstructing the floor and landing behind the stranger, but the floor below his feet was breaking down without his influence. It seemed that the man's gun also could deconstruct objects.

"Dammitdammitdammit . . ." Soleil panted as he scrambled away from the growing hole at his feet. He tried to summon his body out of the hallway but couldn't focus knowing that right below him was a raging fire and a maniac with a spellcasting revolver. He couldn't stay ahead of the growing hole, and when he fell through he landed right at the stranger's feet.

"What are you?" said the stranger as he clicked the switch on the gun's grip and spun the chamber to where he wanted it. Soleil focused on the weapon and tried to deconstruct it, but his magic had no effect. He reached for one of his toxins, but the moment his hand moved, the stranger pulled the trigger, and Soleil began convulsing with pain and numbness. The man was electrocuting him. "Tell me what you are," he shouted.

Soleil's vision was fading, but his fingers found a vial and in a single motion, he pulled it out of its pouch and threw it. He didn't know what was in it or where it went, but apparently it landed close to the attacker, because the pain stopped. Eyes closed, he found the mental strength to summon his body out of the hallway back to his cafe. Feeling safe now, he closed his eyes and waited for the pain of the electric attack to subside.

FLARENCE

Flarence leaned against a tree spinning the loaded Stakehail Colt on his finger. Behind him was Atalissa's headstone, embedded in the ground and surrounded by flowers her friends and family had left.

Her parents had chosen to have the urn buried. Regardless of what happened at the apartment, Florence guessed Darren would go to his wife's burial site to clear his head when it was over. The sound of a snapping twig caught his attention. He peeked around the tree and saw Darren by the grave.

"I know you're there," Darren called out before Florence could shoot. "I can smell you. Claire told me about sense improvement." Florence stepped out from behind the tree with the gun pointed at the ground, level with his waist. "You can put the gun away too, Florence. We both know weapons are useless against people like us."

The revolver turned to metal shavings in Florence's hand, the gas in the cartridge dispersed with a pop, and the icicles in the chambers turned to steam. Darren looked smugly at Florence as he tossed his saw blade on the ground. Florence also grinned. The metal shavings clumped and molded together to form the gun, which he summoned it to his body. "I modified it myself. It's easy to reconstruct objects when you know exactly how every part fits together."

Darren extended his hand and summoned the saw blade back to his body. "Then it's a good thing I chose a simple weapon. It won't take much to reconstruct a flat piece of metal."

Florence deconstructed the saw blade, and Darren instantly reformed it. Just to be irritating, Florence deconstructed it again, and again Darren brought it back to its original form.

"Knock it off," Darren growled. "I don't see Razor Punk anywhere. Did you two have a falling out?"

"She likes to strike from the shadows," said Florence.

"She isn't here," said Darren. "I'd smell her if she was."

"What happened with you and Soleil?" said Florence. "I know he went to see you first."

"That he did," said Darren, "and I wish I knew what happened to him. Last I saw, he was getting pummeled by some nutcase in a bandanna. You should go check on him."

"Soleil can handle himself," said Florence. "I'm here to stop you."

Darren pointed at Flarence's gun. "How? With that? I just had a similar conversation with your brother. Go ahead and shoot me. I'll just heal. Face it: You can't kill me."

"I'll bet I can," said Flarence. "Don't forget, I've been doing this a lot longer than you."

"But you've never fought one of your own kind," said Darren. "You and Soleil can take down humans just as soon as look at them, but you don't know what it takes to kill a Genie."

Flarence chuckled. "I guess Soleil didn't tell you every part of Mohinaux's story. Don't worry. I'll fill you in."

Flarence fired, and Darren ducked. He charged at Flarence, who fired again, but Darren swung the blade into the icicle, shattering it before it hit his body. The third time Flarence fired, Darren let the icicle sink into his chest just below his heart, but now he was close enough to hit back. He swung the saw blade at Flarence's neck, but Flarence avoided it. Darren followed with a kick to the sternum which knocked him down. Darren pinned him to the ground and held the blade high above his head. But Flarence focused on the icicle still embedded in Darren's chest and increased its temperature until it melted and the water boiled. Darren winced, and Flarence could force him off. He went to one knee and fired again. The icicle penetrated Darren's leg, and he fell. Flarence tried to aim at Darren's temple, but he was writhing around too much as he removed the icicle. Flarence stood up and tried to hit Darren with the gun, but it only clanged against the saw blade Darren lifted. Flarence wrestled Darren to the ground and put the Stakehail Colt under his chin, but before he could fire, the gun turned to dust again.

Flarence was about to reconstruct the revolver, but Darren, still underneath, forced his body back into the cold stone wall of a nearby mausoleum. Darren drove his elbow into Flarence's kidney. Flarence grabbed Darren's arm and tried to throw him down. Their feet tangled, and both men fell. Darren pushed away, and swung the saw blade into Flarence's right shoulder. He dragged it across Flarence's body, leaving a long, deep gash. Flarence threw his arms around himself as Darren lifted the blade above his head with both hands and drove it down. Florence rolled, and the blade sank into the dirt. As the cut healed, Florence summoned his body to a tall grave marker near the pile of metal dust in the grass. He reconstructed his gun, summoned it to his body, and reloaded. But by the time he was ready to fire, Darren had disappeared.

As he looked around the cemetery, a dense, gray cloud formed near the ground. It started low but rose quickly and grew thicker. Florence looked up and saw the clouds disappearing. He realized that Darren was summoning water vapor to stone structures in the cemetery and then concentrating it into droplets to create a fog thick enough to hinder their vision. Florence thought about removing the fog with a gust of wind but then decided it could help him too. He raised the Stakehail Colt and slowly advanced through the cemetery.

He improved his eyesight, but no matter how sharp he made it, he couldn't see more than a few feet. The moisture filled the air with a muggy, earthy smell that distorted his olfactory senses in spite of their enhancement. Only his hearing remained useful. When he heard shuffling in the distance, he pointed his gun in that direction and searched the fog for any hint of movement. He was sure Darren was doing the same thing. He backed against a mausoleum wall and stomped his foot, intentionally revealing his position. He counted to fifteen, and when he didn't hear anything, he did it again. This time, he heard what sounded like a footstep in the distance.

Darren darted around the mausoleum wall with his saw blade held high, but Florence was ready. He fired at point blank range. Three shots were grouped into Darren's skull. As Darren staggered back, Florence grabbed a tombstone, made it weightless, and tore it out of the earth. With a shout, he spun around and released it, restoring its weight as the slab of rock struck Darren in the chest like a cannonball. Florence summoned the saw blade to his body as he approached Darren. Mohinaux had said that damaging the Cannibal's brain, then severing its head and limbs had been enough to kill it. He hoped the same would apply to a Genie.

Darren twitched as Florence approached and raised his gun. He fired but missed as Darren leaped up. He ran in circles around nearby graves, kicking headstones and throwing fistfuls of dirt in the air.

Darren was screaming, but it wasn't the bellow of rage he had let out earlier. Instead, he sounded scared. His hands went to his skull, and he ripped out the icicles—but his wounds didn't heal. Instead, the blood quickly clotted as his raging continued.

Florence couldn't decide if he should finish Darren off or let his seeming manic episode run its course. Darren fell to his knees and looked at his hands. The skin was growing pale, flowing from his palms and fingers up his wrist and arms. He lifted his shirt to see the same thing happening on his chest. He lifted his fingers to his carotid artery, and it looked as if he was about to cry. With a final look at Florence, he screamed and ran deeper into the cemetery. Florence tried to follow, but the fog was still thick. He produced a gust of wind which cleared it away. In the distance, he saw the man with damaged skin running, and a few yards away was Darren looking just as confused as Florence as he watched his doppelganger weave through the tombstones. The figure was too far away for the Stakehail Colt, and the grave markers near it were too small for Florence to summon his body to.

"What did you do?" Florence called out as he raised the Stakehail Colt and walked toward Darren, who vanished before Florence reached him.

"No!" Florence shouted. He ran around grave markers and trees looking for any sign of Darren. "What did you do" he called out over and over again into the lonely emptiness of the cemetery. It was no use. Darren was gone, and so was the man with damaged skin.

-14-

DARREN

Darren sat alone in an alley with a stolen bottle of whiskey. He tipped the remaining pool at the bottom past his lips and held it in his mouth to feel the alcohol burn his tongue, then swallowed hard. He had learned that his healing abilities extended to intoxication. Getting drunk had required half the bottle, and even then, it had not lasted long. It had been nearly a month since the confrontation at the graveyard, and twenty of those days had been spent stealing bottles of liquor from convenience stores and consuming them in alleys. He had left Chicago so as not to risk running into Soleil or Flarence, going all over the country instead. Now, he thought, he was in Arizona or possibly Nevada. It was easy to lose track when his days consisted of short-lived drunken stupors.

He still had his saw blade, concealed under his shirt and slung from a shoulder. He slept outside most nights using newspapers for blankets, sometimes in public places like parks until the cops came by in the morning and told him to move along. Occasionally, he would summon his body into a motel room just to feel what it was like to sleep in a bed again.

When the corpse Darren had been controlling came to life, he rejoiced, believing he could repeat the result with Atalissa, but his hope was short-lived. With Atalissa cremated, there was no vein for him to inject his blood into, and recreating her body from the ashes was beyond his skills. Flarence had been able to restore his gun because he'd memorized how all the parts fit together. Darren had no idea how to reconstruct cells. There was nothing anyone could do to bring Atalissa back.

The reality that she was gone for good hit him hard, and he needed to talk to someone. He used an astral projection to look for Mike, Danny, Juan and Josh, only to find them all dead, probably at the hands of Soleil or the stranger with the magic guns. He wondered if he should try to bring them back, but the more he thought about it, the more he decided it was better to wait. It wasn't clear if there were side-effects of being revived, and looking back, it seemed as if the corpse he had Enchanted was in pain as it regained consciousness. It was better to wait until he knew exactly what had happened to the man after his resurrection.

He watched Tyrell through his astral projections. In spite of the paralysis, Tyrell looked happy after leaving the hospital. He immersed himself in his studies, and was staying at Lucy's place. Suddenly, Tyrell's decision to not be Enchanted took on a new meaning. He was moving on, leaving his old life behind, both his experiences with the gang and his discovery of the existence of Genies.

All Darren had ever wanted was to see Tyrell become successful and find a better life than the one Darren and Atalissa had brought him into, and that was exactly what was happening. Tyrell had his whole life ahead of him, but there was no option of moving on for Darren. Ever since he was a teen-ager, all he had had to live for was his wife, his four closest friends, and the gang. Now his wife was a pile of ashes, his friends were dead, and the gang meant nothing to him anymore. All that remained was his grudge against Tymbir. Tyrell needed to move on. As his father, it was Darren's responsibility to do everything in his power to help.

He tossed the empty bottle on the ground and used an astral projection to travel to a university he knew Tyrell had applied to. It was late in the afternoon, and his projection drifted into the Office of Admissions to find it closed and vacant. He summoned his body to a computer there and found a template of an acceptance letter, then typed in Tyrell's name and printed it. He spent the rest of the night uploading Tyrell's information into the system of other offices at the school. In a few hours, Tyrell was an accepted student.

But Darren wasn't done yet. His son deserved the best.

SOLEIL

Soleil had spent the month cooped up in his cafe, back to his old habits of sweeping the floors over and over again to pass the time, with the radio on for background noise. But he didn't have it tuned to his usual oldies. Instead, he was listening to the news for stories that sounded as if they could be related to the stranger he had seen in the apartment. Nothing about a man in black with strange guns was reported, but Soleil worried that the moment he stopped listening, something would happen. He and Flarence wanted to talk to Mohinaux about what had happened and ask his advice, but they found his cave vacant. They waited, but he never showed up. Flarence started looking for Darren while Claire looked for Mohinaux, but neither of them had any luck.

Soleil moved a chair to sweep under it for a fifth time when the door opened and Tyrell rolled in. He had clearly just come from school, and had his backpack resting on his lap. Through the window, Soleil could see Lucy's car pull away.

"You know, I'm sure there are baskets that are designed to be attached to the backs of wheelchairs," said Soleil. "It would be more comfortable than carrying your backpack on your lap everywhere."

Tyrell shrugged as he unzipped a pocket. "I grew up in a shady neighborhood, and I know how easy it is for people to be robbed. I'd rather keep my belongings in sight at all times. Still listening to the radio? Have you tried using a projection to find the guy?"

"Projections only work if I have something to focus on. I need his name, or something he owns. I tried focusing on the guns, but they seem to be Enchanted, and magic doesn't work on them. I won't be able to find him until I have more information.'"

Tyrell took an envelope from his backpack. "Good luck with all that. I'm actually here about my dad. He contacted me last night." Soleil dropped the broom as Tyrell handed him the envelope. "This was in Lucy's mailbox this morning. It was addressed to me." The envelope was already torn open, and Soleil pulled out the letter inside.

> Tyrell,
>   I'm so proud of you. Your mother was, too. You weren't the only kid who grew up in the gang's territory, but you were the only one who didn't let the people around you define who you are. I know you have the potential to do amazing things with your life, and I'm sorry Atalissa won't be around to see the man you become. I just want you to know that I respect your decision to not be Enchanted, and I hope you can respect my decision as well. I'm going back to the way I was before all this started. You and your mother were the best parts of my life, but now I've lost Atalissa for good and I don't want to get in the way of your future. I'm no longer a husband or a father. I'm a loner. I'm the scary man who lurks in the shadows. I know you won't agree with everything that's going to happen. People will talk, and lives will be lost, but I won't bring you into any of it. I don't want you to feel sorry for me. I'm so happy that you're moving on and making something of yourself. I wanted to help you get there. Go to 1414 Wabash Avenue. You're locker number is 348.
>   Keep making people proud,
> Darren

"He's gone," said Tyrell as Soleil finished reading the letter and put it back in the envelope. "He didn't even have the stomach to look me in the face and say goodbye."

Soleil returned the letter. "Does the address mean anything to you?"

"It's a storage unit," said Tyrell. "The key to the locker was in the envelope. I have it with me. Can you give me a lift there?"

"Lucy didn't want to go?"

"To be honest, things have been rough between us lately. I can't really say I blame her. Tymbir left some pretty deep emotional wounds."

Soleil went behind Tyrell's wheelchair, placed a hand on each armrest, and took them to the storage area. They arrived in front of the designated locker. Inside was a backpack, a laptop, a chair, and a mattress resting upright against the back wall. Pieces of paper and a manila envelope were duct taped to it. Tyrell rolled to the mattress and looked at a few of the papers. "These are documents from a university. It looks like Dad got me in."

Soleil pulled off the manila envelope. It was stuffed so full that the top flap barely closed. "This is information for a bank account. There's a balance of . . . wow, Tyrell, you're freaking rich!"

Tyrell snatched the papers and laughed when he looked at them. He wasn't filthy rich, but the several thousand dollars in the account probably was more than Soleil had ever seen at one time. Other than the bank information, the envelope was filled with $20, $50, and $100 bills.

"He left me enough in the bank account for tuition and then gave me another stack to cover my other expenses for the year. It looks like he got the hang of using his magic to rob people. I guess he has you to thank for giving him that idea." Tyrell took some of the cash out of the envelope before he reattached it to the mattress and rolled out of the storage unit. "Let's go. I need to tell Lucy about this."

"I'm not going to give up on him," said Soleil as he gestured to the items in the locker. "You can forget that letter Darren put in Lucy's mailbox. This proves he isn't gone. He hasn't been handling recent events very well, but he's still your dad and he still loves you. Flarence is convinced that Darren is drunk on power and can't come back, but I promise I won't allow anything bad to happen to him. I'm going to bring him to his senses." Soleil walked to Tyrell's chair and put his hands on the armrests. "He was a good father once. He can be a good father again." With that, he summoned them out of the storage building.

FLARENCE

He walked along the nature trail to Soleil's Cafe. He and Claire visited weekly to report on their searches for Mohinaux and Darren, but he had no new information and wasn't in a hurry to see his brother. Winter was in full swing now. Snow coated the trees, and the stream was frozen. He found this time of year beautiful and felt lucky that his health wasn't affected by the cold. He sauntered into the cafe. Soleil was sitting at the counter smoking pot and listening to the news. "You know I hate the smell of that stuff," said Flarence when Soleil offered him a hit.

"Suit yourself," said Soleil who took another puff before he extinguished the tip.

They paused at a story on the radio about a shooting, but the details made clear it was just a typical act of violence unconnected to the stranger Soleil had seen at the apartment. Flarence took a seat at the counter. "I haven't found Darren yet, although that might change if you decided to stop listening to the radio and help."

He turned off the radio and went to the other side of the counter. "Let me get you something to drink. On the house. You must be thirsty after looking for Darren all day."

"You got that right," Flarence sighed. "Get me something with alcohol. Strong alcohol. Enough to give me a buzz for a few seconds."

"I don't serve alcohol here. This is mostly a kid's restaurant."

"You base your menu on your customers? Tyrell and Lucy are the only ones who ever showed an interest in this place."

"Yeah, and both of them are kids."

Flarence felt his phone vibrate, flipped it open, and put it to his ear. "Are you hurt?"

"I'm fine," Claire replied, "but he's not." There was a distant groan. "Where are you?"

"Soleil's Cafe."

The moan on the other end of the line grew louder. "Get us to your son's restaurant, old man. Now!"

Claire appeared in the cafe a moment later. She was fully dressed in her Razor Punk outfit and was sitting on Mohinaux's back. She had her phone in one hand and was twisting his arm with the other.

"Get off," said Soleil who rushed from the counter as Flarence and Claire hung up their phones. "You're hurting him."

"I know," said Claire. "I like it. I dislocate his shoulder, and it pops right back into place. It feels so cool." She pulled on Mohinaux's arm, and he yelped as his shoulder was dislocated again before she eased the pressure and let it realign.

"All right, you got me," said Mohinaux. Claire rose off him. He stood up, and they all sat at a table. "I can't imagine what more you could possibly want to know. Do you think it was easy telling you the truth about our past? The truth hurts both sides. Revisiting those events brought back some old demons I thought I'd conquered."

"Oh, get over yourself," said Flarence.

"Hey, shut up," said Soleil. "Listen, Dad, we don't want to ask you more questions about your past. We need some advice and your help. Flarence and I have both seen things that we can't explain. To be honest, I'm not even sure where to begin."

"I am," said Flarence. "I'll go first." He told Mohinaux what had happened in the cemetery, with great attention to detail about how the man seemed to be in shock when he broke free from Darren's Corpse Puppet spell, and to move at supernatural speed.

"You can't be serious," Mohinaux said when he was finished.

"I am," said Flarence.

"It doesn't work that way," said Mohinaux. "Exposure to magic can Enchant people, but it can't bring someone back to life. Are you absolutely sure the man you saw was dead?"

"His skin changed after he broke free from Darren's influence," said Flarence. "It took on the complexion and texture of dead flesh."

"I know this is a lot to take in," said Soleil, "but there's more you need to hear. It actually gets worse."

"Worse than an Enchanted corpse loose in the city?" grumbled Mohinaux.

"Much worse," said Soleil. He described his encounter with the stranger in the apartment.

"When Soleil first told me that story, I thought it sounded familiar," said Flarence. "Think about it, when else have we seen a man with magical abilities hide his face and attack people?"

"It wasn't me this time," said Mohinaux.

"I believe you," said Soleil. "The man was surprised when he saw me use my powers. He hesitated to ask me what I was. I don't think the man was a Genie. The magic he used came from his guns. He's something else entirely. Before any of you start asking me about astral projections, I've already explored that option. I don't know enough to find him that way."

"And yet you're sitting in here all day listening to the radio instead of getting outside and looking," said Flarence.

Soleil leaned over the table to look Mohinaux in the eye. "The point, Dad, is that this is more your field than ours. You told us you spent a large chunk of your life creating monsters and then destroying them. There are two new monsters loose in the world, and we're going to need your expertise hunting them down."

Mohinaux seemed to consider it for a moment, and then disappeared.

"You've got to be kidding me," said Flarence. "Some help he was. Where do you think he went now?"

Mohinaux reappeared in the room with a pen and paper in his left hand and his ink-covered shirt in his right. "I'm in," he said as he slipped his shirt on and sat at the table. "Walk me through your stories again. I'd like to take notes this time."

FROM BOOK 2 OF THE MYSTIC RAMPAGE SERIES

Up next: Problems in Chicago keep getting bigger

Meet Inspector R.E.D and the Old Ticker

INSPECTOR R.E.D.

He couldn't remember who he was, which didn't scare him as much as not knowing what he was. He remembered feeling numb, and then seeing light, but filtered light, as if he was looking through a fog. Then he became aware of the smell of wet grass, and the feeling of damp dirt on his hands. The last thing he became aware of was the man standing in front of him with a gun.

His first instinct was to run, but he couldn't seem to control his legs. It was as if someone else was making his body move. He tried to scream, but his voice was dry and hoarse, as if he hadn't used it in a while. He started recognizing shapes of objects around him, and saw he was surrounded by tombstones. He panicked. He thrashed and pounded his fists into the dirt as he tried to swear at whatever was making this happen to him. Suddenly, whatever was trying to control his body released its hold, and he was free.

He didn't know where he was going, but he was moving fast, much too fasy for a normal person. He wanted to go home, but didn't remember where that was. He barreled past people on the street, passed bicyclists, and even kept pace with cars. He stopped for a moment to get his bearings, but as he stood still, a young boy looked at him and screamed. He didn't know what had frightened the child so much, but he ran again.

Eventually muscle memory took over and guided him. While he didn't recognize all the scenery around him, the street felt right, as if he had walked down it a million times before and could recall every crack in the cement. Finally, something familiar caught his eye: a building that was closed but looked as if it used to be a store of some kind. Cardboard in the windows blocked the view of anyone looking inside, and the small parking lot in front of the building was empty. He rushed to the door, but it was locked, and when he pounded on it, nobody answered. In frustration, he kicked it, and the door swung inward. He hadn't meant to kick it so hard, but somehow he was stronger than he knew.

He went in and straightened the door as best he could. There was only one large room, and the floor was covered with a thin layer of dust. In a far corner, a small workspace had been set up, and not too far away was what appeared to be a shabby living area. The workspace had a desk, a lamp, and a laptop connected to a multi-outlet plugged into the wall; in the living area, a cot with a single blanket was next to a coat hanger and a bucket.

He opened the laptop, but the screen and keyboard were smashed and useless. All the drawers were all empty, but the desk was surrounded by shreds of papers. Some had been torn, others burned. He read what he could of them, and the information seemed familiar, but details escaped him. He could see names on some of the papers and a fragment of a job description on others. Some of the scattered shreds of paper described medical problems. On one he read "heart attac . . ." and on another "respiratory complic . . ."

He turned to what seemed to be the sleeping area. The cot was dark green with a check-patterned quilt on it. A red baseball cap and a white lab coat with the letters R.E.D. on the left side were on a hook. He was sure the coat was his but couldn't remember what the letters stood for. He saw that the bucket was full of water; next to it was a disposable razor, a red towel, and a handheld mirror. Again, he was positive they were his. He worked in this building, and took his job seriously. He stayed here overnight to accomplish his tasks, but he couldn't remember what he did that was so important.

He picked up the mirror to look at his face, and realized instantly what had made the boy scream. He was a freak. His skin was a mask of different colors. Splotches of dark stuck out in some places while others were deathly pale. All of it had a sickly blue tint, like a man who was starved for oxygen. He looked like he was nearly dead but somehow clinging to life. He could see fine, but his eyes were glassy, and when he stuck out his tongue, it was the same pale blue as his skin. He lifted up his shirt and pants legs, and saw that his skin was the same everywhere. He also noticed four deep holes in his chest, directly over his heart. At one point, they had bled but now were only scabs. When he moved his left shoulder, he could feel a weight in his chest. It wasn't painful, just discomforting. He placed his hand on his chest but couldn't feel a heartbeat.

He stayed in the store for days, fearing someone might see him and be frightened. Strangely, he never became hungry, thirsty, or tired, and never even had the urge to use the bathroom. He simply existed. He paced around the vacant room with the tattered remains of his work lay scattered about.

Eventually, as if his brain was slowly healing and restoring his memories, he began to recall flashes of life. He couldn't remember everything, but he was beginning to remember how he'd gotten the chest wounds.

It had happened in this very room, working late transferring information from his papers to his computer. A group of people burst in. Some of them went through his desk and destroyed his work, and one with a silencer on his gun shot him four times in the heart. When he moved, he could feel the bullets still inside him. He still didn't know who he was or what had happened after he was shot, but slowly, as the days went by, he remembered more and more from that night. Soon the names of his killers would come to him, and he would go to them. He would have revenge. He would make them bleed as he had bled.

THE OLD TICKER

His experiment had worked. His hypothesis was correct. He beamed as he walked the streets of Chicago, armed with the discovery that made him the most dangerous man in the world. For him, bullets and bombs were child's play. With the pull of a trigger, he could deconstruct buildings, burn people to death, or produce electric currents from a distance. What he had seen at the apartment, though, was beyond even his understanding.

Apparently, he wasn't the only one who had made a groundbreaking discovery. The man in the poncho and the one with the saw had walked away from his attacks unharmed. His gun's voltage could stop the average person's heart instantly, but he'd zapped the man in the poncho for several seconds and he still didn't die. What was more bizarre was the man in the poncho leaping straight through the ceiling as if he had become intangible. To the man thinking back on this, it seemed his pride was blinding him to crucial information. He'd missed something. But he would worry about that later. At the moment he had work to do.

It was night. He walked down the street with a wool coat covering the guns in his shoulder holsters as well as the shirt and its symbols. In the back pocket of his jeans was his black bandanna with the circular image. At first it might seem to be a clock permanently set to two minutes before twelve, but it actually portrayed something else entirely.

The man turned down an alley and walked to the back entrance of the house his target was staying in. His target was Jeremy Clancy, who had escaped with his life from the apartment that had been burned to the ground earlier in the day. It had taken a few weeks to track Jeremy down, but he had eventually found the kid staying with a friend.

He tied the bandanna around his face, the clock image draped over his nose and mouth, then pulled off the coat and took his guns from their holsters.

He thought he probably could climb over the tall iron gate bordering the back yard, but he didn't have to. He clicked the switch on the grip of his gun to deconstruct the latch and let him nudge open the gate with his foot. He went to the house and turned the wooden door to sawdust. He walked inside as quietly as possible and found Jeremy asleep on a couch in the living room with no blanket. He didn't hunt for sport, but he also didn't find any joy killing a man in his sleep.

He set one of his guns to freeze and switched on the light, which made Jeremy groan and roll over. His eyes cracked open, and when his gaze drifted to the wall switch he jumped upright, fully awake. Jeremy opened his mouth to scream, but it was too late. The trigger had been pressed, and his voice came out as a gasp as he was frozen solid from the inside out. The gun's energy sank to his bones first and froze his joints, which immobilized him. The fluids were affected next, and his blood cells burst as the water in them froze. Jeremy's body shook as he succumbed to instant frostbite. The man had targeted Jeremy's neck first to silence his scream but then swept the gun up and down until his body was completely destroyed. Finally, Jeremy stopped moving and collapsed back onto the couch.

The man holstered his gun and reached into the back pocket of his jeans. He pulled out a piece of paper that was folded into quarters, and contained a list of names. After the attack at the apartment, many names had been crossed off: He had killed Mike, Josh, Juan, Danny, and others. Now he crossed out Jeremy's name and looked over the rest of his list: the ones who had not been in the apartment but still must die at his hand.

He pocketed his list and took one of his guns out of its holster as he crossed the room to the window, then smashed out the glass with the butt of the gun. Then he hopped up onto the windowsill, set the gun to attract, and fired at a car in the distance. There were footsteps behind him. The owners of the house heard the breaking glass and woke up to investigate. He pointed the gun to his head and pulled the trigger, which made him fly out the window and land near the car as a blood-curdling scream told the world that the owners had discovered Jeremy's body. The man holstered his guns and pocketed the bandanna as he circled around to recover his wool coat. He slipped it on and walked calmly down the street as if nothing had happened. *You think you're scared now?* he thought. *Just wait. You'll be screaming a lot louder than that soon enough, along with everyone else in this city.*

TYRELL

He didn't want to talk, but he also knew he couldn't let his last moments with his best friend consist of the two of them listening to the radio while seemingly endless stretches of corn fields passed them by. Lucy was driving, and he was in the passenger's seat with the back of the car filled with boxes, suitcases, and Tyrell's folded-up wheelchair. There was a time when the two of them could talk all day long, but now, just turning his head to look at Lucy was painful. In spite of her disapproving parents and the negative things other kids at school said about Tyrell, the two of them had been so close the past three years. They said they would be friends forever, and for a while, it felt like they were becoming more than friends, but the last year had driven them apart. The marks Lucy received the night she was kidnapped were long gone and she was mostly back to her pleasant self, but when she was around Tyrell, she became distant.

They tried to keep spending time together. Lucy let him stay at her house after Darren disappeared. They would eat dinner and watch movies together, but things had changed. It seemed as if Lucy didn't want to lose Tyrell as a friend but couldn't move on from all that had happened. Today was the last opportunity to revive the relationship they once had. Lucy's bags were packed, and she was ready to move on campus. Her parents, who had more of Lucy's things in their car, had passed them on the road miles ago. Though Lucy drove much slower than her parents to make the trip with Tyrell as long as possible, eventually, a sign told them their destination was a few miles away.

"We're almost there," said Tyrell. Lucy didn't say anything, so he turned up the radio. "I'll visit you sometime. Soleil probably won't mind bringing me here every once in a while."

Lucy kept her eyes on the road when she spoke. "I don't want to see Soleil. I need time away from him and his family. I need time away from everything."

"Even me?" said Tyrell. Now Lucy did look at him. Their eyes locked for a moment, and then she took her hand off the wheel and held his before turning her attention back to the road. "I'm sorry things got so out of hand," he said. "I never wanted you to get hurt."

"You were never the problem. Your neighborhood was a problem, and so were the people you spent time with. Your dad was a problem too, no offense."

"None taken."

"I just want you to know that I'm not mad at you. But I need a fresh start and some time to myself."

Tyrell squeezed her hand. They were silent until Lucy pulled into the parking lot of her dorm. People were moving in and out, but Lucy's parents were nowhere in sight. While she fished her phone out of her purse, Tyrell thought about their relationship and couldn't shake the feeling that saying she needed time alone was her way of saying goodbye. He knew the experience as a captive had changed her, and he was the one responsible. Even though she said she wasn't mad, it was looking likely that their friendship was about to end.

It wasn't what he wanted. A part of him wanted to respect Lucy's wishes and let her have her fresh start and her space, but another part wanted to make one last effort to save what they had had before the door closed for good. Over the years, the two had done lots of things together, but Tyrell had never verbalized his feelings for her. Maybe the reason he and Lucy had never become more than friends was that she was waiting for him to make the first move. If that was the case, then the window was closing—but the opportunity was not gone yet.

Lucy hung up her phone and dropped it back in her purse. "They knew they were far ahead and didn't feel like waiting, so they went to get lunch. They'll be here in a few minutes."

Tyrell leaned toward Lucy a little, though he didn't know if it was noticeable. He suddenly felt like his whole body broke out in a cold sweat, even though his mouth had gone dry. He tried to lean in again, but now he was paralyzed from the waist up as well below. Lucy took the keys out of the ignition, but when she turned him, she froze. He was about to lean in and meet her lips, but still had a shred of doubt. A lot had changed between them. He reminded himself there would not be another chance. It was now or never.

He chose never. Their eyes remained locked but the moment passed, and eventually Lucy turned away. She opened her door and insisted that they get started. Tyrell could offer minimal assistance, only able to carry a box or two on his lap. The pace increased when her parents showed up, and when they were finished, Lucy hugged him and said goodbye one last time.

Tyrell rolled through the campus, burning Lucy's last words and her hug into his mind, grateful for the contact with her. He explored the campus until he found an empty spot, then called Soleil and told him he was ready to be picked up.

"So how did it go," Soleil asked when he arrived. "Is everything good between you two?"

"No," said Tyrell. "Things aren't good between us at all."

ABOUT THE AUTHOR

Hugh Fritz is a fan of monsters, mad scientists, sorcerers, and anything that involves beings with incredible powers beating each other senseless. After years of writing research papers, he decided it was time to give reality a rest and let his imagination run wild. This is his first book, and it has been an illuminating experience making the transition from reader to author.

He was born in Chicago where he spent most of his life until moving to the Southwest four years ago. He finds inspiration bouncing ideas off other novelists in a critique group, but hours of television and finding the right songs to put him in the writing mood play an important role as well. He has no plans to end the Genies' adventures here, so be on the lookout for more magical mischief in the next book of the Mystic Rampage series.